Contraband

By John Sandel

ACKNOWLEDGMENTS

Of all the many pilots, flight attendants and ticket agents who contributed their expertise to this book, I'd particularly like to mention the retired Delta Airlines Captain who was always ready to help. Jim Gregg lives around the corner from me, and he spent hours feeding me technical information while providing treats for my West Highland Terrier Fergie as we passed by on dog walks. Before Jim flew for Delta he piloted a Sabre Jet fighter on combat runs over Korea, and he has an encyclopedic knowledge of aviation data.

Deadly Contraband

To Brenda –

My fellow Stephen Minister and book lover

John Hansen

Copyright © 2016 John Sandel All rights reserved.
ISBN-13: 978-1539954262
ISBN-10: 1539954269

CHAPTER ONE

TransGlobal First Officer Lori Fyfer was hurrying down the ramp at Gate 12 on DFW's International Concourse when she spotted the maintenance pickup parked under the huge silver airliner sitting at the gate.

Oh no, she thought, *not today! Surely there isn't something wrong with this big beautiful bird this morning!*

She'd only flown domestic TransGlobal flights until today, and was so eager to take this next step in her flying career she had trekked down to the gate just to look over the empty aircraft a few hours before the crew collected to take off for Kloten Airport in Zurich, Switzerland.

Fyfer knew these wonderful airplanes were such complicated, high-tech flying machines; it was only very skilled mechanics who kept things from going wrong all the time. But surely not on her very first 'hop over the pond' as part of a flight crew!

She began to imagine the possible delays that might occur. *Was the flight about to be cancelled entirely?* She had been looking forward to today for months. She stepped into the airliner and looked left into the cockpit. *Great ... no one in there, so probably no major problems affecting flight controls or navigation.* Turning to her right, Fyfer looked down the long central aisle of the airliner. Nothing moved. She seemed to be completely alone on the huge airplane.

* * *

But F/O Fyfer was not alone. Standing in the Business Class restroom peering through a crack in the door was a large burly man wearing a TransGlobal mechanic's burgundy overalls. He was bald, with deep, dark eyes, one of which had a golden fleck in the iris. He clenched his teeth and glared at Fyfer. *It's too early for the crew to arrive!* He had heard this little woman as soon as she entered the airplane, and now stared through the slit in the door wondering what to do with her.

Oh, no. Of all times to have a pilot wander aboard. I may have to kill her, he thought. *Can I convince her I'm supposed to be here? I certainly can't let her find the hydrogen cyanide. Nobody's supposed to be here for hours,* he raged. *I didn't even write up a fake work order telling me to fix the Business Class toilet. What if she asks to see it? I might indeed have to kill her. But finding somewhere to dump a body in an airliner about to take off for Europe would be a problem. Pretty little thing. Can't be much over five feet tall. She won't be a problem to kill. The problem will be finding a place to put her body. I've got to be more careful.*

The hulking man frowned as he puzzled over the small figure. She somehow looked familiar. But he couldn't place where he had seen her. It had been somewhere close and personal.

But the man standing in the restroom had been so many different people when he needed to be, his biggest worry was that she might remember him as someone else; that he had not been dressed as an airline mechanic ... and he could have been doing something very illegal at the time. But maybe she wouldn't remember him at all, so he'd better act like he was just doing his job as a mechanic. If things went south, he'd do whatever he had to do with her.

* * *

F/O Lori Fyfer had turned to the cockpit, and leaned in the door to get a better view of the interior of the spacious flight deck laden with high tech instruments and dials on both walls and overhead. Suddenly she heard scuffling sounds from behind her in the rear of Business Class, and turned to see a large man wearing TransGlobal mechanics' overalls backing out of the rest room dragging a large tool bag into the corridor. She was relieved. Problems in the restroom? Good ... that could be handled quickly.

"Good morning," she called as she walked back into the aircraft toward the man. With a grin she added hopefully, "Is everything working all right this morning?"

The man turned around to face her, and drug the tool kit around the floor in front of him, smiling awkwardly at her. "You surprised me!" he said. "I thought I was all alone. Just working in the Business Class restroom ... uh, toilet acting up. But I got it fixed now. Just finished. You're ready to go!"

The man's faint accent that Lori had heard in so many nightmares sent chills through her body. She remembered the same crisp, educated sound of his voice from her hotel room in Istanbul all those years ago, and she shivered with fear. Then she caught sight of his eye. That same golden fleck she'd seen in that monster's eye as he beat her senseless so very long ago.

Lori froze where she stood. Her mouth dropped open. *It's really him!* She felt light-headed as she stared at the monster. The maniac who had haunted her fitful sleep for years. She had started thinking of him as the Turkish Madman, because she had no other name for him. The one who had nearly killed her.

Her right hand rose slowly to the scar on her cheek, and felt of her square jaw where he had broken it. She couldn't believe she was actually standing here looking at him after all these years!

But wait a minute. She stopped herself as she fought to control her emotions. The monster had worn a TransGlobal pilot's uniform, not mechanic's overalls ... and then he had had a mop of black curly hair and a bushy black moustache. And the attack happened halfway around the world eight years ago. Am I just going crazy paranoid?

But no, no, no she screamed at herself ferociously! This man's same golden eye fleck is in the same right eye, he's still connected to TransGlobal Airlines, and I haven't seen another such eye irregularity on anybody in the ensuing eight years, or heard that hateful voice. This has to be the monster who beat me so badly.

Lori opened her mouth and screamed with all her might, "Help, help ... somebody help me!" Only silence met her cries in the empty aircraft. The man just stared at her, bewilderment on his face.

"You monster," she screamed. "You're the man who tried to kill me in my hotel room eight years ago in Istanbul." She dragged in a wheezy breath shakily, and reached deep in her pocket for her cell phone. "I'm reporting you NOW! You won't get away this time, you maniac!"

Recognition widened the big man's dark, sunken eyes when Lori mentioned the hotel room in Istanbul. And then anger.

"Well, well," he growled. "You got in my way then, and you're doing it again, aren't you, little woman? You would show up at a time like this! You should have learned better that night in Istanbul, because you're not going to survive this time around.!" The man lunged forward, stumbling over the large tool bag, staggering a bit as he tried to get around and over the heavy canvas container. "I'm going to finish you now like I should have eight years ago," he raged in a guttural voice. "You're dead! *This time* I swear you're dead!"

But Lori was already moving. She had turned and fled toward the entrance of the airliner, frantic to get away from this monster.

Can I make it up the ramp to the concourse? No agent at the counter yet. Maybe no one even close in the terminal.

He's probably right, I probably am dead, she told herself in horror as she sprinted through First Class. *Thank God for the shiny black flat-heeled loafers I'm wearing with my manly uniform.*

Then she noticed just ahead of her the door ajar to the cockpit. Instead of running out of the airplane, she leaned to the right and fell through the cockpit door, hearing the man right behind her, and expecting to feel his hand on her arm or shoulder at any second. She went down to her knees in the cockpit before swiveling around to rise from the floor. She threw her shoulder against the door. Too late! She couldn't close it. The monster on the other side had placed his much larger shoulder against it, and was slowly pushing it open.

Even with all Lori's strength fighting to close the door, the man was pushing her and the door backward across the floor of the flight deck. Even her foot braced against the jump seat at the back of the flight deck failed to stop the door from slowly opening inch by inch. Lori had no weapons. What would she do when he pushed into the cockpit? She looked frantically around the flight deck. There was nothing.

"But it's not really so bad for you, little woman," taunted the man in an educated accent that contrasted so strangely with his dirty coveralls. Lori saw his left foot slip between the door and the wall of the cockpit, and felt the force against the door increase even more. He was beginning to enjoy this. "You would have been dead a week from now, anyway. This airplane is never coming back to DFW. It's going to drop into the deepest part of the North Atlantic, and everybody on it is going to be as dead as you're going to be today." Then he added with an evil chuckle, "Of course, that might be a better way to die than what I'm about to do to you right now!" The pressure on the door lessened for a moment as the man turned slightly to draw a folded knife from his coveralls pocket.

That reminded Lori ... in her pocket ... her canister of MACE!

Straining to keep her shoulder pushing as hard against the door as she could, Lori twisted to her side and ran her right hand down her right pants pocket. There it was ... thank God!

She frantically congratulated herself for being so cowardly she had kept it in her pocket even though she knew it was illegal in Zurich. She fought to twist back around, and then thumb back the safety tab. Her contortions had allowed the man to push much faster and farther into the cockpit. The door was now halfway open, and moving steadily inward against her best efforts. Lori was exhausted and almost hysterical, but she raised the canister of MACE and pointed it directly where she expected the man's strange eyes to appear just as he pushed his face around the door rim with a victorious grin.

Lori shot the searing liquid into his eyes from a distance of less than three inches. In the instant before he screamed and disappeared behind the door, Lori could see the acrid spray splatter against that golden fleck in his right eye ... and then he was gone. Lori could hear the man continue to scream as she lunged against the door with all the strength she had left, and felt it slam close, and then ... thank God, she felt it latch.

Lori turned and grabbed the mike on the control panel as she heard pounding on the door. "DFW Tower, this is TransGlobal aircraft parked at Gate 12 on Concourse D. I'm First Officer Lori Fyfer." Lori was panting so hard she could barely speak coherently. "I ... I've just been attacked by a TransGlobal mechanic here in the aircraft. I've locked myself in the cockpit! Please send the airport police before this maniac gets in here! Please hurry! Do you copy?"

The pounding grew heavier and Lori heard the madman yelling hoarsely through the door. Then it stopped.

The radio crackled. "This is DFW tower. I'm calling police now, and sending them to Gate 12, D Concourse ... repeat, Gate 12. Confirm?"

"Yes," said Lori, with a relieved sigh. "Yes, Gate 12. Thank you!"

CHAPTER TWO

Lori listened to the muted roar of the two huge General Electric GE90115B engines as they drew Flight 4416 across the white carpet of clouds above Tennessee. When the airport police discovered that her attacker had been a suspected smuggler eight years ago, they declared her aircraft a crime scene. They were currently searching it carefully from nose to tail.

That forced TransGlobal to bring in another 777 from Phoenix, which delayed the departure of Flight 4416 by two hours. The new aircraft happened to be a 777-200ER, an extended range 777 with a pilots' lounge area above business class, and a flight attendant crew lounge above tourist class. Both lounges were small, but they boasted beds and easy chairs.

The pilots' lounge was currently empty, as Lori and both captains sat in silence in the cockpit, all busy with their own thoughts. Lori had told them of her experiences with the mechanic, and exactly what the man had said, including the man's remarks about bringing this airplane down before it could ever return to DFW. After the initial lively conversation, full of uneasy laughter and assertions of disbelief, talk had dwindled to the fewest words needed to maintain the aircraft.

Bill Travers sat on the left. As the senior captain, a fit, middle-aged pilot with a salt-and-pepper crew cut, Travers was in charge of the airplane. Lori sat on the right, in the co-pilot seat, and the other captain, Jack Willow, very plump and bald with a bushy white moustache, sat in the jump seat at the rear of the flight deck. One of the captains had to be in the cockpit at all times, while Lori was needed only when things got busy, especially during take-offs and landings.

Lori had also told the other pilots about sitting in the airport police office for the rest of the morning and the early afternoon studying every photo ID in the police computer of all the TransGlobal mechanics, fuelers and baggage handlers at DFW. Lori recognized some of them, but none as her attacker. By this time Lori was so bleary-eyed she wondered if she'd recognize the maniac even if she *did* find him among the dizzying sea of faces. *Was that what had happened? Did I pass over his picture, not recognizing him?* she asked herself anxiously. But she didn't believe she had. She felt sure she would have spotted him if he were there. *What other lists were there?* Lori had given her last fifteen minutes of free time to scanning photos of DFW TransGlobal pilots before rising from the computer to get busy doing her preflight walk-around looking at the underside of the new airplane from Phoenix.

From the lists she'd perused, her attacker didn't seem to exist! But he *did* exist. Lori had seen this monster in a pilot's uniform with curly black hair and moustache in Istanbul, and in TransGlobal coveralls this morning. At least one of those outfits was fake, but which one ... or was he not even a TransGlobal employe at all? And he had told her he was going to bring her flight down in the North Atlantic on its last leg of this trip eight days from now! He wasn't even threatening her. He was just taunting her with news about what was going to happen nearly a week after he killed her in that cockpit!

This was too much! Being beaten so badly by this man had literally changed Lori's life. Eight years ago Lori decided she would never again be a victim of this monster or anyone else, and she started focusing on everything she'd ever wanted to achieve. She had been a flight attendant when that animal attacked her all those years ago, and now she was a pilot, a TransGlobal First Officer. She used to be afraid of everything, becoming a flight attendant because she couldn't imagine ever being an actual airline pilot. But refusing to be a victim after this maniac attacked her had led her to doing some incredible things.

Many of her fellow pilots now called her Mighty Mite because of the enthusiastic way she attacked things that needed to be done. Lori felt her bosom swell as she considered what she had managed to achieve in the last few years ... her commercial pilot's license, her multi-engine rating, and getting hired by TransGlobal. She was exactly the minimum height ... five-feet, one-inch-tall, and able ... just barely ... to reach the foot controls below her while touching the overhead controls above.

She'd been afraid she'd fail many times, but the anger she felt for that man who attacked her and hurt her so badly brought her through. And now he was back, planning to destroy her airplane and all her passengers ... and her, too! Well, that was one good thing that had come from Lori's one experience with violence and evil. It had knocked her life out of neutral gear. In refusing to think of herself as a victim, Lori had changed her whole self-image. *That is,* she told herself, *she was at least beginning to change ... at least some of the time!*

And there had been one victory that morning in the airport police office that might make all the difference in catching this guy! She had suddenly remembered Aspen Mohr! Back in Istanbul on that horrible day when Lori first encountered him, Lori had wondered if Aspen Mohr ... her own fellow flight attendant ... was involved with that criminal! Being suspicious of Aspen was really the only lead she had, and she had suddenly remembered it as she scanned the ID Pictures in the police office.

Back all those years ago Aspen was the flight attendant in Lori's crew who had talked the others into visiting that Istanbul bath where Lori first saw the man who later attacked her. Aspen Mohr was a stunner. She was so tall and willowy, and so blonde and beautiful, that she turned heads in every airport in the world as the flight attendants passed through. Once when they were plodding through an airport after working all day and all night, Lori still noticed a wave of heads turning in Aspen's wake like spectators at a tennis match whose eyes were following the ball. Even in her zombie state a silly smile had spread across Lori's face. She wondered if anyone would have noticed if all the other girls had been lumbering along stark naked, as long as Aspen was in their midst.

What had first caught Lori's attention when all eight of them had arrived at the public bath was that they were met inside by a very elderly topless and toothless woman who seemed to know Aspen. She showed them to the disrobing room, and handed out towels like she wore herself, wrapped around her waist.

Aspen called her an *odaci*, Turkish for "attendant", and told the girls that she would guard their things until they returned. They all hung their uniforms in the open closets, and swaddled themselves in their brightly colored p*eshtemals*, as Aspen called their towels. The girls also all placed their uniform purses in the closets, except for Aspen, who was still rummaging for something in hers. All the others, including Lori, clomped out of the disrobing room on the raised plastic clogs that the *hamam*, as Aspen called the public bath, had provided to keep their feet dry and uncontaminated by the wet floors. At the time Lori hadn't paid attention to the fact that Aspen was the last to finally join them in the Hot Room.

Lori had been beckoned by a large, sweaty woman wearing flowery panties who spread Lori's naked body across the hot, wet surface of an octagonal marble platform ... face down at first

... and poured nearly scalding water over Lori's calves and thighs. Lori let out a screech as the woman began scouring her bright pink legs and backside with a rough, soapy hand mitt, obviously intent on removing every ounce of dead skin or grime accumulated since she was born. Lori clenched her teeth and tried to breathe through the bubbles on the smooth surface of hot marble, finding herself wondering how many other flushed pink chins had rubbed the same spot on the soapy stone in the past four hundred years or so Aspen claimed this *hamam* had served Istanbul.

Occasionally, as much as her ordeal allowed, Lori raised up slightly to look for her friends. The hot room's thick fog of steam softened Lori's view of the other girls, who had been deposited haphazardly about the octagonal raised surface of marble that spread some twenty feet across the center of the room.

The writhing bathers were all being drenched and scoured by female bath attendants, and their gasps and protests mixed with the giggles of the Turkish *natirs*, as Aspen called the hot room attendants. The oldest woman of Lori's group was Elsie Ponder, her head flight attendant, who had two natirs scrubbing her down, one positioned by her head, and one scrubbing her legs, as her body turned a bright pink.

But what mattered most in that experience was that as she saw the first girls being released from the marble platform to soak in whirlpool baths, Lori decided that she would get a great picture of all of them peering over the edge of the tub in the *hamam*, with their heads only visible. When the sweaty Turkish amazon working on Lori splattered more steamy hot water on her and declared her clean, Lori grabbed her towel and clomped to the disrobing room on her elevated clogs. She was surprised to find no sign of the *odaci,* and one uniform purse left out on the bench where the girls had disrobed. She opened it, found it was Aspen's, and returned it to the somewhat dubious security of Aspen's closet. With the *odaci* gone, nothing was very safe. Lori decided to find the *odaci* as soon as she took her picture. She removed her camera phone from her own purse, leaving the purse temporarily on the bench as she clomped rapidly back to the steamy Hot Room. She found all the girls in the tub except Aspen, who had been last. Lori could barely see the bottoms of Aspen's feet through the steamy mist as her *natir* scrubbed her back vigorously.

Anxious to locate the missing *odaci,* Lori decided to get a picture of the girls in the tub, and take shots of herself and Aspen later somewhere else. Lori squatted low to the floor and photographed the giggling *hamam* survivors grinning at her over the edge of the tub, all looking like drowned rats.

Lori hurried from the hot room as quickly as she could, and clomped to the disrobing room. She stopped short just as she reached the entrance, where she saw a burly man wearing only a *peshtemal* around his waist looking through her purse, the only one left on the bench. He held it in his lap as he pulled her billfold out of it. He was only some three feet away from Lori, and had thick black curly hair and a bushy black moustache. In his right eye there was a golden fleck. He glanced up as Lori grabbed at her towel and flinched backward, screaming with all her might, and looking left and right for the still missing *odaci*. Then he threw down the purse, and ran.

CHAPTER THREE

As Lori sat in the co-pilot's right seat on the 777's flight deck, she was deep in thought, remembering the very first time she had laid eyes on the monster who later attacked her in her hotel room.

Would anything have gone differently if I had spoken to him instead of screaming at the man in the disrobing room of the hamam in Istanbul eight years ago, then ... Lori was suddenly startled back to the present by loud static on the cockpit radio. A tinny voice began speaking to all three pilots through their head sets: "TransGlobal heavy 4416, this is TransGlobal Operations. Do you copy, over?"

Lori's mouth opened reflexively as she watched Captain Travers lean forward and click his mike button. 'TransGlobal Operations' meant the Director of Operations for the entire airline. His name was Fitzgerald, she thought. Lori had never even seen him in person.

"Hear you five by five, sir," responded Travers. "This is TransGlobal heavy 4416, Captain Travers speaking." Lori loved finally crewing an airliner big enough to be designated "TransGlobal heavy". It was a warning to other aircraft that the 777 was so large that the vortex of air that followed it through the sky could bounce smaller aircraft about.

"Good evening, Captain," the voice replied. "Are First Officer Fyfer and Captain Willow on the horn, also?"

Travers glanced at both Lori and Willow with raised eye brows, and replied, "Yes sir, right here."

"I actually need to talk with all three of you, Captain. This is Fitzgerald, TransGlobal DO. You're all involved in this. Did First Officer Fyfer tell you about this morning's events?"

"Yes, sir."

"Well, the airport police have searched the aircraft you were originally going to fly to Zurich, and they found some interesting contraband. In the restroom where Fyfer first encountered the mystery man, they found a cache built into the wall that held a gas cylinder about two feet long. They took it to a Dallas lab where the gas inside was identified as hydrogen cyanide. It's a powerful insecticide also used in U.S. gas chambers, and was the gas used in Nazi gas chambers. Very nasty stuff. When the tiny dry pellets are exposed to the oxygen in air, they turn into a toxic gas that will kill everyone exposed to it within a few minutes. In other words, we have evidence this guy is very serious and very dangerous. Did you get all that?"

"Yes, sir," responded all three pilots quietly into their mikes.

"Hydrogen cyanide is also very unstable," said Fitzgerald. "If it's tossed around too much it can actually explode, so there's a federal law against transporting hydrogen cyanide on any airplane."

"Sounds like the mystery man isn't too concerned about breaking aviation safety rules," said Captain Travers.

"Not as long as he isn't riding on the airplane. I'm glad your crew has a day's layover in Zurich," continued Fitzgerald. "That will give us time to search other aircraft to see if there's any more gas around, and time for me to get there for a meeting in our offices at Kloten Airport in Zurich with the authorities. I'm even bringing a couple of FBI agents with me. We intend to manage this crisis vigorously, and to prosecute whoever is involved. I'll want the three of you at the meeting at 9 a.m. Zurich time the day after tomorrow in one of our airport offices. Plenty of time for you all to attend the meeting before you take off for Istanbul. Considering what the man told Fyfer, he apparently intends to strike on your return flight from Zurich to DFW. That gives us eight days to get to the bottom of all this, protect your flight, and arrest this guy. I'll see you day after tomorrow!"

"Yes, sir," the pilots repeated.

"TransGlobal Operations, over and out."
"TransGlobal heavy 4416, out" said Travers, as he leaned back and stared straight ahead, deep thoughtfulness on his face. Captain Willow and Lori also drew into themselves and thought about the deadly gas that had been hidden on their airplane, and what might still lie ahead for them.

Lori thought about all she had just heard. Back in the days before she first met the smuggler in Istanbul she would have been scared to death, and would have just sat back hoping to be saved. Now she began to plan what she could do. She thought of the first time she had confronted this maniac. What a wuss she had been. If she had helped the Istanbul police find the monster instead of just leaving the hospital and flying home, maybe he wouldn't be around to threaten her passengers and herself now. She didn't plan to act like a helpless victim ever again.

Why does this maniac want to destroy my aircraft? she asked herself. *He had been a smuggler who wanted to kill me when I first met him eight years ago. I'm sure he was trying to pass along some sort of contraband, and got into my purse by mistake. That's why he broke into my room later. But by now he obviously didn't even remember who I was until I told him, so that wasn't why this airplane was in his sights. Was it because someone else is going to be on board for the trip back to DFW ... or something else? Or was it all just random? The answer had to be one of those reasons ... there was nothing else. Or at least I can't think of anything else*, she told herself.

I can't do anything about several of the possible reasons, decided Lori. *But I can check the airplane roster for the trip back to DFW to see if any of the names of passengers or crew members aboard sound familiar.*

Hey, she reminded herself, *this substitute aircraft I'm on right now had also been en route to Zurich ... just a day later than the one I met the monster on. What are the chances I might find something in the business class restrooms of this airplane? The DO is having other airplanes searched, but I doubt anyone had time to look this one over in the rush to get it to DFW.*

"Anyone need to visit the john?" Lori asked the other pilots. Head shakes and negative grunts were the only responses. "Mind if I take off an hour or so?" she asked Travers.

"Just be back by two a.m. DFW time," said Travers. "One of us may be beginning to nod off by then. Although," he added with a grin and a glance back at Lori, "I'm not sure I'm ever going to feel sleepy again after that conversation we had with Fitzgerald

"Me, too," agreed Lori with a smile, "I'll be back." She now had over two hours to snoop around the aircraft. *Good time, too. It was now almost midnight DFW time, and there shouldn't be all that many folks visiting the restrooms.* Lori walked back through the darkened airplane between seats of sleeping travelers and squirming night owls who wished they could go to sleep. Bleary eyes followed her professional-looking black uniform through the airliner, but lost interest when she turned into the Business-Class restroom. *Hope this guy hides things in the same place on all airplanes,* thought Lori. *Now what on earth does a cache look like?*

The four interior walls of the Business Class restroom were all a silver plastic. However, the wall holding a mirror had brushed aluminum panels on both sides of the mirror. There were four small screws in the four corners of both panels apparently holding them to the wall.

Lori pulled her beloved Swiss Army knife from her pocket and extended the small screwdriver from the knife. She got the knife through security claiming it was a utensil she sometimes needed to repair small electronics on the flight deck, but she actually more often used the tiny scissors to nip off stray threads she found clinging to her uniform, or the ivory toothpick to remove stubborn bits of food from her teeth when she found herself alone.

The small screwdriver fit the screw heads well enough that she was able to remove them slowly, one by one, without touching the surface of the panel, which she hoped would yield fingerprints to the police if there was anything in the cache. When she pulled out the last one, she was able to use her handkerchief to remove the panel without disturbing any fingerprint clues. She found the panel was also magnetized to the frame below. The same screwdriver she'd been using to remove screws was the perfect lever to pop the plate away from the frame.

Beneath was a hidden vault about two feet tall by six inches deep and wide. Lori let out her breath gratefully as she realized there was no cylinder of toxic gas resting in the hidden space. But there was a small twice-folded sheet of paper at the bottom of the vault. It was held in a folded position by what looked like a short strip of transparent tape. Lori started to reach for it, then stopped. Were there fingerprints on the paper, as well? She pulled out her handkerchief again, and carefully removed the note. She held it in her handkerchief, and ran her Swiss Army knife blade under the tape to free the folds of paper. Eagerly, she opened the note ... and stared at what looked like German and the Cyrillic alphabet of Russian. The note was apparently typed on a computer, and was about half in German and half in Russian. *Is nothing easy about this detective stuff?*

Lori pulled her I-phone from her pocket, spread out the note on the toilet top, and took several pictures. Then she refolded the note and re-secured the tape, then dropped it in the cache and carefully put the panel back in place, trying to avoid smearing fingerprints anywhere. For the first time she wondered if the people attending the meeting with the TransGlobal DO tomorrow might disapprove of her activities tonight. *After all*, she realized, *I'm not a policeman, and I need to be careful not to mess things up. But a pilot protects her passengers,* she told herself, *and while I was a wuss before, I'm not a wuss any longer! I've got to do everything I can to keep the folks travelling with me safe, or turn in my wings!*

CHAPTER FOUR

Lori furtively departed the restroom and crossed the darkened First Class section. It was so dark, in fact, she almost plowed into a figure standing in the entryway to First Class. Lori recognized that the dark shape was a TransGlobal flight attendant, but when she spotted the stripes on her sleeves that identified her as the airliner's head flight attendant, or purser, she stiffened. Lori had forgotten that after she told Sergeant Wilton of the DFW airport police about Aspen that morning, he had checked TransGlobal's records and found her. She was listed as the purser on Lori's first European flight!

So Aspen was still bidding the same flight plan she had been flying when Lori was hurt in Istanbul eight years ago. Lori had been so sure that there was some connection between Aspen and the man Lori caught going through her things in the Turkish bath, the DFW police had been willing to contact Interpol officers who were now waiting at Kloten Airport in Zurich to follow Aspen. What an ominous coincidence that Aspen would be on this airplane. Did she still work with that criminal? If she did, he must surely have mentioned to her that he was going to destroy this aircraft on its way back over the North Atlantic! So Aspen's sudden absence would be a warning to watch for. If Aspen failed to show up for the last leg of the trip, Lori would be forewarned ... if it wasn't too late by then. She also didn't seem terribly surprised to see Lori after all those years.

Lori saw her mainly as a silhouette in the gloom of the First Class cabin, but as her eyes adjusted to the darkness, she could make out long blond hair and the beautiful face of an angel. She hadn't changed in all these years! Lori stopped short, and her mouth dropped open. She was careful to act surprised. "Aspen Mohr!" she whispered as they stood amid rows of mostly sleeping passengers.

"Hello, Lori," whispered Aspen in that nasal voice Lori remembered so well, even after eight years. "I haven't seen you since that terrible night you got hurt. I can still remember what a bloody mess you were, too. And I heard you actually became a pilot! You should have just kept flying across the pond with your buddies. Here you've been flying domestic flights in the States earning pilot seniority, while we've been enjoying adventures in Europe all these years. Was it really worth it?"

Aspen was several inches taller than Lori, and she lifted her chin to the point that she was looking down her long, lovely nose at her exactly as she had done so many times all those years ago. Maybe she was still associated with that violent man she had been helping eight years ago, and he'd already told her who the First Officer of this flight would be.

"Oh, I think so," said Lori quietly. "I love my job." She gestured toward the curtain dividing first class from the galley area, and farther from the sleeping passengers. She brushed the curtain aside, followed by Aspen. "Did you enjoy the *hamam* we visited on that trip?" asked Aspen, watching Lori closely.

You mean, have I figured out exactly what happened in that place? thought Lori.

"Yes, it was very educational", she said, "and I was so clean I didn't need to take a bath for two months ... which was good ... because I was so beaten, bruised and broken I could hardly stand to touch any part of my body for at least that long!"

"You poor thing, you were really hurt, weren't you?" said Aspen, still studying Lori's eyes. "So awful that that man caught sight of you wearing nothing but that *peshtemal* at the *hamam*, and liked what he saw enough to follow you to the hotel and attack you!"

"Being sexy is a curse sometimes," said Lori with a wry smile. *But the reason that man attacked me was that he wanted three uncut gemstones back that he had put in my bag instead of yours,* she thought as she gazed up into Aspen's angelic face. *And you're going to help me find him, Aspen Mohr*, Lori decided.

"Did you see the man that night?" asked Lori. "I'd probably be dead right now if it weren't for Mary Lou McDaniel. She happened to be in the hall passing my room, and heard me screaming through the door. She started banging on the door and screaming, herself, and pretty soon the hallway was full of screaming flight attendants. All that racket must have spooked the maniac who had me on the floor by that time, dead to the world. He brushed past Mary Lou and the others, and ran for the stairs. They all stood in shock for an instant because he was wearing a TransGlobal pilot's uniform. By the time they began to try to find him, he was gone. The Istanbul police never found any sign of him, either. And I was so gutless, I never even filed any charges. I just wanted out of the hospital, and back home."

"No, I never saw him," answered Aspen slowly as if she were carefully considering her words. "No, I think I had gone to bed early that night. All the noise in the hallway woke me up, but he must have gotten away before my brain was working well enough to open the door to the corridor."

"Well, let's get together when we're in Zurich, or Moscow at the latest," offered Lori. "I'll tell you all about him, and how the police are probably going to catch him!" *That information should sound interesting enough to get Aspen to talk with me,* thought Lori. *Now all I have to do is make up something to tell her!*

"I'm going to get some shut-eye up in the lounge," Lori added, pointing up the stairway. "Talk to you soon!" *And the cops are following you to be sure we talk to you again soon,* thought Lori, wondering who the DFW cops had arranged to watch Aspen. "I'm looking forward to it, dear," said Aspen with a thin smile, gazing down her nose at Lori in that irritating manner she did so well.

Lori tried to ascend the steps to the pilots' lounge with slow dignity, but her telephone was burning a hole in her pocket. *It looked like a foreign language!* she told herself as she remembered what she saw of the note through the viewfinder of her telephone camera. Lori just hoped enough was in English to give her a better idea of what was going on. She pulled her key fob from a back pocket, and opened the lounge door. *I wonder if, being an airline pilot, I'm going to start looking at the world like a man, she* thought, *since I wear manly uniforms and distribute possessions around my body in pockets like men do, instead of carrying them in a purse! But hopefully the frilly underwear hugging the curves beneath my uniform will ward off any major concept changes.*

Inside the lounge, Lori peeled out of her coat, tossed her hat on the bed, slipped out of her loafers, and flopped in the easy chair to look at her I-phone. As her eyes swept over the lines of typed words in the pictures she had taken of the note, she confirmed in her own mind that about half was Russian, and the other half must be Swiss German, a dialect of the German language spoken in northern Switzerland. What a downer! She couldn't learn anything tonight. She didn't speak either language, so she'd have to get the material translated before presenting it in the meeting the morning after tomorrow morning.

But somebody had done a lot of writing, so hopefully there were important clues in there. But wait ... not all the writing was in a foreign language. She hadn't noticed the English name in the first paragraph amid all the Cyrillic words. Eric McEllen! If the smuggler was the man who wrote the letter, then McEllen must be an associate of some kind. The words didn't seem to be *to* him, but *about* him. Or maybe ... since both his first and last names were written ... perhaps the smuggler is introducing him to his fellow smugglers for some reason. Of course, he may be a good guy whom the smuggler is warning them about. But Lori hoped he was another villain. That way, she'd finally have another name of a conspirator besides Aspen. So she did have new evidence to present at the meeting. Maybe a few quick arrests could be made, and this horror would all be over in a few days.

* * *

"How does she do that?' fumed Aspen Mohr. *"The most irritating thing about that irritating woman is that she turns up at the worst times in the worst places, again and again! How could I have known that surrounding myself with those giggling idiots while I received a diamond drop from the Skipper at the same time would turn out like it did? The Skipper almost dropped me because Lori saw him, and now, once again, I've got this frustrating female on my case at the worst possible time ever!*

At least it was his fault that she got away when she spotted him in the airplane this morning, thought Aspen. *Unbelievable! A little woman like her ... and the Skipper couldn't kill her when they were alone in an empty airplane. And then he barely got away himself!*

I've just got to make sure all the mistakes are his from now on through Tuesday, when he dies ... otherwise, he may decide to kill me before I kill him! Aspen stood still and thought about her responsibilities as a smuggler. Was she on top of everything? Her only current job would be to get anything the Skipper had put in the restroom cache into the hands of the recipient as soon as she landed. She'd do that a few hours from now.

Wait a minute! Lori had first discovered the Skipper this morning as he came out of the Business Class rest room where the police later discovered the gas cylinder! Was there any chance Lori would think about checking the Business Class restroom cache on this airplane? What were the chances of her doing that? wondered Aspen. *Almost none*, she told herself, but she felt a sickening feeling in her stomach. She hadn't intended to remove any message hidden there for another three or four hours, when most of the passengers sitting around the restroom would be asleep. *But she couldn't wait now ... not with that feeling of dread in her stomach.* Aspen turned and walked quickly down the aisle toward Business Class.

I'm getting paranoid, she thought. *The Skipper may not even have hidden anything there this trip. But chances are, he did,* she told herself. As Aspen approached the restroom, the stares that followed her multiplied. One man even leaned out of his seat to watch her trim figure hurry down the aisle. But no one thought to question her entering the Business Class restroom as Aspen feared. The sign on the door read UNOCCUPIED, and she ducked inside. The little red adhesive label was still stuck high on the wall, so something was indeed hidden inside the cache. She'd been right to come check. Aspen pulled a tiny screwdriver from her uniform pocket, and quickly removed the screws holding the silver panel to the wall. Then she felt inside, brushing her fingers across the bottom.

It's still here! But could that infuriating woman have read it, then left it behind so we wouldn't know? wondered Aspen. *She probably can't read German or Russian, so the chances are she still can't know whatever the note says, even if she did think to look in here. Could she have photographed it? The Skipper had better kill her tonight just in case she has something to show the police. He should have warned me that there was a message or contraband on the very airplane that witch is flying to Zurich! I could have gotten it even before we took off. This is his fault entirely. Not that it will affect him. He'll be dead, whatever happens. But the trouble is, that beautiful gem will never be <u>my</u> diamond if <u>he</u> keeps making mistakes!*

CHAPTER FIVE

Lori stared at herself in the bathroom mirror of her hotel room inside Zurich's Kloten Airport. She decided she was still operating on adrenalin, because she didn't think she looked too haggard yet. She had gotten only two or three hours' sleep last night, and some of that was spent having a nightmare about a monster in mechanic's overalls chasing her through an empty airplane that was flying itself.

When the Swiss police checked the cache in the airplane, it was empty, so Lori was very glad she had photographed the note. *Who could have taken the note?* Lori asked herself. The police had looked for it as soon as the airliner landed.

Could it have been someone who flew in on the airplane, or could it have been one of the baggage workers or mechanics who swarmed around the aircraft as soon as it parked at the gate? It disappeared so soon, it was probably someone already on the aircraft. Was it Aspen? And whoever it was, had they any idea that I found the note, also?

Lori tried reading the translated words one more time. Leaning against the marble surface of her bathroom sink, she was wearing pajama shorts and a short sleeved pajama top. She was so weary, all she could think of was getting to bed, and sinking into oblivion after spending some 30 hours with only a couple of hours' sleep. She'd left a call with the desk to be awakened at six so she could get breakfast, and have plenty of time to get to the meeting with the TransGlobal Director of Operations. Surely he would take care of everything at tomorrow's meeting, get the bad guys all arrested, and puncture the huge balloon of fear and panic that Lori felt growing in her as she moved farther and farther into this horrible situation. She was an airline pilot. *I don't want to worry about anything more than weather fronts and fuel levels and baggage weights and engine performance*, she told herself.

The translated note had left Lori with more questions than answers. It was a series of instructions, along with a message that the writer wanted read to the largest Zurich television station. It began with general instructions, none of which Lori found easy to understand:

1. From Skipper to Purser: Have Co-Pilot meet Eric McEllen at the safe house in Istanbul Thursday at one p.m.. Give him a complete tour. Also take him to the house near the bridge over the Bosporus where we met with the Russians, and give him some small African stones as examples of normal merchandise. Explain deals we make with pilots who work with us.

2. From Skipper to Navigator: Have Engineer use a pay phone to call the local number of Zurich television station Schweizer Fernsehen SRF at two p.m. local time Wednesday, ask for the news desk in Swiss German, and tell the editor

to record the following message from the Armed Defense Brigade of the Siberian People. Read it first in Swiss German, then in Russian. Then get away from the pay phone quickly in case they can track the call.

Read to the television editor as follows: On Friday the Armed Defense Brigade of the Siberian people will carry out heroically the assassination of an American CIA agent who is assisting the Russian secret police in stealing a priceless gem ripped from the depths of the Siberian steppes. This monster has torn this national treasure away from the Siberian people to be displayed for the curiosity of the rest of the world in a foreign museum, and as a result of his callous greed the American CIA agent will die in the historic waters of the Bosporus in Istanbul Friday at the hands of the Armed Defense Brigade of the Siberian People. Two days later he will be joined in death, this time in Zurich, by the Commander of the Russian Secret Police who is assisting him in stealing the Star of Yakutsk from the Siberian people. And four days afterwards, the aircraft carrying away the Star of Yakutsk to be housed in museums in the Western World will fall from the sky, and be totally destroyed. The loss of this incredible Siberian diamond is tragic, but Siberian treasures may no longer be torn from Siberian soil for the entertainment of foreigners. Long live the culture and the fierce pride of the people of the Siberian heartland!

Lori had re-read the note three times. Reading the part about the airliner 'falling from the sky' caused a shiver to run through her body.

Was this message about a TransGlobal airliner? Was it about her airliner?! Are these guys smugglers or terrorists? she asked herself. *I certainly didn't see this coming! I noticed that evil man's accent, but thought he was just a hood. However, they're also talking about seducing a pilot into helping them smuggle! They seem to be both smugglers and terrorists! How crazy is this?*

And the airline job titles referred to in the note, like "pilot" and "co-pilot" must be aliases for gang members, she decided. *So the maniac who attacked me must be "Skipper" to his cohorts. And this Eric McEllen sounds like an airline pilot who wants to join the gang of smugglers. Too bad he sounds so new. He may not have even done anything illegal yet*, thought Lori with chagrin. *He'd be a much better source of information if he'd been involved with the other villains for a long time. I've got to get this note to the police who are going to be at the meeting tomorrow morning!*

As Lori wearily put the note back into her makeup case where she'd be sure to find it tomorrow, she suddenly froze, and focused on listening as carefully as she could. She thought she had heard the faintest sound from the bedroom area of her hotel room. She stood frozen and listened to the silence. Nothing now. She tip-toed to the slightly ajar bathroom door, and leaned out so she could peer around the corner into the room.

There he was! The man ... it had to be the Skipper, himself ... wearing the black, double-breasted uniform of a TransGlobal pilot ... bent over her luggage, systematically going through her things. He had a mop of black, curly hair and a moustache again ... just like he did in Istanbul. Lori felt panic well up in her until she thought she would burst. But she tried to think .... *She had to think!* She looked frantically around the bathroom. There were no weapons. The canister of MACE that had saved her before was on the desk top in the bedroom, much closer to the maniac than to Lori. Should she lock herself in the bathroom? But if he kicked in the door, she'd be totally helpless ... with no weapons at all. The last time they'd met, the man seemed completely intent on killing her. She felt sure he would come in the bathroom after her when he was finished looking through her luggage. He still hadn't looked up from her bag. He must have known Lori was in the restroom. Apparently, he felt she was trapped, and wanted to ransack her things before he attacked her personally.

The note! Maybe he knows I saw it, and he wants me dead! He just opened the last section of my bag. He'll head for the bathroom next. Lori decided getting a weapon was the best plan. She had to have a weapon!

She took a deep breath and bolted through the bathroom door. She ran directly at the large man, leaping over her shoes on the floor, almost on top of him when he suddenly looked up. Lori couldn't see his eyes because of the dark glasses he wore. But for a moment there was obvious surprise and uncertainty on the man's face, because his mouth dropped open beneath that black bushy moustache on his upper lip. Lori may have kept him immobile for an extra second or two, because she started screaming with all her might right in his face, and the burly brute even cringed backward. Lori grabbed the MACE canister from the desk, only a couple of feet from the man.

He let out a roar and bounded to his feet, his arms outstretched toward her. But Lori was no longer there. She had recoiled backward toward the bathroom, and managed to bounce off the door and into the small tiled room well ahead of the man. In fact, she had slammed the door, and secured the lock by the time he reached the door.

Déjà vu, thought Lori. *I seem to always be running into small rooms or airliner cockpits, and slamming the door on this monster! Only this time there is no radio to call for help. My cell phone!*

No, it's in the bedroom, realized Lori in horror. She had put it on the desk not far from her MACE canister. But she had been too busy grabbing the MACE to even think to get the cell phone, also.

The whole bathroom seemed to reverberate to Lori's shrill screams and the noisy slamming against the bathroom door. Lori heard splintering wood around the lock, and noticed cracks spreading across the mirror attached to the back of the door. The second blow made even more noise. Lori decided the maniac had turned to kicking in the door rather than slamming against it with his shoulder. There was more cracking and splintering, and the door pushed an inch or so into the bathroom.

Lori flipped the cover back on her MACE canister to prepare it to fire. *This is going to be Fyfer's Last Stand,* Lori thought. *But I know last stands never work out well for the standees. Even if I can get to his eyes with the MACE, in spite of those sunglasses,* she asked herself, *how am I going to get past him, and out of the bathroom? Lori hoped the answer to that question would occur to her in the very near future.* She tensed her muscles and dropped into a defensive crouch, staring at her own defiant image in the floor length mirror on the nearly destroyed door. This is the way she wanted to go down ... the defiant glare in her eyes as she braced her trim, fit body swaddled in baggy shorty pajamas alone with a murderous criminal in a Swiss hotel room, prepared for a fight she couldn't possibly win. She might die, but she was a wuss no longer.

What happened next occurred so rapidly it seemed like a blur to Lori, and when she thought back to it later, she could barely sort out what happened in the next several seconds. Lori's screaming and the battering of the door went on, as the Skipper kicked the splintered door again and again, and it finally swung open, slamming against the towel shelves. Lori pressed the trigger on the MACE canister, and it sprayed its noxious mist up toward the Skipper's massive head. However, he ducked barely in time, and his left uniform sleeve absorbed most of the spray as he blocked it with his arm. He reached out and grabbed Lori's wrist in a painful grip that turned the spray canister back at her. Her own face was in exactly the wrong place, and the immobilizing spray filled her own eyes. They squinted closed automatically, and she convulsed in pain as if a thousand needles were being plunged into her face and eyes.

But the cracking and battering of the door seemed to go on forever as Lori dropped hard against the bathroom floor, still trying to spray with the now empty MACE canister. Only now the noise in her head seemed to include deep men's voices yelling from every direction, along with more banging and crashing sounds. She even thought her own screams were still jangling around in her head, but she could no longer be sure.

Lori suddenly felt a man's strong arms beneath her body lifting her, then lowering her against a hard, smooth ceramic surface. It was the tub! She was now lying in the tub. The man was going to drown her! The crash of water from the shower overhead splashed hard against her face, and she gagged and fought for breath. The man was pulling on her eye lashes, pulling her eye lids away from her eyes! Was he going to torture her? The stinging pain from the MACE was intense.

She gasped and sputtered, and tried to keep screaming. But now the only noises she could make were gagging and gurgling and spluttering. And the pain was diminishing as her eyes were washed by the cold water cascading down on her face.

Then Lori realized that the water was gone, and the man was rubbing her head and face with a soft towel. He pulled her up to a standing position, and supported her there, as Lori felt her legs wobble like spaghetti. She clung to the pilot's black double-breasted uniform coat, and tried to hit him with one clenched fist. But she had no strength at all, and her fist just left damp marks on his coat. Then she realized that he was speaking.

"Glad I got in early tonight," he was saying. "It sounded like World War III going on over here, and I managed to get through the connecting door between our rooms ... doing a little damage on the way, I'm afraid. But I wouldn't have wanted to waste time banging on your hall door. That jerk was really giving you a rough time. Have I intruded into some sort of domestic dispute?"

"Domestic ... no ... no, not domestic," gasped Lori, still shivering. "I was being attacked. I'm so glad you intruded. Thank you!" Lori was staring up at the tall, lanky pilot towering over her. He certainly wasn't the Skipper, even though he wore the same black TransGlobal uniform complete with Captain's stripes. He was clean-shaven, though, and he had hair ... just not a lot of it. He wore it in a military style, clipped almost mirror over the sink, and she watched her entire body blush red. Her hair was wet and matted around her face, her eyes were beet red in the areas that had been white, and the silk shorty pajamas she was wearing were so drenched they clung to her body like a second skin, leaving her more naked-looking than if she'd been naked.

The tall pilot's eyes followed hers, and he obviously noted her embarrassment. "Uh ... here, let me help you get a little drier," he stammered, as he covered her wet pajamas with more towels. He gently released her, waited a second or two to be sure she could stay upright, and turned away. "I'll bring your bag in so you can find something else to wear," he said.

"But before you go," pleaded Lori, covering herself with more towels, "tell me who you are. I think you just saved my life." "Oh, I don't know about that," said the pilot. "Just glad I could help. Anyway, my name is McEllen. Eric McEllen".

CHAPTER SIX

I can't do this, Lori told herself, staring at the disorder in her recently invaded hotel room. *I need help. I run into a guy who I think is a hero, and he turns out to be another villain! I can't tell them apart! How can I identify these people and protect my passengers!*

She suddenly sat up erect on the bed. *Elsie Ponder,* she thought suddenly! *Of course. Elsie knows everybody in the airline ... well, almost everybody. Why didn't I think of Elsie before! And she can be researching this business while I'm flying! And I know I can trust her!* Then Lori hesitated. *Will she want to do it? Elsie's the busiest person in the airline. What have they got her doing now? She's in Europe. She's checking out internet ticket facilities. What country is she in? I think it's Norway. I wonder if we're in the same time zone? What difference does it make?! It's midnight here ... so it can't be worse, where ever she is!*

Lori got off the bed and found her global cell phone. *And in a way, she's already involved in this mess,* Lori told herself, trying to convince herself she was doing the right thing to disturb her old friend in the middle of the night. Elsie Ponder was the Purser ... the head flight attendant ... on Lori's momentous flight to Istanbul eight long years ago. She had allowed herself to be scraped and prodded on the same hot, sweaty marble slabs with her girls, and had visited Lori in the hospital before flying back to DFW airport without her. She had encouraged Lori when she was struggling to become a pilot, and had herself risen to become Manager of Passenger Relations for the entire airline in those eight years.

With a personality that never met a stranger, Elsie Ponder knew an overwhelming number of the airline's personnel by their first name. And in turn, she was an airline legend, herself.

But isn't she too old for me to drag her into this mess now? Lori asked herself guiltily. *I guess she must be middle-aged by now,* Lori decided. *But she's still young enough to have the best pair of legs in the entire airline,* Lori recalled, *and a smile that still warms the world. But I won't push if she sounds like she doesn't want to do this.* Lori found Elsie's cell phone number and punched in the buttons.

"Good evening, … err … Good morning. Uhh …."

"Elsie, this is Lori Fyfer. I'm so sorry to wake you up in the middle of the night!"

"Dearest Lori, is that you?" asked a happy but fuzzy voice.

That's Elsie, all right, Lori told herself. *So precise that when she gets a call at midnight she struggles to come up with the exactly correct response, and recognizes it's me seconds after rousing from the deepest slumber when she hasn't spoken to me in months. I should have called Elsie much sooner!*

"It's me, Elsie! I'm so sorry to call you in the middle of the night. Where are you?"

"I'm in Norway ... wait a minute; today's Thursday, isn't it?" asked Elsie, sounding more awake now. "Yes, I'm in Norway! But where are you, and how are you?" she asked, sounding more anxious now. "I love talking with you at any time, but midnight calls make me nervous. Are you OK?"

"No, Elsie, I'm not really OK. Do you have a few minutes?" *What a stupid thing to ask,* Lori berated herself, *after awakening Elsie in the middle of the night.*

"I've got all night, Honeybunch," Elsie assured her. "Lay it on me."

"I've met that maniac again ... the one who almost killed me eight years ago in Istanbul," began Lori.

There was only silence on Elsie's end, so Lori continued with the whole story. Elsie said very little as Lori told her tale, only asking terse questions now and then when Lori didn't include enough details.

"And that's where I am now," finished Lori. "Can you find out who this villain Eric McEllen is, and what's going on around here?"

"If he works for TransGlobal I can find out how he takes his coffee, and whether he wears shorts or briefs," Elsie assured her. "As for what else is going on; that may take a little longer. I've known that something is wrong with this airline for a long time. It has a dark side somehow."

"A lot of employees are not growing old gracefully. I mean, they're more and more anxious as they get closer to retirement. They have more than enough money. In fact, I'm amazed at how much they've managed to save. Some of them are just awash in money."

"But a large number of them are not happy folks. And a lot of them have ... have resigned early, and walked away from their really great jobs. Or gotten beaten up in bar fights or maimed in accidents or killed in other crazy ways. And a few have ... have actually *disappeared* down through the years. Just disappeared. More than I hear about through any other airline. This is a very unlucky organization."

"And I've heard so many whispers about smuggling, I think some of it has to be true. I don't know if your mystery has anything to do with all this other stuff or not, but it's all very ... well, very violent and mysterious and altogether very sad." "And yet you're still here," said Lori.

"I've been here since high school," said Elsie thoughtfully, "and had some wonderful times with people I'll always love. I don't guess I'll leave, if I have a choice. This is the only family I have, and I want to take care of it. You and I are both sitting in our beds alone tonight, aren't we? Where would we go?"

"You're a pretty good philosopher, old buddy," said Lori. "And I'm with you. We're going to find out what's happening in our airline no matter what it takes. If you'll start by finding out who Eric McEllen is, I'll attend the security meeting tomorrow, and find out what the experts are doing. I'll call you as soon as I know anything."

"By the way," said Elsie slowly, "do you remember Aspen Mohr, the flight attendant who flew with us in the old days? In fact, she was with us when you got hurt on that trip to Istanbul."

"I certainly do remember her," said Lori, feeling a chill climb up her back bone. "In fact, she's the purser on the flight I'm flying right now!"

There was a long pause. Finally Elsie said, "How strange. Several of the people who bailed out of the airline visited with her just before they left. None of them had anything to say about her, but I kept hearing that she had been talking with the people when they were last seen at work. I never asked her about it. In fact, I guess I haven't really talked to her once in all the years since that Istanbul trip."

"Since I'm already here, I get to sleep for a few hours "Well, I guess I'm going to talk to her soon to see if I can find anything out. I'll probably see her in Istanbul," said Lori reluctantly. "You know, she's always kind of spooked me somehow. I guess the spookiest thing was that I've never met anyone so focused on whatever they want that they'll do anything to win ... and I really mean *anything!*"

"I know what you mean," said Elsie. "Just thinking about her, I'm wide awake. And I'm getting out of bed right now! I'm due like a year of vacation time, and I can surely take a few days. I'll call it in to Human Resources at DFW, get my gear together, and catch the first flight out of *Gardermoen* here in Oslo. I should be in Zurich by early afternoon. I think we need to be fairly close together to support each other when we need to!"

"Since I'm already here, I get to sleep for a few hours," said Lori. She hesitated a moment, then added, "I know we're David, and the bad guys are Goliath several times bigger. But we're the good guys, so I expect to pull this off just the way David won his fight the first time around! Call me when you get here! See you soon, girl!"

* * *

On the same floor of the hotel, and only three doors down the hall from Lori's room, Aspen Mohr had just received a telephone call from the man known as the Skipper. He often called her in the middle of the night, but she never gotten used to it. She had once thought of it as exciting, as part of the mystery of the man. Now it enraged her.

"Yes, Emil," she answered pleasantly between clenched teeth. It was her only revenge.

"Stop using my name," growled the Skipper. "I won't tell you again! It's not safe."

"I'm sorry, Skipper," said Aspen, knowing that she could go only so far with this animal. "What is happening tonight?"

"I did not tell you before", he said, "but the Siberian activists will arrive tomorrow by Aeroflot from Moscow. We want the authorities to be aware that there are Siberian 'terrorists' in both Istanbul and Zurich. We e-mailed your room number to the two coming to Istanbul, and told them that you will bring them to a conference where we will all synchronize our plans so that our combined forces will be stronger and more effective. They didn't know anything about us, of course, but they will come because we sent them paid round-trip tickets, and they've probably never left Siberia in their whole lives. I'm also sure their own government pays little attention to them, so they weren't concerned about a trap of some kind. Russia has few worries about these harmless men. That is obvious by how easy it was for me to get them passports. They are country men, and would probably be flattered if their government would pay them more attention."

"And you say I'm supposed to bring these yokels to you?" asked Aspen.

"No, you will never see them," explained the Skipper. "They will both die on the escalator near the baggage claim area. We want the Turkish government to find them in their country and believe that they are involved in this affair. I'm just telling you this so that if they write down your room number or bring the e-mail, and Turkish police do come to your door, you'll know to claim that you've never heard of them."

"But I'm probably already suspected of some involvement in this affair," argued Aspen.

"I'm sure Lori Fyfer has told them about her switching bags with me in the Turkish hamam eight years ago, and the police will be very suspicious. They may even take me to the police station."

"All they can do is ask you questions," said the Skipper, his voice raised and hostile. "And you can answer them better than anyone in our organization. I have no one else to do this. I am calling you so that if some mistake is made, and these yokels do show up at your door, you can make them comfortable and call me. But you know how rarely my men make mistakes. You will not see these Siberian men."

"Unless Lori Fyfer is involved," said Aspen with a wicked smirk on her face that the Skipper couldn't see. "When she's around, everyone seems to make mistakes."

The Skipper slammed down his telephone.

CHAPTER SEVEN

TransGlobal Director of Operations Thomas Fitzgerald looked around the meeting room table, and began introducing people. He explained that the two nattily dressed FBI Special Agents on his left were experts in terrorism. The next attendee to Fitzgerald's left was a tall, older man with a large beak of a nose. His name was Inspector Ian Lodge, and he was from Interpol, the international police organization that spans the globe. He was also a terrorist expert specializing in European cadres. Pilot Claude von Schpritz sat on Fitzgerald's right, representing the airline locally. Two Zurich policemen in the grey uniforms of the *Stadtpolizei* were next, one of them older and heavier, and the other a burly young bull of a man.

And then there were the flight crew of TransGlobal Flight 4416 across from Fitzgerald ... all except Captain Jack Willow. Captain Travers and Lori were very aware of the empty seat between them, and stole questioning looks at each other as Fitzgerald introduced them. They hadn't seen Willow since the day before when they all had dinner and went to their rooms ... where Lori promptly got attacked by the villain who calls himself Skipper.

"Events continue to transpire almost faster than we can react to them," began a frustrated Fitzgerald.

"One inexplicable coincidence First Officer Fyfer has told me about is that the purser on her current flight is the same Aspen Mohr who was the flight attendant involved with the smuggler who nearly killed Fyfer eight years ago, and who introduced the entire cabin crew to the Turkish Bath, and Fyfer imagines that Mohr still is involved, eight years later. We have police agents following this woman to observe if she gets together again with this villain, the Skipper. If we can pick up both of these persons together, we might solve a lot of our problems in one move!"

"That we will do," Fitzgerald assured him, "Now I'm sure you all noted that there is only one TransGlobal Captain at the table this morning," continued Fitzgerald. "That's because Captain Willow called in sick yesterday," he explained with a frown. "We immediately replaced Captain Willow with Captain Eric McEllen who was on 'Stand-By' here at Kloten."

That certainly was convenient, thought Fyfer. *I wonder who arranged that?* But as Lori pondered how Eric McEllen became one of her crew, Fitzgerald continued as if there were no questions about that quick personnel change.

"First Officer Fyfer got to meet McEllen last night when this Skipper person somehow managed to get into her airport hotel room, and attacked her around midnight. He was apparently doing his best once more to murder her when

Captain McEllen broke in through the connecting door from his room, and apparently saved the day. This Skipper man seems to be able to pop up anywhere, and do anything he wants. I'm wondering if he flew from DFW in disguise on Fyfer's 777!"

"However," he added, shaking his head, "this all continues to get crazier, because First Officer Fyfer notified me yesterday as I flew here from DFW that she had found a contraband note in a hidden cache on her aircraft that implicated McEllen in the alleged smuggling activities of this man we are calling the Skipper. If McEllen has joined the smugglers, his introduction must have been a little awkward when they learned that he was the one who saved the person the Skipper was trying to kill!"

Fitzgerald continued to shake his head as everyone else at the table turned and stared at Lori. However, no one said anything, and Fitzgerald continued. "By the way, Fyfer," he said, "we still don't know how this man got into your hotel room last night. Apparently, he somehow got a key. I think I'm going to replace you, also, and send you home. This whole thing is getting too dangerous for you."

"Sir," responded Lori, "you forget that I'm the only one who has actually seen this man. Actually," she added with a slight smile, "I've seen him several times now in his different costumes ... and I might be a significant asset in catching this guy."

Fitzgerald stared at Lori for a few seconds, a frown on his face. "All right, Fyfer. Very courageous to want to stay on board after what you've been through. However, I'm going to ask Interpol to provide bodyguards from local police departments to stay with you all through the flight back to the point when you take off for home."

"OK, back to the note," ordered Fitzgerald. "A photocopy of the note is in front of each of you. Fyfer took the picture and left the original in place so the perpetrators hopefully don't know we ever found their note. An undercover officer entered the rest room about a half hour after the plane landed, and found the note gone ... so, it was picked up by someone, either just before the plane landed, or during the melee of offloading, on-loading and maintenance activities that took place just after the plane touched down."

"The first part of the note appears to be an introduction of McEllen to the rest of the perpetrators, and the second part is a script to be read to a television station in Zurich. It is written in both Swiss German and in Russian, and includes English translations we added ourselves."

"Crew Scheduling assures me that there is nothing special about Captain McEllen," continued Fitzgerald with another slow shake of his head, as if he couldn't quite believe it himself. "He was just the next pilot to be assigned. In hopes that the terrorists don't know that we intercepted their note, these gentlemen believe it best for us to keep Captain McEllen in this crew," said Fitzgerald, nodding at the two FBI agents.

"We'll be watching every move Captain McEllen makes," said the man with KIRKLAND, FBI written on a paper tag on his suit coat lapel. "You know the saying," he added with a smile, "Keep your friends close, and your enemies closer."

"I ordered McEllen to inspect his aircraft from nose to tail while we are in this meeting," said Fitzgerald, "since it is being held among 'need to know' people only, and he is not yet involved ... even though he apparently is, according to this note." Fitzgerald shook his head and stared down at the note Lori had found.

"In fact," allowed Fitzgerald, "he may have a better idea what we're talking about at this meeting than we do. It's very important that McEllen not be told that we found his name mentioned by the smugglers, nor that we found a note of any kind on that aircraft," he added with a stern glare at Travers and Fyfer. "No one here will tell McEllen or anyone else either in the airline or not part of the airline anything about the note we intercepted, or anything about this meeting," continued Fitzgerald, never taking his eyes off Fyfer and Travers.

"Sir," began Lori hesitantly, "I have already briefed one other airline employee on the events that led up to this meeting, and what it was to cover."

"And who is that?" asked Fitzgerald, his voice rising in a threatening tone.

"TransGlobal Customer Service Manager Elsie Ponder," Lori replied, in as even a tone as she could manage under Fitzgerald's withering glare.

Fitzgerald relaxed slightly. "Well ...," he said thoughtfully, "I suppose Elsie would be one of the least dangerous persons in the whole airline to have aware of this problem. In her job she certainly knows what this could cost us if the nature of this terrorist threat became public knowledge. How did you happen to tell her about all this?"

I can't believe it, Lori said to herself. *Even the Director of Operations for the whole airline knows Elsie by her first name!*

"She was my head flight attendant on that trip to Istanbul eight years ago when I was first attacked by this 'Skipper' man," said Lori. "And I thought she might be able to tell me more about Eric McEllen, and help me identify this smuggling gang."

Fitzgerald actually managed a small smile. "Why am I not surprised?" he asked. "So she was your purser. That woman always seems to be present wherever the action is."

He stared at the table for a moment, thinking. "You and Elsie may certainly ask around among our employees all you want to about any smuggling activities taking place inside this airline. Anyone who doesn't like it can call me! But you two are not policemen, and I don't want you investigating terrorism, or making comments of any kind to anyone in the airline or outside it about terrorists. It's dangerous, and it could cost us millions if the word gets out that terrorists might be targeting this airline!"

Lori wondered whether Fitzgerald was more concerned about losing living, breathing passengers, or about losing incoming ticket fares to terrorism.

Fitzgerald sat back in his padded leather chair, and looked around the table. "Gentlemen," he said, "I think we'd better attack this problem on two fronts. Customer Service Manager Ponder and Flight Officer Fyfer can delve into this smuggling question, while the rest of us begin planning our steps to fight terrorism. We'll continue calling meetings to discuss strategies as TransGlobal 4416 makes its way to Istanbul, Moscow, back here to Zurich, and then to the States. We'll keep Captain Travers in attendance, because his airplane is being threatened, and he needs to know what is going on at all times. And Flight Officer Fyfer may attend future meetings if she and Elsie have found anything out that affects our terrorism investigation. If it's just smuggling, she can talk with me alone. Are there any questions before I turn the meeting over to Inspector Lodge?"

While the others at the table looked at each other questioningly, Lori stared at Fitzgerald, thinking about what he had just said. *He doesn't even believe there are any smugglers,* she decided. *He thinks these evil people are terrorists, and he just wants to get rid of the two women in the group.*

Well, I'm glad he gave Elsie and me the smugglers, she decided. *I'm absolutely sure they're smugglers, and I'm not so sure they're terrorists. So, that works for both of us. But if they're also terrorists, I certainly hope he and these cops know what they're doing. It would be mighty scary to have to take my seat on the flight deck of 4416 flying back to the United States in a few days knowing only what I know right now.*

"I was not familiar with the Armed Defense Brigade of the Siberian People," began Inspector Lodge in a very British accent, "until I queried the Russian Federal Security Service ... the FSB ... which handles internal intelligence matters within Russia.

They say there is such an organization," he continued. "But they claim it isn't very large or very sophisticated; just some loud local nationalists who enjoy protesting against those who they think have insulted their beloved Siberian steppes. The FSB haven't even encountered any 'armed' terrorists from the group." A faint smile spread across Lodge's face. "I could tell the agent with whom I spoke was actually surprised that I had ever heard of the 'Brigade'."

"Well, they must be fairly sophisticated to come up with that cylinder of hydrogen cyanide," piped up the other FBI agent, whose paper tag read WALKER, FBI. "It's a two-threat device. It can explode if handled roughly, with more than enough 'bang' to bring down an airliner, and if released in even minute amounts, it will fatally gas everyone on the airplane in a few minutes." He looked down at a notebook in front of him. "It's a powerful insecticide that was also used in Nazi gas chambers, where it was called *Zyklon B*'. It's very deadly stuff, and not easy to obtain. We're assuming it was secured in the United States, since we found it as it was being sent from there to Zurich, where this terrorist attack is apparently being planned. We're looking into all sales of the substance, and any reports of thefts of cylinders. Even though we have the only cylinder of gas we know about, it's very likely they sent multiple cylinders to be sure they had at least one to do the job when and where they need it."

"I think we can forget about the use of *Zyklon B* as an explosive," said Inspector Lodge. "Activating it is too uncertain. It will surely be used by the perpetrators in some way as a toxic gas."

"But how will they introduce it as a gas?" asked Fitzgerald. "They can't activate it before take-off, because it would kill the pilots before they could get the airplane in the air. To activate it in flight, they'd have to have some sort of timer connected to it, because anyone doing the job manually would also be killed." Fitzgerald glanced across the table at Lori and Captain Travers. "Captain Travers and Flight Officer Fyfer, I know you both have to get ready for your flight to Istanbul in a few hours. The police officers and I will plan our anti-terrorism strategy now. I'll call you in your hotel rooms tonight, and let you know if we're going to meet in Istanbul tomorrow. In the meantime, if you find anything that might help us, call Inspector Lodge at a number he'll give you. And remember ... do not talk to Captain McEllen about any of this!"

"Yes, sir," said Travers and Lori simultaneously, as they rose and pushed back their chairs.

* * *

Lori and Captain Travers left the TransGlobal headquarters building at Kloten Airport, and both returned to their airport hotel rooms.

"See you in a couple of hours,"Lori called to Travers as she turned down her own corridor. They would actually be taking off for Istanbul in a little more than three hours.

As Lori headed toward her new hotel room, she passed her room of last night, which was now a locked crime scene. No one had yet been able to explain to her how the 'Skipper' had managed to enter her hotel room either last night or eight years ago, and she was taking no chances. Lori unlocked her door, drew her newly loaded canister of MACE from her coat pocket, and held it at the ready as she pushed the door open, and gazed around the room. The room was empty, and all seemed to be in order.

Suddenly her cell phone rang, shocking Lori. She shook her head slowly, willing herself to relax. Sinking down on the sofa, she raised the cell phone to her ear, wondering with dread if she might hear the Skipper's voice. If he could get her room number and somehow enter it, he could surely find her telephone number. It was Elsie. "Hello, Doll," Elsie began with an obvious yawn.

"You poor sleepy creature," said Lori. "You must be exhausted."

"I've been more chipper," Elsie said, "but I thought you might be out of your meeting, so I called to tell you I've solved the whole mystery. Are you ready to hear what's going on?"

"Yes, please, please, please!" said Lori.

"I was talking to Millie Banks in Kloten Operations this morning when an operation order came across her desk advising that the government of Russia is transporting via TransGlobal Airlines a huge uncut diamond they just dug up in ... you won't believe it ... in the diamond mines of Siberia! It's a blue diamond, according to the memo ... the largest raw, uncut diamond ever found; worth many millions ... and guarded by four armed guards who have just been approved to keep their firearms on the aircraft!"

"Wow!" breathed Lori in awe. "Wow!" she repeated.

"There is one confusing drawback," said Elsie. "The diamond is traveling on another aircraft, Flight 4427 from Zurich to New York City. However, it is taking off only two hours after you do on Wednesday afternoon from the same airport. So this has still got to be the answer to everything! Now, if we only knew whether we're dealing with smugglers who want to steal the diamond, or terrorists who want to blow up our aircraft because we're carrying a local treasure out of Siberia!"

"Why is nothing ever easy?" sighed Lori.

CHAPTER EIGHT

"Have you considered all the great opportunities an overseas airline pilot has to supplement his ... or her ... income?" asked Eric McEllen suddenly as he and Lori sat alone on the flight deck of Flight 4416. The two had been working together silently since Captain Travers had retreated to the Flight Crew Lounge to read his *USA Today*. It was a bright sunny day, and 4416 was soaring above the Apennine Mountains at 30,000 feet down the backbone of Italy en route to Istanbul. Eric's question jerked Lori out of her jumble of thoughts about diamonds and villains and dangers to her aircraft.

What is he planning to talk about? wondered Lori. *Diamond smuggling? Would he do that in a cockpit where every word is recorded on our black box? Of course, if we don't crash, probably no one will ever listen to it. But how does he know I won't turn him in, and have the authorities listen to our conversation as evidence?*

"What sort of opportunities, Captain?" asked Lori slowly.

"Please call me Eric. May I call you Lori? Business opportunities like moving goods around. Goods you are in place to analyze in Europe or Africa or Asia, for instance, and then are able to ship free to the States without going through customs, where you can receive them yourself as you move around the world at no cost. Wonderful situation!"

"Please do call me Lori." *What a con man!* she thought, *He must be in solid with the smugglers, in spite of saving me from the Skipper, and now he wants to recruit me into the program. How can that be, though? Does the Skipper think I might make him enough money that he could forgive me for getting in his way, or does he just want to lure me into a meeting so he can kill me? He certainly hasn't learned much about me if he thinks I'd work with him.*

The question is, Lori told herself, *can I lure the Skipper into a meeting where I can deliver <u>him</u> into <u>Fitzgerald's</u> arms? Maybe there's some way I can make it look like I can make money for that monster,* thought Lori, *so I can seem to become part of the gang, and end up finding a way to prove who he is and what he's guilty of.*

"What sort of goods were you thinking of, uh ... Eric?" asked Lori.

"Items you can obtain at very low cost in one place, and sell at a high price somewhere else," said Eric casually.

"By joining this airline you access a smuggling organization so good, all you have to do is obey some simple orders, and do some very simple "And without paying the duty in between," said Lori, managing to giggle a little. *But I'm not going to sit here and let him be coy with me,* she decided, beginning to feel a little angry. *When is he going to mention the 'D' word?*

"Were you thinking of something like diamonds?" she asked demurely.

"Oh, diamonds would be good," Eric replied with a smiling glance at Lori. "The cost of transportation is always critical in any business, and with diamonds it would be very small. Also, with all the business activity going on in Europe, Asia and Africa, obtaining them in the first place could be very inexpensive."

Lori could feel her face getting red. *Be careful*, she told herself. *Stay cool, or you're going to blow this whole thing, and maybe never get a chance to talk to this contemptable smuggler again.*

"By business and military activity, you mean all the gem thefts and smuggling ... and the shooting wars being fought in the areas where they dig up diamonds in Africa!"

Eric hesitated a moment. "Yep," he said finally. "But you can't worry so much about the moral element in such purchases. You may never know exactly where the diamonds come from. The only thing you can ever know for sure in transactions like that is whether the cost of the diamonds is low enough to make the deal profitable for you. And if you choose not to buy the gems, someone else will!"

"Well, I can see your point there," said Lori. "But the whole thing gets black and white fast when you start secreting contraband around your aircraft. . It doesn't matter to the authorities where you got the stuff; it just matters that you're trying to bring goods through customs without paying taxes. And I'm not interested in going to prison!"

"And who have you noticed going to prison, Darlin'?" asked Eric with a grin. "You've been around this airline off and on for the past ten years, at least, and you've never seen anyone indicted for smuggling. I can assure you that customs and the executives of this airline know next to nothing about the huge amount of contraband being transported right under their noses in this airline ... probably more than in any airline flying around the world today.

The employees cooperate with what they call the 'Association' headed by an old professional called the 'Skipper', and everybody gets paid, but nobody gets caught. That's probably the very best perk available, working for this airline."

"Please don't call me Darlin'," said Lori through clenched teeth.

Eric glanced again at Lori, and chuckled. "Smuggling ought to be promoted by Human Resources at hiring interviews. The Association will throw more money your way than you've ever seen in your entire life. You just can't afford to work for this airline," he concluded with a grin, "and not belong to the Association."

"So you work for this Association, and you're willing to talk about it like this while being recorded by our cockpit black box," said Lori sarcastically. "I don't think you guys sound so professional!"

Eric looked over at Lori, a smug look on his face. "I didn't say I worked for the Association," he said. "I'm just telling you about them. As a good friend, I want you to know all the opportunities available to you. However, it's been hard finding a convenient time for us to get together alone like this, so the Association enhanced the environment a little bit for me, which just shows you how efficient and professional the Association is. They ask you to fly very carefully today, because our black box seems to be broken. If we go down, the authorities will have no idea what was done or said up here before the crash. And no one will ever be able to decide whose fault it was that one tiny but essential wire somehow got disconnected from the black box. However, very shortly after we touch down at Istanbul Ataturk in a few hours I'm told it will be working perfectly again."

"And that," concluded Eric with an arm held high in a flourish, "is an example of why working for the Association is such a wonderful career opportunity!"

CHAPTER NINE

Lori was the first crewmember off the 777 after it taxied to a gate at Ataturk Airport in Istanbul. As she strode briskly up the ramp toward TransGlobal operations where she had to debrief after the flight, Lori called Elsie on her cell phone with one hand, pulling her luggage wheelie behind her with the other. Maybe Elsie could watch the rear galley to see if any mechanics showed up to work on the two black boxes located in the ceiling above the galley.

"Can you talk?" Lori asked when Elsie answered. "Tell me if you're in the process of pulling your luggage out of an overhead bin!"

"Nope. I'm just sitting in the rear of the aircraft watching everybody scramble to get theirs. But you won't believe what I've got! I was just getting ready to call you! I've been searching the company database on the whole flight from Zurich, and found four very interesting names of passengers, two *en route* from Moscow to Istanbul, and another two heading to Zurich."

"Interesting how?" asked Lori.

"Oh, my gosh," said Elsie suddenly. "I didn't notice the time! We may already be too blooming late! Two men, named Ivanev and Gorski, just landed at this airport from Moscow about twenty minutes ago. They're probably down at the Gate 10 luggage carousel right now. Don't you remember those names? They're on the list you showed me of Siberian extremists the Interpol guy at your meeting got from the Russians. They're here!"

"Listen!" said Lori. "Eric McEllen gave me a big sales pitch on becoming a smuggler while we were alone on the flight deck. I told him he was a fool to say something like that in the cockpit with the black boxes recording, and he told me the black boxes were disabled, and the Association would repair them in short order. I'm going to try to find your extremists at baggage claim, and then I've got to debrief at Operations. Would you watch for anyone to show up in the galley to repair the black boxes while I'm doing that? And please call Lodge to be sure he knows the bad guys are here from Russia, just in case the cops aren't as sharp as you are! I'll get back as soon as I can. And in the meantime, don't do anything dangerous!"

"You got it, girl. And you be safe yourself!"

It took Elsie another ten minutes to clear the ramp, and glance out the plate glass window at the aircraft she had just left on her way to the coffee bistro one gate down the concourse.

A TransGlobal maintenance truck had already pulled up under the 777, and two men in burgundy TransGlobal mechanics' jumpsuits were getting out of the cab. One of the men was a muscular blond, while the other was slender, with thick black hair and bushy black eyebrows. Both had tools hanging from their tool belts, and both looked legitimate in every way. Elsie glanced around the concourse first, then pulled out her cell phone and came to a complete halt in front of the window as she began taking photos of the two. No one else seemed to be paying any attention as the men climbed up the entry ladder where it joined the ramp, and entered the aircraft. *Gotta hand it to them,* thought Elsie. *They do move fast!*

Elsie got more and more frustrated as she flipped through the pictures she had just taken. *What good are they? I'm pretty sure they can't be blown up enough to read the numbers on the tarmac passes clipped to these characters' TransGlobal coveralls. I have to get closer for these pictures to be worth anything!*

Elsie retraced her steps back down the ramp, and into the aircraft she had just left. She knew the men had to be all the way back in the rear galley if they were working on the black boxes. *The road out of here is sure a long one*, she told herself as she glanced back down the long corridor leading to the exit door next to the cockpit, *and I sure hope I don't have to retreat all that distance at full speed with my life in my hands!"* She could hear the men muttering to each other as they worked in the galley ahead. She and the two men seemed to be alone on the aircraft. *Well,* she told herself, *I've never seen either of them before, so hopefully they have no idea who I am. Maybe I can make this work.*

The two men stopped talking as soon as she stepped into the galley. Both turned to stare at her as she held her tarmac pass up in front of them, then shoved it quickly into her top left blazer pocket.

"Hi, guys," Elsie said with a smile. "I'm with TransGlobal Public Relations. Let me get a couple of shots of you guys working."

"Just look natural, and pretend I'm not even here. I'll just take two or three pictures and then get out of your hair."

By the time Elsie had finished her greeting, she had already taken two flash pictures with her tiny cell phone camera. Both men still stood staring at her and the little cell phone. At least one of the pictures showed both men's faces and close-ups of the tarmac passes clipped to their overalls.

Are they wondering whether a PR photographer would ever take publicity pictures with a cell phone? Elsie anxiously asked herself. *I sure hope not."*

"Please, guys!" Elsie said to the two men, who were still standing transfixed. "I need some action shots. You were looking great! Just go back to working on whatever you were doing. OK?"

The slender man with the black hair frowned ferociously at Elsie. "No. You are not authorized," he said in a heavy accent. He stepped toward her and put on hand on her shoulder. "Who are you?" he asked gruffly, his other hand hovering vaguely above her ample bosom where her ID card rested in her blazer pocket.

He won't try for that card as long as he's trying to appear legit, reasoned Elsie.

"I'll be back with the flight line supervisor," claimed Elsie. "You fellows stay right where you are. This is very important. I need these pictures!"

What I really need is to get out of here, Elsie told herself, turning and walking rapidly down the aisle toward the cockpit. She forced herself to keep her rapid steps slower than a run, and not to look over her shoulder. With every step she took, Elsie expected to feel a hand grabbing her from the rear, but she kept going until she passed through the aircraft door and down the stairway to the tarmac below where she would have found the flight line supervisor ... had she intended to talk to one. At the bottom of the stairway, Elsie looked back up at the entryway to the airliner to see if she was being followed. She saw the mechanic braced against the doorway, pointing his own cell phone down at her.

Oops! I think I'm busted. Elsie dropped her chin and quickly turned away in hopes the mechanic hadn't gotten a shot of her face. She snapped a picture of the maintenance pickup that included its license plate, and broke into a run for the TransGlobal offices on the lower level of the concourse. *Thank the Lord*, she whispered to herself, *I managed to bail out of that airplane.*

CHAPTER TEN

After talking with Elsie and stuffing her cell phone back in her jacket pocket, Lori turned quickly to race to baggage claim, but collided with two Istanbul policewomen who had been standing right behind her. Both were taller than Lori, and built solidly. They wore navy blue uniforms, baseball caps with POLIS written across the front, and both were armed with semi-automatic pistols holstered at their waists. "Miss Lori Fyfer?" said the taller of the two, with a pronounced accent.

What have I done now? Lori asked herself automatically.

"Inspector Lodge say be with you," said the same officer, who seemed to be senior.

"You're the bodyguards Mr. Fitzgerald and Inspector Lodge arranged for me," exclaimed Lori. "Please ... come with me quickly. Quickly", she repeated, pointing down the concourse toward baggage claim. Waving her arm for the officers to follow, Lori began jogging toward the baggage carousels one level below. Her baggage carrier bounced along behind her as Lori pounded down the concourse. The two female officers looked at each other, then hurried after Lori. Travelers stared at the three women, quickly moving out of their way to both sides of the concourse. Lori wondered if the people they were passing thought the two officers were assisting her, or trying to catch her!

Thank goodness for these little black loafers, thought Lori. *I'd probably kill myself in high heels at this speed.* By the time the trio reached the escalator at the end of the International concourse, Lori was breathing heavily. *But I'm not more winded than these two very athletic ladies who are breathing as heavily as I am,* she thought with satisfaction.

People were travelling up and down the escalators to and from the baggage areas below in steady streams as the international flights arrived. *Where is that photo list Inspector Lodge gave me?* Lori asked herself as she frantically patted the pockets of her coat. She found it in her left inner coat pocket, unfolded it quickly, and began scanning the names and faces on it. *There's Ivanev,* Lori told herself as she studied the photo of a bald headed man with a full beard, and there ... just below Ivanev ... the picture was labeled Gorski, a much younger, rather burly man with a very short haircut and thick eyebrows. Still breathing heavily, Lori leaned against the railing and watched the travelers coming up the escalator toward her.

"Nope! They're not on the escalator yet, but ... there they are!" Lori cried aloud as she spotted the two men, both in suits and ties, approaching the escalator from the closest baggage carousel. Both carried bulky bags, which they placed on the escalator step in front of themselves, as they stood side by side on the step w and leaned against their luggage with one d and steadied themselves with the other on e handrail beside them. "Inspector Lodge" said one of the two Istanbul policewomen standing behind Lori. She pointed to Lodge and two other men in civilian clothes who had just entered the baggage claim area, and were walking quickly toward the two Siberians on the escalator.

Two TransGlobal pilots in black uniforms, and carrying chart cases, had stepped on the escalator immediately behind the two Siberians, and were now standing closely behind them. As the men were slowly drawn up toward the upper level where Lori was standing, she was trying to decide what to do.

But she decided the right thing to do was nothing. *Just let them go by and ignore them,* she told herself. *They're terrorists, and not for me to get involved with in any way. Fitzgerald made that clear enough. Inspector Lodge and the two men with him can take care of terrorists,* she decided as she leaned over the rail to meet the eyes of Lodge, who was just now getting on the bottom steps of the escalator, and looking up at her.

Lori looked up the escalator to where the two Siberians, with the two pilots right behind them, were nearing the upper level. She noticed the two pilots first glance at each other, then look down at their chart cases. Suddenly the two Siberians in front of them jerked upward, with the older man actually flinging his arms up, while the younger merely slumped sideways against the handrail. Then both men fell loosely down the escalator, slamming into the people below and creating an ever growing mass of bodies falling, tumbling and cart-wheeling down the moving stairway.

People on the down escalator stared in horror at the screaming and yelling mass of humanity falling over each other and tumbling down the escalator next to them. Both pilots had stepped to the side, and had clung tightly to the hand rails to let the men's bodies ahead of them fall past them. Now they reached the upper level and quickly stepped off the escalator to join the rest who had turned and stood staring down the moving stairs that had delivered them to the top.

The two policewomen standing with Lori wore expressions of bewildered horror just like everyone else, but the younger woman was the first to act. She had noticed movement on the front of one of the pilot's cases as he belatedly pressed a button on the case handle to draw the gleaming hypodermic needle back into his case. The two pilots had been immediately behind the two Siberians who were now sprawled motionless at the bottom of the escalator. The policewoman knew they must have caused the two men in front of them to fall by stabbing them with the needles being shot out of the fake chart cases. She put out a hand against the chest of the pilot nearest her, and she drew her automatic pistol from its holster.

The pilot pressed his chart case forward against the policewoman's torso, and pulled a trigger concealed in the handle of the case. A second needle popped out of the other side of the front panel of the case and plunged into her stomach. *The needle must be firing some sort of nerve agent into people's bodies*, thought Lori, who had also seen the needle explode from an innocent-looking travel sticker attached to the front of the pilot's leather bag. But before Lori could move, the pilot reached forward with his free hand and grabbed the policewoman's leather pistol belt, and threw her body forward down the escalator steps. The officer's body tumbled down the steps, cart-wheeled over the left-side hand rail, and down to the floor below. The second policewoman acted instinctively, and drew her weapon even before the first officer's body disappeared over the side of the escalator. But the pilot was even quicker.

    He grabbed the pistol in her hand, twisting it to point it away from himself, and with both their hands still on the pistol, yanked her forward down the escalator. As the policewoman fell, she fired two shots into space that exploded deafeningly next to Lori's ear. The officer slid down the stairs still strewn with bodies, some still squirming, and others lying still. She landed at the bottom next to Inspector Lodge, who was sitting on the floor, drawing his own weapon. The policewoman rolled over and grasped her right leg, a grimace of pain on her face.

CHAPTER ELEVEN

The elevated AirTrans train that provided transportation between all the airport concourses and the centrally located airport hotel had swooshed into its station on the second level of the concourse as Lori watched the two murderous pilots wrestle with the Istanbul policewomen. The train consisted of two trams joined together nose to nose, with hydraulic air pressure operating the two sliding doors on each tram.

Deafened and disoriented by the gun shots, Lori fell to one knee and turned left and right, trying to find the two murderous pilots. There they were, running toward the airport tram! She couldn't let them get away. *They know what's going on!* She kept telling herself.

The hydraulic doors on the two tram cars joined nose to nose on the track opened in a great swoosh. The people getting off the AirTrans had flinched as the shots echoed through the concourse, then dove back into the two tram cars, crouching down as low as they could behind the seats. Those who had been waiting for the trams piled into them and prostrated themselves on the floors, crawling as quickly as they could away from the violence.

The two men dressed as pilots started running toward the two AirTrans cars as the automated doors of both trams began closing slowly with a loud, drawn-out hydraulic swoosh. Both seemed to want to get as far from the officers on the escalator as possible, and they managed to run past the slowly accelerating tram on the tail end of the two connected cars. The first assassin was able to grab the handles beside the slowly closing door of the forward tram, and pull himself in.

The second man did the same, and both dropped to the floor, breathing heavily. Lori sprinted with all her might as she saw the two trams slowly moving faster away from her. She gritted her teeth and frantically managed one last burst of speed that brought her alongside the last car. She leaned forward, just as she had so many times trying to grab the baton on her high school relay track team, and she grasped the handle alongside the door of the last tram, and pulled herself into it and dropped to the floor.

The AirTrans must have been in their getaway plan all along, Lori realized, as she raised her head cautiously to look for the pilots in the AirTrans car ahead of her. Now if she could only stay hidden from the two men in the next car ahead until they got off, she could tell the police where they went.

The dozen or so people in the two cars lay anxiously on the floors of the cars, bouncing lightly as the AirTrans climbed long rises and dropped into low areas between buildings. They stared at the two pilots in the leading car, and Lori in the back tram, not sure whether any of the strangers wearing pilots' uniforms were involved in the violence on the escalator, or were just unlucky bystanders as they were. The shrill roar of the electrical motors beneath the AirTrans cars increased as the cars accelerated along the track to the next station.

The two pilots looked around themselves, holding their brainbags as if they were ready to use them, then walked back to where their car's rear-facing nose was connected to Lori's tram. Standing there, they glared through the glass windows at the passengers hiding behind seats and sprawled on the floor.

For the first time, Lori noticed that one of the pilots wearing dark aviation glasses looked familiar, and her heart sank. She tried to burrow into the floor behind the seat in front of her, but it was no good. The pilot with dark glasses was staring directly at Lori. A triumphant leer spread across his face. Then he took off his dark glasses, and Lori knew it was the Skipper. She wasn't close enough to see the golden fleck in his eye, but she recognized who he was.

Lori got to her feet and stood swaying as the AirTrans cars hurtled through the airport. She wasn't sure if she had decided to stand because the Skipper had obviously seen her, or because she just refused to continue quaking in front of this evil man. She kept her head high and her face emotionless as she slowly made her way among the huddled passengers lying on the floor all the way forward to the window in the nose of her car across from the Skipper's window.

From the smugglers' position in the rear-facing nose of their car to the dashboard of the last car where Lori stood, the distance was only some six feet. The two bouncing, clattering cars rumbled along the track, forcing both Lori and the Skipper to cling to the nearest seats and supports as they stood staring at each other.

The Skipper raised his brainbag to rest on the dashboard of his tram, and pointed the bag at Lori. Only one of the needles had pierced the red and green label on the leather front panel of the bag when he used it to kill one of the Siberians. He worked the mechanism in the handle so that the already used hypodermic needle was thrust out and back in several times. The needle projected from the left side of the front panel of the bag when it was extended, so Lori assumed, as apparently the Skipper intended her to, that there were two such needles built into the bag, one still rigged to fire when the Skipper was ready.

Apparently, just to be sure Lori understood what he was telling her, the Skipper took the brainbag from his companion, and showed her the two used needles which he extended from the bag. Then he returned that bag to the man next to him, and showed Lori his bag again. He pointed to where the unfired needle would pierce a small but colorful label showing the Egyptian sphinx on the front of his bag, then pointed his finger at Lori's stomach, ending the movement with a quick, hard stab toward Lori's midsection. The evil grin spread farther across his face as he continued to stare at Lori.

Lori kept her face emotionless. Her mind was frantically considering all the possibilities she could think of. The next station was only three or four minutes away. But there probably wouldn't be any security people there. Maybe just two or three more passengers, if that.

When the trams stopped and the doors opened hydraulically, there would be no place to hide from these maniacs ... no defense at all. She looked around her. Several of the passengers on her car were elderly, and there were more women than men. And none of the people on either tram looked eager to cross these two men in pilots' uniforms.

Inspector Lodge and the policemen with him knew where they were, but Lori had no hope they could get transportation to reach the next station before these two AirTrans cars did. The two men would do whatever they wanted and flee the scene before anyone would be able to arrive to help Lori.

Lori turned her head slowly to scan her own car and look past the two men in front of her to their car and the elevated track ahead of them. She paused for a moment staring at the Skipper's smug, grinning face. He obviously intended that Lori had only moments to live. She glanced down, and her heart leaped.

Below the window in front of her, there were several safety mechanisms. She knew that depressing the electrical button on the left would call the AirTrans supervisor in the airport headquarters, and that the device on the right was an emergency stop lever.

Lori weighed her options quickly. There were only minutes until the two trams would decelerate into the next station, and stop, and open their doors ... and then it would be too late, and Lori would die. Calling the AirTrans supervisor by pushing the button on the left would alert him to stop the trams anywhere he wanted. But even if he could keep the doors closed, and thus protect Lori until the police arrived, the bad guys might still break a window, climb in and stab Lori with one of those murderous brainbags, and disappear.

But if she hit the emergency stop lever, the same things could happen ... except that perhaps Lori could surprise the thugs in the car ahead of her ... and maybe Lori could escape before they could recover from the surprise. Lori knew she could run like the wind, and that decided it. Ever since she had noticed the emergency stop lever, Lori had kept her eyes moving, and she swept them around the two cars one more time. She couldn't let the Skipper have even an inkling of what she was about to do. This had to really be a surprise! She felt the two AirTrans cars slow as they climbed around a high point in the airport topography, then speed up as the trams swept around a corner between two buildings.

It was now or never! She lunged forward, pushing down on the Emergency Stop lever with all her strength, throwing it forward against the tram's dashboard. The two trams screeched to a halt like they had hit a wall, with showers of sparks shooting from the rails and the metallic scream of brakes grabbing rails deafening Lori.

The two cars were yanked from furious speed to a sudden stop. Even knowing what was going to happen and holding tightly to the tram dashboard, Lori was slammed into the dashboard by the enormous force of the sudden halt, and cracked her forehead on the hard metal surface. The people on her tram yelled and screamed as their bodies were thrown down the length of the car, some becoming airborne before crashing against the end of the tram next to Lori.

But none were as surprised as the two pilots in the other tram. Both of them had been raised off their feet and thrown violently backwards. The Skipper barely seemed to touch the ground as he flew backwards the length of his tram. The other man slammed against a seat about half way down the length of the car, was thrown across the aisle with great force, and then slid the rest of the way on the floor, crashing into the Skipper's body.

The hydraulic doors opened with a great swoosh of air as a dazed Lori staggered to her feet holding her bleeding forehead. She knew every second was precious. She had to get away before the two men recovered. She held on to a seat back next to the open door and tried to focus her eyes on the ground outside.

The ground was a good thirty feet below her. The trams were poised above a concrete street between two buildings. Most of the AirTrans track ran alongside buildings and through elevated concourses around the airport, but she had managed to stop the two trams high above a paved street!

Lori glanced through her tram and forward to the interior of the tram attached to hers. The Skipper was lying at the far end of the vehicle, unmoving. He had apparently slammed his head against the wall of his car, and his black curly wig lay on the floor next to him, exposing his bald head. The moustache beneath his nose was still attached, but askew.

The other man was on his hands and knees next to the Skipper, his brainbag nowhere to be seen. He grabbed the Skipper's brainbag with its one remaining unfired hypodermic needle, and turned back toward Lori. He staggered to the open door of his tram, pulling the brainbag with him. His face appeared at the door of the tram, swollen and splotched with darkening bruises and a bloody nose as he peered out of the door down at the street below. He turned to stare at Lori, some 20 feet away, and his expression was one of pure hatred.

Holding the deadly chart case in one hand, and favoring his right leg, the man pulled himself awkwardly out of his tram car, then back toward Lori by stepping gingerly on the rails beneath his feet, and grabbing parts of his tram with his one free hand to steady himself as he passed them.

The police should be here soon, Lori told herself. *But I need to wait for them as far away from these monsters as I can!* She turned and looked down the track away from the man pulling his way toward her. Lori stepped onto the rails, but cringed back against the side of her tram.

I have two free hands, though, she told herself, *and I should be able to pull myself along the track faster than that murderer by holding on to the side of the tram. But I hate heights.* Her breaths were rapid and shallow as she moved along the rail. *I'm an airline pilot, and yet somehow I'm panicked to be tip-toeing along an overpass thirty feet above a concrete road!*

Suddenly Lori heard a scream. She wrenched herself around to face the TransGlobal pilot making his way toward her, and saw him desperately trying to grab a handhold he couldn't reach with his one free hand on the side of Lori's AirTrans car. He let go of the handle of the brainbag, and tried to reach the next hand-hold with both hands, but it was too late.

As he fell away from the car into space, Lori leaned out trying instinctively to reach his hand, never thinking how quickly she would be yanked from her own perch if the man had managed to grab that hand. But the man in the pilot's uniform fell past her, and dropped to the hard concrete surface of the road below. He landed on his head and shoulder so hard it seemed to Lori that he bounced. His brainbag *did* bounce, and skittered along the concrete to land in trees alongside the road. And then all was quiet in the roadway below.

Lori stared down in horror for a second, then raised herself to see where the Skipper had been lying at the other end of the other AirTrans tram. He was gone.

* * *

Elsie grabbed her cell phone, and brought it to her ear as soon as it rang. She was riding in the back seat of an Istanbul police car following the AirTrans tracks looking for the two trams.

"There they are," she said in response to Inspector Lodge's questions on her cell phone. She could see the two trams parked on the elevated tracks above her, with passengers milling about the area. The Inspector was farther down the line, also looking for the spot where the AirTrans cars had stopped.

"Don't approach them," said the Inspector. We don't know the condition of the two TransGlobal pilots who escaped the escalator scene on the AirTrans" trams. You might be in danger." The Inspector was also concerned about the welfare of Lori Fyfer. He knew that she had been in close contact with at least two of the smugglers for some time, and he was very afraid that Elsie might come across Lori's body herself. He certainly didn't want that to happen.

"Inspector, said Elsie quietly. "I know where one of the murderers is located. I'm looking at his body right now lying on a concrete road where he apparently fell from the tracks up above. He's not moving, and I'm pretty sure he's dead. His brainbag is here on the road, also."

"I'm on my way," said the Inspector. "Don't touch anything."

Elsie walked slowly toward the body in the pilot's uniform, and the brainbag lying across the road. As she reached the body, she heard stealthy steps approaching her from the shadow of the elevated track stations nearest to her. A large, bulky man with black, curly hair and a black moustache that was strangely askew, and wearing a TransGlobal pilot's uniform stepped out of the darkness under the track and walked toward her. He was limping slightly, apparently had a terrible headache beneath the hand he held to the back of his head ... and he looked angrier than anyone Elsie had ever seen.

Elsie quickly walked over and picked up the black brainbag. It was dusty and scraped, and Elsie decided it must have dropped from the tracks above alongside the body of the man at her feet. The inspector had mentioned what the two pilots had done on the escalator, and Elsie knew this must be one of their weapons. She wondered if it still worked, or if it's internal mechanism had been broken by the fall. She could see where one of the hypodermic needles had been extended, and had broken off in the drop from the elevated tracks. But the other was still covered by the adhesive labels that had been attached to the front side of the brainbag. *With only one needle left, I have no chance of practicing with this thing*, Elsie knew. *It'll either work or it won't.*

Elsie held the bag by its handle, carefully avoiding touching the leather-covered button next to the handle. *That has to be what activates the mechanism inside that hurls the needle out of the bag,* she decided. *So I either drop this thing and run, or I attack him with it.*

"Lady" said the Skipper, who was now glaring at Elsie from some ten steps away, "I think you have something that belongs to me." He spit the words at her, and his face was now red with anger. He seemed barely able to control himself.

Elsie thrust the bag toward the Skipper, holding it in front of her. Her extended arms shook with the weight of the bag, which Elsie hoped was the only reason they shook. Her left thumb rested lightly on the leather covered button. *I wonder if it will take a light squeeze or a heavy squeeze,* Elsie wondered. *I'd better do it right the first time.*

"If you don't give me that bag," the Skipper said, "I'm going to take it away from you and stick the needle inside it in your stomach, and you're going to die!"

Elsie suddenly realized that the police siren she could hear faintly was getting closer and closer. Thank God for Inspector Lodge. "If you think you can take this away from me without getting stabbed, you'd better do it now", she said slowly, "because you don't have much time left!"

The Skipper raised his arms slowly as if to grab Elsie, and slowly stepped two paces closer. But Elsie didn't budge. *I can't hold this thing out toward him much longer*, she told herself as she watched the tremor in her arms increase.

Suddenly the Skipper turned and ran beneath the tracks and disappeared behind a concrete building as an Istanbul police car pulled up, and Inspector Lodge got out of the back seat. He sent the policeman who drove the car after the Skipper, and turned to face Elsie, who had lowered the brainbag, but was still standing there shaking.

"Was that the Skipper?" he asked. She nodded.

"You held him off with that leather chart case?" She nodded again. "Oh, my dear!" said the Inspector, stepping forward and wrapping his arms around her. He held her tightly for a long moment before releasing her and stepping back. Then he stood staring at her and clearing his throat, his face turning red.

"Please don't ever do that again," he said.

CHAPTER TWELVE

Lori was perched in front of a laptop computer surrounded by books and scattered pages of American newspapers in the tousled bed she occupied in the American Hospital in Istanbul. She glared at Elsie, who had just been passed into the room by the new Istanbul police officers arranged for by Inspector Lodge. "I shouldn't be here. I don't have a concussion!" she complained, raising her hand to feel of the butterfly bandage on her forehead.

"You know the rules for airline pilots who get big bumps on their foreheads" said Elsie. "Good thing, too. You could easily be dead after all you just went through!"

"And several people actually *are* dead," said Lori quietly, "including one of my police bodyguards, and I don't even know her name. Elsie, I don't know if I can handle any more of this horror."

"You should go home," said Elsie. "This isn't what you're trained for or used to. Mr. Fitzgerald understands that. That's why he told you to go home!"

"But I'm closer to this than anybody else, even if I don't want to be. There might be something I can do to save lives," said Lori slowly and quietly. "Look at these English language newspaper stories. All of them are reporting on terrorist attacks on American property in Istanbul by Russian extremists.

They barely mention the diamond except to say it's the reason for the terrorism. But I don't think that's what's going on. I think these people are smugglers, not terrorists. Yet ... yet, why are they killing people?" asked Lori with frustration. "For a gigantic diamond," said Elsie, but without conviction. "But how does killing people help the smugglers get the gigantic diamond?"

"Well," said Elsie, "maybe I've got the answers to your questions without even knowing it. I come bearing evidence."

"Really?"

"Yep. Just got back from Inspector Lodge's office. The first stuff he gave me was initially uncovered by ... me," she concluded with a grin. "One of the two mechanics I caught working on the black boxes on your flight was legit, and works for the TransGlobal maintenance office. He even had a work order to check the black box written by the maintenance supervisor, who said it was just time to replace the boxes ... he says. But the other one, the skinny kid with the black hair, doesn't exist, according to maintenance records, and he's disappeared. Yet, the first mechanic says the fake guy is legit, he just doesn't know him well, and doesn't know where he is right now."

"The photo I took of the number on the fake guy's tarmac ID was that of an ID destroyed here at Ataturk because it was damaged when printed, according to the lady who issues the ID's for TransGlobal. The license on the maintenance pickup I photographed under the airplane identifies it as a vehicle that was sitting at the maintenance office all day ... or so says the maintenance supervisor."

"So, all we know so far is that a lot of legitimate airline people are involved in this affair. They're in it for the big money they get for doing almost nothing, and because the really bad guys do all the really dirty work, and the airline folks are trying their best to cover for the bad guys and themselves. I'd say that when this is all investigated completely, the jails are going to be full, and this airline is going to need a ton of new-hires."

"Oh, and about the two dead Siberians who got skewered by brainbags on the escalator," added Elsie, "they were fresh in from Russia, all right. But neither of them had any sort of weapon on him. They both just appeared to be tourists, although those dress coats and ties they wore suggest they were here for a meeting or conference of some sort."

Has Lodge come up with anything on the pilot who got killed falling off the AirTrans overpass?" asked Lori in frustration.

"Well, if the pseudo pilot were still talking," replied Elsie, "he'd probably have as thick an accent as the rest. His body was covered with Russian gang and prison tattoos, and Inspector Lodge found an instruction sheet in his pocket from 'Skipper' to 'Purser' with pictures of the two Siberians, and instructions to kill them and escape on the AirTrans."

"Apparently no one was supposed to notice the hypodermic needles or see them stab the Siberians. They were just supposed to get on the AirTrans and calmly ride to the airport hotel. The cops also found a car registered to a Yurii Tamisov – that's the 'Purser' – in the hotel parking lot. They've also got an address in the hotel, and are investigating that now."

"If the code names mentioned in that message you found from the Skipper ... Co-pilot, Engineer, Navigator and Purser ... were all the professional thugs the Skipper had working with him, then he's down to only three henchmen left ... Copilot, Navigator and Engineer." Elsie hesitated, then added, "There is one more piece of evidence. The pilot who fell had a sheet of paper on him with some kind of a schedule on it. It was all in Russian, which Inspector Lodge is having translated right now. He's supposed to scan an English version and e-mail it to me any time now."

"Well, tell me about those brainbags with needles coming out of them!"

"The chart cases with needles look like the chart cases all pilots carry that allow the thugs to walk around in airport uniforms armed with deadly weapons that nobody pays any attention to. Do you remember the spy who got killed in Europe back a few years ago by being jabbed with a needle on the end of an umbrella?" asked Elsie.

"Same idea, just more sophisticated. The cases are standard, 'made in America'. But the metal framework inside, and the machinery that fires the needles is suspected to have been made in Russia." Elsie raised one palm toward Lori and shook her head. And I have no idea how Lodge decided that."

"My head's spinning," said Lori. "So what's actually going on here?"

"I think we're somehow fighting Russian spies for a big diamond," Elsie suggested. Rolling her eyes, she added, "And we're about to head to Moscow, where we'll be totally outnumbered and on their turf."

"What are the police doing about that note I found on the airplane about assassinating an American CIA officer tonight somewhere along the Bosporus?" Lori asked.

"Well, I guess the whole world is waiting and watching," Elsie said with awe in her voice. "That note you found was read on the Zurich radio last night exactly like the version you brought us, and then it got picked up by the media around the world, and big time in the States. Now everybody is waiting to see what happens. It has everything to make it exciting -- CIA operative facing death from unknown terrorists along the mysterious, exotic banks of the Bosporus River."

"And I imagine half the Istanbul police force is going to be stationed along the banks of the Bosporus tonight," Elsie added. "It would be embarrassing to have a murder take place a day after the police are notified who is going to get killed and where it's going to happen, and then have the whole world watching. And even worse, for it to be a CIA officer! Which, of course, actually makes it even more mysterious, because according to Inspector Lodge, the CIA says it doesn't have any agents in Istanbul. That's probably a lie, of course, and the Turkish government knows it, so nobody trusts anyone else, and everyone is just hoping to get through tonight on the world stage with their dignity intact. Whatever happens, the whole world is talking about a huge diamond no one knew existed yesterday ... the Star of Yakutsk, as well as the terrorists who are killing people because of it."

"Exactly how huge is it?" Lori asked.

"No one has said, since it's a raw stone. I don't think they even measure it in carats until all the foreign material is scraped off, and it's cut in its final shape. You know, if I were the Russkies, I'd have some other airline transport the diamond after all the publicity and the violence against TransGlobal because of it. Yet, they seem to think that it would be the same no matter which airline was transporting it, so nobody asks many questions."

Lori concentrated thoughtfully on Elsie's laptop open on her lap. "Elsie, you mentioned that these spies ... or smugglers, or whoever they are ... seem to prefer to smuggle diamonds above all else. Why is that?"

"Well," said Elsie, "they're small and easy to hide, and there's probably nothing else worth so much by the pound or the inch as diamonds."

"And you were going to find out where they can get diamonds."

"I did," said Elsie. She ticked off each location on her fingers. "They come from India, Brazil, Australia, Russia, Africa, and the US."

"Forget the US," Lori said. "That's where people can most afford to buy them, so that's where they'll be smuggled *to*, not *from*. And forget India and Australia and Brazil. That's the other side of the world from this smuggling operation. It's probably also going on there, but probably not by these guys. Tell me more about Africa."

"Forty-nine percent of all the world's natural diamonds are found in central and southern Africa."

"But TransGlobal only serves the largest urban centers," Lori said. "We fly into Cairo in the north, and Capetown in the south, but hardly anywhere in between."

"That's where our regional airline partners like AfricanAir come in," Elsie explained. "Little two engine prop planes that carry a dozen or so passengers each."

"OK, we're in Istanbul," Lori replied. "These books say that Istanbul has been the center of smuggling of African and Asian goods going to Europe and the United States for centuries. How many of these regional flights connect with Ataturk airport, here in Istanbul?"

"Some three or four a day," Elsie said. "The regional guys are parked down at the very end of the International concourse. I don't know exactly where they come from, but I called an old buddy who supervises their maintenance. He used to be stationed at Zurich, but got a promotion four years ago to come here. He says he's the TransGlobal expert", she added with a grin, "on the 'low and slow' parts of the airline."

"The only problem is that if this guy is a buddy of yours, I imagine he's as honest as President Abe was. He's not going to know anything about terrorists or diamonds or anything shady."

"He's a rough old codger with a heart of gold, all right" said Elsie. "But he runs his gang of mechanics like the military -- which is where he comes from -- and he can't stand inefficiency … which is all he wanted to talk about when I mentioned AfricanAir!"

"What do you mean, inefficiency?"

"Well, he kept describing how inefficient the refueling guys are. The fuel group is a different organization entirely. Hershell … my buddy … kept telling me how they fuel those turboprops twice every time before using them. Doesn't make sense to him. In fact, it drives him crazy. He can't figure out why they can't get their act together."

"Can you check with him now?" asked Lori. "This is the only afternoon we have left before we head for Moscow tomorrow morning. We still don't have anything, and Flight 4416 and 4427 depart Zurich for the US Tuesday afternoon. I feel sure Fitzgerald intends that we take off Tuesday for the States unless we know some good reason not to -- and I don't have one -- unless this business about the AfricanAir turboprops is somehow worthwhile."

"We do have the threat you heard the Skipper make in the cockpit back at DFW when he thought you were sure to be dead in a few seconds, and we did find a canister of poison gas on the aircraft," Elsie pointed out.

"I think Fitzgerald will search our airplane from stem to stern, then have us take off for the States if he doesn't find anything," Lori said.

"Will you fly 4416?"

"Yep," said Lori. "If I don't have a good reason to tell my passengers to stay away, then I don't have a good reason to stay on the ground, myself."

"Sounds like you've been thinking about this," said Elsie.

"Just every waking moment of the last few days."

At that moment Elsie's cell phone emitted a chirping sound. "This may be that evidence they found on the Russian hood." She began tapping buttons. She nodded at Lori as she listened, then said "Gas ... like in 'gasoline'?" In a minute, however, she looked even more confused than before, and began writing something on the napkin on the tray beside Lori on the bed. "Thanks," she told the policeman she was talking to. "Thank you so much!"

Putting her hand over the telephone speaker and turning to Lori, Elsie said, "Nothing interesting among his possessions except a notebook in his shirt breast pocket."

"It's a list of dates and times and names, and I've got it all right here," she said finally, scanning her cell phone face. "Several lines with the Russian word for 'gas' on each line. Then dates ... the dates go on for months ... and the names aren't Russian, but they're not English, either. There are only three names listed among all the dates and times -- Moloobi, Ganesh and Olamoot. Here's one for today. It says 'gas' dash, 'Moloobi' dash, then today's date, and the time 6:47 p.m., which is three hours or so from now."

"What's 'gas' all about, and could the names be places ... or maybe people?" asked Lori thoughtfully. "I've never heard of any of them. I'll bet they're people! Elsie, can you check the rosters of this airline for any of those names?"

"Even as we speak," said Elsie. Then she frowned. "It should be faster if I just give the names to Samantha Arnold, and let her check them on her PC." She punched in a number on her cell phone, then said, "Hey, Sam. This is Elsie, and I'm down in Istanbul! Would you do me a quick favor? I'd appreciate it, girl. Would you try to find these names in our system?" She carefully spelled all three, then grinned and replied, "Yep. Easier than trying to pronounce them."

A full minute went by before Elsie looked up at Lori with disappointment on her face. "Did you try all the different employees in the whole system?" she asked into the cell phone. "Right, wait a minute... please look at our associated commuter airlines, as well ... like AfricanAir ... Pilots, mechanics, secretaries ... everybody." With a smile on her face, Elsie added, "I know, girl. I'm going to owe you big time!"

Now the smile spread across Elsie's face, and became a howl! "Yes," she exclaimed! "Sam, please e-mail me the head shots of Moloobi and whoever his co-pilot is! I'll talk to you soon. Come up with something that we'll both love, Sam, and can do together. It's all on me! I haven't seen you in months! Bye, girl! I'll get back to you soon!"

Still grinning, Elsie turned back to Lori. "They're all three Captains for our commuter airline AfricanAir. They fly those little twin turboprop Beechcraft KingAirs that serve the smaller airports in Central Africa, and carry about 15 passengers at a time to the larger TransGlobal airports that connect with the rest of the world. AfricanAir has a fleet of some twenty airplanes. Just pilots and copilots on each one ... no flight attendants, unless the co-pilot is willing to go back and pass out sandwiches," she added with a grin.

"Check the AfricanAir schedule -- please!" asked Lori, who was beginning to get excited. "Are any flying into Istanbul this afternoon, and are any of those three pilots on the airplanes?"

"Bingo," said Elsie finally. "Moloobi's going to drop in. And guess what time! 6:47 sharp!

"Elsie!" cried Lori as she pushed back her bedding, "Get me out of here! If you have to, tell the doctor I want to sign myself out. But use that only if nothing else works. It might get me in trouble with the airline, and I might not be allowed to continue on 4416."

An hour later, Lori was again wearing her uniform, and sitting with Elsie in the back seat of a police car racing through heavy traffic toward Ataturk Airport. The doctor had been willing enough to sign her out after a night in the hospital, but just finding him to get his approval had taken the rest of the afternoon.

The Istanbul police had increased Lori's attending officers to four after one of their policewomen had been killed on the airport escalator. Inspector Lodge had told them that she was involved in the terror investigation along the Bosporus, and they agreed to take her where she needed to go as long as their officers went with her. The traffic was intense and chaotic, but it seemed to open up for them like the Red Sea as the police car sped through Istanbul, it's siren blaring "dee-dah, dee-dah" as it raced toward the airport.

CHAPTER THIRTEEN

The sun was setting in a red haze above the Bosporus River when Lori and Elsie arrived in a police car at the airport. Darkness had settled on Istanbul by the time the group had entered the vast terminal. The AfricanAir commuter should have landed ten minutes ago. The two women ran down the nearly deserted International Concourse with the four Istanbul policemen now assigned to them at their heels. Lori guessed that the more fatalities there were among the officers assigned to guard her, the more would be assigned ... in spite of the huge draw of officers watching the streets along the Bosporus ... and she welcomed every one of them. By the time they reached Gate 8, the aircraft sitting at the gates were smaller turboprop aircraft like the AfricanAir Beechcraft KingAir they found parked below them at Gate 4.

"Can you find a second spot from which to view what's happening on the tarmac at Gate 4?" asked Lori of the senior policeman.

"Okay. We go down past Gate 4, and we look back," said the officer. "And we have your number, as you have ours," he added, as he pointed to Lori's cell phone. He and the other officer turned and ran toward Gate 3. The senior policeman carried a pair of large gray binoculars, and the other cradled a video camera against his chest as he ran. The two policemen who stayed with Lori and Elsie were equipped the same way. The concourse in which they stood was well lit, but the tarmac below was ablaze with flood lights, so Lori didn't feel conspicuous as they gazed down at the silver KingAir parked below them.

All was quiet on the tarmac. Whatever passengers there had been had all de-planed and gone through Customs, including the two crewmen. Nothing moved on the tarmac for nearly a minute as the women and the police officers all stood watching at the plate glass window.

Suddenly, a squat little fuel truck came into view driving alongside the concourse. It was exactly on time to refuel the aircraft for its early take-off tomorrow morning. Lori turned to the policeman with the auto-cam and asked, "Can you get where you can photograph all this without being seen?" The officer nodded, and knelt behind a plush leather seat, then aimed his camera at the tarmac below. The others moved back from the window, finding as much cover as possible among the furniture and foliage and advertising signage that lined the concourse. *These policemen are acting like I'm the police chief,* thought Lori. *I wonder exactly what Inspector Lodge told them when he asked them to take care of me. They seem to think I'm a terror expert; maybe that I'm undercover as an airline pilot!*

There was movement on the first floor of the terminal building below Lori and Elsie and the two policemen. Two men in khaki uniforms casually walked toward the aircraft, where they stood watching the refuelers. "Those have to be the AfricanAir pilots," Lori told Elsie.

The driver and his assistant both got out of the fuel truck, and began uncoiling a long three inch diameter hose that reached from the tank of the truck along the concrete tarmac to the wing of the KingAir. The hose was attached to the underside of the wing by one of the men, and twisted, to secure it in place. The refueling technician then pulled down on two levers on both sides of the hose to lock it into place attached beneath the wing. Then both fuel technicians walked back to their truck and climbed into the cab. The driver adjusted something on the truck's dashboard, and both men seemed to sit back and relax, apparently waiting for fuel to fill the gas tanks in the wings of the KingAir.

A TransGlobal pickup truck drove up to the KingAir aircraft and the tanker down on the tarmac below. Eric McEllen got out of the cab and walked over to the two AfricanAir pilots. The two black pilots both wore semi military uniforms that consisted of khaki bush jackets and pants, and both wore burgundy berets on their heads. One stood and talked with McEllen while the other climbed into the KingAir's cabin.

"Must be going inside to check the level of fuel in the KingAir's wing tanks," Lori told Elsie and the policemen. "They should be full about now", she added softly. Lori blushed as she realized she was almost whispering. After all, McEllen and the two AfricanAir pilots couldn't have heard her through the plate glass observation windows even if she'd been yelling.

The AfricanAir pilot in the airplane appeared at the door, and climbed down to the tarmac. First he, McEllen, and the other pilot all walked to the fuel truck and seemed to study the controls on the side of the tank while the refueling helper disconnected the hose from the wing of the KingAir. Then they climbed into the cab of the TransGlobal pickup truck, and started the engine.

The tanker truck pulled away first, closely followed by the pickup. Lori was surprised. She had expected some sort of exchange of diamonds or other contraband among the men on the tarmac below her. As she watched the fuel truck pull away from the airplane and drive across the tarmac along the concourse toward the maintenance offices, she wondered, *What are they doing? No one has removed anything from the airplane.* Were the smugglers leaving the airplane behind with the contraband in it?

"Let's check out that airplane," said Lori. "Can anyone here act as lookout to warn us if they return?" The policemen would be best at doing that, she decided, but both were looking at her with blank faces. "Tell me," she said to them, pointing at herself and raising her voice a little, "if truck comes back! Stay here," she added, pointing at the floor, "and watch!" How funny, she realized, that people trying to converse with those who speak a different language, always raise their voices, as if that would help understanding.

"Okay," finally replied the senior officer. "But this police officer go with you!"

"Okay ... thank you!" agreed Lori, as she turned and ran down the concourse with Elsie and the Istanbul police officer just behind her.

They found an unlocked door that looked like it would lead in the right direction, and pushed through it. They made so many missteps through different doors and down various short corridors that Lori wondered if they'd get to the tarmac before the AfricanAir pilots returned ... if they were going to return. But finally they opened a door that led outside. The AfricanAir regional passenger airplane stood some 20 yards away, and was still unoccupied.

Lori and Elsie and the police officer all searched the aircraft from tail to propellers. Nothing. They opened all the baggage areas, felt under seats and carefully examined all exterior features. They had to be smuggling contraband. Probably diamonds. Everything pointed to it.

Finally Lori climbed into the command pilot's seat and began searching both seats and the floor beneath them, and all the niches and shelves around the control panels. She had to look at everything and get out of this airplane before the pilots returned.

In fact, she was moving so fast she almost missed it. Her hand stopped in mid-air over the fuel tank readings on the console. She flipped from the reading on the left wing tank to the right wing tank. They were both empty! *The instruments say they're totally dry!* she told herself in amazement. She sat in the pilot's seat and just stared ahead.

They were just refueled, but these fuel tanks are empty, she told herself.

They don't even contain the half-a-tank loads they should have come in with a few minutes ago. That means the fuel truck must have removed fuel, not added it! If they came in with the requisite half-tank or so, then that half-tank was siphoned into the fuel truck. And what else came with it?

Lori didn't know enough about fuel trucks to know whether the bottoms of the fuel trucks' tanks and the aircraft fuel tanks were flat or rounded down to the fuel holes in the bottoms of the tanks. Could they be rounded so that all small objects inside slid to the fuel hole in the bottom as the fuel was removed, or could they be modified to that shape? Lori decided the answer to that question had to be in the affirmative.

"Let's get out of here!" called Lori to the officer and Elsie, who were still searching the passenger cabin of the aircraft. "The tanks are empty. They've smuggled diamonds or whatever into Istanbul, drained the tanks and the diamonds into the fuel truck, and driven off to inspect their loot! We've got to find where they went."

Then Lori cried, "The tower! Maybe they'll let us look around the airport for that little fuel truck from above. Officer, if you can get us into the tower, we may be able to discover where it went. Leave everything here looking the same! This KingAir is supposed to fly out of here tomorrow morning, so I'll bet that fuel truck will be back here sometime tonight to actually fill this airplane with aviation gas. And for the second time, Elsie, as your buddy in maintenance would say. Come on, guys, let's move!"

The Ataturk tower was adjacent to the International Concourse, so the two women and the policeman ran from the AfricanAir aircraft along the tarmac beside the International Concourse to the tower entrance. The entrance door to the tower was locked, but the Istanbul officer punched a button on the security panel next to the door, and a voice queried them in Turkish. The officer yelled something in Turkish at the panel, then listened for a moment to the reply, then yelled into the panel again.

H*e certainly sounds authoritative to me,* decided Lori. *I'd let him in.*

In a few minutes a dark Turkish face appeared in the small glass window next to the security panel and stared grumpily at the officer for a few seconds before the man opened the door. There were a few more seconds of grumbling before the man stood aside, and allowed them entry. Lori raced for the elevator, and stood at the back as the group all filed in and faced front. In just a few seconds the elevator doors opened, and Lori waited as the others moved into the open, spacious office surrounded by plate glass windows that looked out on the well-lit airport and the dark neighborhoods that surrounded it. Dividing the darkness to the north was the hazy ribbon of reflective light that was the Bosporus, the river that divided Europe and Asia.

Since Lori knew that all official aviation conversations around the world had to be in English, she expected she'd be better able to converse with the tower controllers than she had with the police, and they quickly proved her right. A buzz of conversations ... all in English ... emanated busily from the desks arranged in a huge circle around the room. Not a man or woman looked up or interrupted their chatter as Lori and the other visitors walked in.

A bushy-haired man with horn-rimmed glasses and a bow tie who seemed to be in charge of the tower's air traffic controllers spoke first in Turkish to the Istanbul policeman with Lori, and the officer responded in the same language. As he spoke, the policeman made sweeping hand signals toward Lori that looked like he was introducing her. But it was his last remarks that earned the greatest reaction from the tower supervisor. The man's eyebrows rose, and he raised his heavily-rimmed eyeglasses to rest in his bushy hair as he stared unaided at Lori. "This has to do with the anti-terror activities that are going on along the Bosporus?" he asked in English. "I'm Ahmet Tamuk. How can we help you?"

"A fuel truck just refueled an AfricanAir turbo prop aircraft at Gate 4 on the International Concourse. It has a red cab and a cylindrical silver tank with red lettering in Turkish along both sides of the tank. Do you know where the refuelers are headquartered that serve AfricanAir? The truck drove away, and we need to find it as quickly as possible!"

Mr. Tamuk looked around the circular room, then called to two men from one area, and another from across the room. He spoke to them in Turkish, and they all picked up binoculars lying on desks around the room, and began searching the airport tarmac on all sides. The one studying the International Concourse was the first to turn back to the Supervisor and speak in Turkish to him. The supervisor waved to Lori, and pointed down to the International Concourse below. "There he goes," said the man. "He's already back at Gate 4. He must not have refueled the AfricanAir flight completely the first time."

"As soon as that aircraft is refueled," the man added, "it will be taking off."

"It's going to take off tonight?" asked Lori. "I didn't think it would leave until tomorrow morning."

"I just got a proposed flight plan from TransGlobal operations," replied the tower supervisor. "They're requesting a short flight away from the city to test some of their aircraft's flight characteristics. Apparently the aircraft received minimal repairs here at Ataturk right after they landed this evening from the Sudan. Something must have been giving them trouble on the flight. They'll just take off in a few minutes to fly over unpopulated areas for a quarter hour or so to try different maneuvers to see if we cured their troubles so they can fly back tomorrow morning."

"Mr. Tamuk, what areas do you think they'll fly over?" asked Lori, a dark premonition suddenly occurring to her. "Oh, he'll probably fly low over the Bosporus toward the west out over the Mediterranean, and back. Most of our land areas here are heavily populated. The Bosporus would be the safest area to overfly in this neighborhood."

"No wonder they weren't afraid of alerting the police that they were going to kill some CIA agent and drop him in the Bosporus," Lori said slowly and quietly, horrified at what she had just guessed. "It won't matter that there are police patrolling the streets in the areas around the Bosporus. They're going to drop his body at night from that AfricanAir commuter airplane!"

"Try to delay that aircraft from taking off for as long as you can, Mr. Tamuk" Lori said, "but don't give them any idea that there's anything wrong. Maybe they haven't killed the CIA agent yet, and just maybe we can sneak up and save him before they do. Here's my cell phone number, so you and I can communicate. Please give me yours."

"But this all sounds incredible! Do you have any proof that this AfricanAir flight has a hostage on board?" asked the tower supervisor, beginning to look argumentative.

"No, Mr. Tamuk, only grave suspicion at this point. The police authorities may want to talk to you during their rescue operation." "Then have them call me," relented the tower supervisor, apparently mollified by the idea of conversing with top police leaders, as he handed Lori a scribbled number on a memo notebook page. "But they must understand, I have to go by the rules here."

"Yes, sir," said Lori, looking back at the man over her shoulder as she hurried to the elevator. "I understand. But just about everyone in Turkey, and maybe around the world, is going to feel very badly tomorrow that you are unable to save the hostage we are so sure is there."

On the way down in the elevator with Lori and the policeman, Elsie asked quietly, "Will you really tell the world it's that guy's fault if there is a CIA man in there, and we fail to save him?"

"Probably not," said Lori. "But if there is someone about to be killed in that airplane, I'm sure that person would like for Mr. Tamuk to be as motivated as possible to save him!"

"Little mighty mite," said Elsie affectionately, "you know you could get fired if you irritate too many of these airport VIP's around the world."

"I may already be there," said Lori. "But even that isn't as bad as something happening to 4416 ... or any human beings involved, when we might have saved them! And we don't have time to wait for anybody, but we'd better keep the authorities informed. Please call Inspector Lodge, Elsie, and tell him we've got some policemen and two trucks, and we're about to attack an airplane!"

CHAPTER FOURTEEN

The metallic-sounding airport tower radio delivered information to all airplanes and vehicles moving on the airport tarmac and runways, and was always 'on' in those vehicles. "AfricanAir 1612 taxi for takeoff and hold at east end of runway 40," Lori heard it order as she hurried out of the tower. "Oh no, oh no, not so soon," she moaned. She poked Mr. Tamuk's number into her phone as she ran out of the Ataturk tower building.

"Mr. Tamuk, this is Lori Fyfer," she began breathlessly as she ran out of the tower building. She could see the fuel truck and the TransGlobal pickup truck still parked down the tarmac at the next gate where the AfricanAir turboprop had been, and the small Istanbul police car even farther away. She raced toward them as she gasped into the cell phone she held bumping against her ear.

"One of your people just cleared the AfricanAir commuter to taxi for takeoff. We *must* stop them! But police units cannot pursue him without crossing active runways. Is there any traffic on runways 40 and 34 left or right?"

"No, not at the moment" answered Tamuk hesitantly. "But in only some 20 minutes there will be a heavy incoming passenger plane landing on 34 left."

"Please notify AfricanAir that it must hold for takeoff until after that aircraft has landed," begged Lori. "That will give us time to intercept them. And I'm afraid that they'll take off without permission if they know we're pursuing them. The hostage on board will prove kidnapping, along with the smuggling, which will put both these guys away for a long time. They may prefer to run."

"I can't hold an aircraft on the runway for 20 minutes," protested the tower supervisor.

"I've been held for that long for all sorts of reasons," replied Lori, gasping for air as she ran along the tarmac, the cell phone jiggling against her ear, with Elsie trying to keep up in her high heels.

"Perhaps we're more efficient here than where you were operating," complained Tamuk stiffly. "We've never held an aircraft that long."

"Come up with a reason you can later tell the media about," suggested Lori breathlessly as she ran. "No one will blame you. Quite the opposite. The whole world will congratulate you on how you saved the situation and the human life involved."

Tamuk's "Hmmmm" stretched for a long moment as he considered. "I'll come up with something."

"Request permission for two vehicles to cross runways 43 left and right. We have to approach the AfricanAir commuter from directly behind the aircraft so they can't see us coming. If they spot us I believe they'll try to take off."

"Permission granted," said Tamuk hesitantly.

"Roger," confirmed Lori. "We're on our way."

Lori had to slow down to a fast walk as she looked for the telephone number of the officer in the Istanbul police car ahead of her. She punched in the numbers by the glare of the airport flood lights far above her.

"Stop the refueling truck," she gasped. "It's pulling away from the gate area now. Stop them!"

Ahead, she saw the blue lights on the top of the Istanbul police cruiser flash on, and the police car pulled out onto the tarmac to pursue the fuel truck. It was a very short chase alongside the concourse before the police car swerved in front of the fuel truck, with one policeman brandishing a machine gun out his window at the two men in the cab.

The fuel truck stopped. When she ran up to the vehicles, the Istanbul police were already pointing short-barrelled little submachine guns at the two fuel technicians who were leaning against the truck before being hand-cuffed.

"I need the pickup truck. I'll drive it." Lori gasped at the policemen. "Leave one officer with these men in the fuel truck," she called to the senior officer. "Take me to the pickup truck, then follow me in the police car with the other officers."

The officer remaining with the fuel truck drivers had handcuffed both of them to the door handles of the fuel truck, and stood watching as Lori and Elsie, along with three officers, crammed themselves into the police car and drove away. The binoculars and camera once carried by the officers in the police car were now in the trunk, replaced by small black machine guns.

Thank the Lord those AfricanAir guys left the keys in the pickup, said Lori thankfully to herself when she got to the pickup, and crawled in. *That may be their one most fatal mistake tonight.* She wondered if the police officers with her would have known how to hot wire the little truck.

Elsie, her eyes huge and her open mouth straining to breathe, jumped in the truck alongside Lori. Trying to speak as she gasped for breath, Elsie was holding her high heeled shoes clasped to her chest and staring down below the dashboard at the runner in the left leg of her panty hose. "I called Inspector Lodge," gasped Elsie, still breathless. "He said to wait for him."

"I knew he would," said Lori, "but we just can't."

"Wonder who's going to jail? The bad guys or us?" murmured Elsie.

Seven minutes had passed since Lori received permission from the tower supervisor to cross runway 43 left and right. Lori, in the pickup truck with Elsie, bumped across the grass as she cleared the runways, keeping the tail assembly of the AfricanAir commuter aircraft straight ahead of her. "Elsie, call the police car driver," called Lori across the noisy pickup cab.

"Tell him to come up behind the aircraft, blocking them in from the rear.

Otherwise, they can put reverse thrust on those engines, and back away from our truck in front of them."

"Got it, Mighty Mite," yelled Elsie with a grin.

Thank goodness airplanes don't have rear view mirrors, thought Lori as she bounced toward a new set of runways between them and the aircraft ahead.

She called Mr. Tamuk. "Request permission for two vehicles to cross runways 10 and 12," she said.

"Permission granted," said Mr. Tamuk, his eyes studying Lori's progress through the lens of a large pair of binoculars. "I see you are nearly there now, but the incoming aircraft I mentioned will be landing very shortly!"

Lori found the little pickup truck harder to drive than a 777 as she climbed a mound of turf alongside runway 10 and raced across its smooth surface toward runway 12. She could see the reflection on the hood of the truck of the blinking lights above her head that were required of all vehicles moving about among the runways, while behind her blinked the blue lights atop the Istanbul police car that followed.

Ahead of her the AfricanAir commuter was sitting a good 50 feet from the active runway where the incoming passenger jet would soon be landing. Keeping the pickup truck bumping across the grass at least 20 feet from the active runway, she drove up behind the airplane as it sat waiting for permission to take off.

Well, here goes nothing, Lori told herself as she yanked hard left on the steering wheel, and pulled the pickup around the left wing of the KingAir and in front of the aircraft. The pickup truck tires screeched to a halt in front of the racing propellers of the turboprop commuter aircraft, and Lori stared up into the faces of the shocked pilots. She was close enough to watch the expressions on the pilot's faces change from surprise to rage as they stared down at her.

That was when Lori noticed the lights of the landing aircraft several miles behind her in the truck's rear view mirror. The lights raced closer, and the jet engines on the wings of the incoming passenger airplane roared louder and louder as the aircraft rushed down the runway above them and to Lori's left. Soon the roar was louder than a dozen freight trains, and the ground itself shook as the passenger jet touched down with a shriek of burning rubber against the runway surface. The roaring fury of the jet engines faded rapidly as the airplane rushed on down the runway. "Elsie, get out on my side," yelled Lori, warning her to stay away from the roaring engines of the AfricanAir turboprop just in case the pilots tried to get by the pickup truck somehow.

Suddenly, the two engines of the turboprop aircraft slowed, then rebounded with a new and different sound as they gained power again.

"They've reversed thrust on their engines," called Lori above the roar. "They're trying to back up. They must not see the police car."

Lori marched around the front of the pickup and stared up at the two pilots in the KingAir. She pointed to her right at a policeman who had appeared around the side of the aircraft, and who was now pointing a machine gun at the pilots in the cockpit. The two pilots in the aircraft stared for a moment at the policeman, then both raised their hands, letting their heads slump forward dejectedly.

One of the policemen unlatched the door and climbed into the KingAir. He held the two men at gun-point until the other policeman joined him. Then they hand-cuffed the pilots, and helped them out of the aircraft a few minutes later. As he passed Lori holding one of the two AfricanAir pilots, the first policeman said to her, "Hostage there," and pointed back in the airplane cabin. Lori let out a breath of thankfulness, and hurried through the door. She turned left to see one man in a TransGlobal pilot's black doublebreasted uniform sitting on the first seat with his hands cuffed behind him, and a white cotton sack pulled down over his head. The gleaming silver name tag on his chest read CAPTAIN ERIC McELLEN.

"Eric," cried Lori, as she pulled the sack off his head. One of the policeman used a universal handcuff key to free McEllen. "Are you a CIA officer?" Lori asked.

"Lori Fyfer ... I should have known it would be you!" sighed McEllen with a relieved chuckle. "No, of course I'm not CIA. I think these 'terrorists' are also a little confused about who I am. Somehow they've lost confidence in what a great value I would have been to their organization, and decided to lay me off, as it were. Mighty glad you made them reconsider, Darlin'."

"Darling?" repeated Lori. "I asked you to stop calling me that! Doesn't my saving your hide earn me that one favor? But the more I know about you, the more natural you look wearing those handcuffs, and I bet it won't be the last time I see you in them!"

"Sorry, sugar," said Eric. "I suppose there are some negative aspects to a career in smuggling that I didn't mention on the flight deck the other day. One doesn't always associate with the nicest people."

CHAPTER FIFTEEN

"Highly placed sources in Washington announced today that the American CIA agent reportedly to be targeted last night somewhere along the Bosporus River in Istanbul by Siberian terrorists does not exist, and never did," reported the British anchor in a clipped accent. "In response to the story initiated by Zurich TV station Schweizer Fernsehen SRF, Istanbul police units blanketed both sides of the Bosporus River last night to insure that no such assassination would occur, but found no American agent or Siberian terrorists, either. Sources at the CIA speculate that the false alarm was raised to promote the activities of the Armed Defense Brigade of the Siberian People, a very small, and until now obscure terrorist force in Siberia."

The reporter smiled slightly then, and added, "Turkish authorities assure reporters that they were always able and ready to keep the peace had there been any need."

Lori Fyfer glared across the cockpit of the 777 at Eric McEllen. "I should have stayed completely out of that news story," said Lori. "That way it would have had a much more exciting ending."

"Yep," allowed Eric, "and the news story ending would have been all about *my* ending if you hadn't swooped in to save my bacon!"

"Thanks again, by the way!"

"Stop thanking me!" growled Lori. She added reluctantly, "You'd have done the same for me." Then she pointed out quietly, "In fact, you did. You saved me from that monster who calls himself the Skipper in that hotel bathroom." *But I wonder if that could have all been scripted,* she thought. *Could that Skipper monster have been helping McEllen look good by letting him win the day?* Lori gave Eric another withering glance as she added, "So anyway, now we're even. Let's leave it that way."

With a small smile on his face, senior Captain Bill Travers glanced over at Eric, then back at Lori. "I hope the powers that be never listen to the black box tape of what's been said on this flight deck," he said, grinning. "They might never let you two fly together again!" In the quietness that ensued, he added, "And you both can have all the adventures you want without involving me in any way. Those stories are the scariest tales I've ever heard in all the years I've flown this trip! Maybe you two should just settle down and fly airplanes."

"Lots of bad people around, doing really bad things," replied Lori with a pointed look at Eric McEllen. "Well, I imagine our Director of Operations, Mr. Fitzgerald, is eager to hear how you're taking care of that," said Travers with a smile. "Ataturk Operations passed me a note from

Mr. Thomas Fitzgerald, himself, this morning inviting me to another meeting like the one we had in Zurich. It seems like that meeting was a month ago, even though it's actually been less than a week."

But they still didn't include Eric, considered Lori thoughtfully. *I guess Fitzgerald isn't any surer of him than I am. But they must not be watching him anymore, or they'd have known when the AfricanAir pilots kidnapped him. Maybe he is a good guy. I just can't tell who's on which side any more. But I can certainly tell how Fitzgerald feels about Elsie and me as a team. Nobody tells us anything.*

"Yes", acknowledged Lori. "I also got a note from him when I signed in this morning. Maybe he and his policemen have solved this thing … I hope, I hope."

"Didn't Fitzgerald include you in this shindig?" Travers asked McEllen.

"No, but I'm not at all offended," claimed Eric. "I just want to fly airplanes, and let others deal with smuggling and other such shady activities," he added with a grin.

"Well, you've certainly changed your tune about the merry life of smuggling," observed Lori with a frown.

"Not at all," countered Eric. "I'm just a simple airplane pilot, not a detective like some of the more intellectual airline people."

"I just hope I'm intellectual enough to help put away all the smugglers or terrorists, or whoever they are, who threaten my airliner or the passengers in it," stated Lori with a glare at Eric. "And I hope I help bury them so deep they never again see the light of day," she added emphatically, never taking her eyes off him.

"You two *are* on the same side, aren't you?" groaned Travers. "I'll be at the meeting, of course," he said, looking supportively at Eric, "but I, too, just want to fly airplanes, not tussle with terrorists along the way." He glanced back at Lori and added diplomatically, "And I'll be rooting for the good guys, whoever they may be."

Lori rolled her eyes and flattened her lips into a short straight line. There were terrible dangers here, but no one seemed to be taking her seriously. Yet, as irritated as she was with Eric, she was having more and more trouble imagining him as a terrorist. She had interpreted Eric's getting kidnapped and almost killed by the terrorists to mean that he wasn't willing to be as bad as they were. Lori sighed, and turned her attention to the envelope in the pocket of her coat. It was an invitation, as Captain Travers said, and a mandatory one at that, to appear in the conference room of the TransGlobal Airlines offices at Domodedova Airport when they landed in Moscow. It was signed by TransGlobal D/O Thomas Fitzgerald, and Lori was sure he'd be in charge of the meeting. *I pray somebody has figured out something, and that this mess is about over with,* Lori thought. *We're getting awfully close to that return trip, which all the clues point to being an awful catastrophe for some airliner. He and his policemen just seem to talk about these mysteries, but no one ever seems to solve anything.*

* * *

"We will destroy them!" shouted the Russian Colonel. The face of the high ranking officer of the Russian Federal Security Service had turned red, and Lori noticed that a vein in his forehead was beginning to bulge. Colonel Damitrov appeared to consider the publicity being given to the Siberian terrorists a personal insult to himself. He seemed enraged that the small, obscure activist group in Siberia had managed to come to the attention of newspaper readers and TV news recipients around the world by threatening a single CIA agent in Istanbul, and then failing to carry through on their threat.

The rest of the people sitting at the long table in the conference room at Domodedova Airport sat silently and waited for Damitrov's wrathful indignation to diminish. It was the same group who had met around the conference table in Zurich, except that Colonel Damitrov and two Russian militia officers had taken the places of the Swiss policemen.

The Russian Colonel had been introduced as the officer in charge of the transportation of the Star of Yakutsk from Russia to the United States. When he had calmed himself a bit, one of the FBI agents present asked Damitrov if he had considered transporting the diamond on an airline other than TransGlobal.

"Not really," said Damitrov. "The terrorists are only an annoyance. "You notice that in the case of the American CIA agent. The terrorists got everything wrong. There apparently never was such an agent, and if there was, they were unable to do him any harm."

"Colonel Damitrov," began Fitzgerald, who was reading from a printed schedule in front of him. "I've seen the schedule of exhibits you set up with museums in the United States, and I notice that the first place you'll show the Star of Yakutsk is the Metropolitan Museum in New York City. I know you have to negotiate with museums to determine what dates they will agree to house different exhibits months in advance, and you can't change them. Yet the flights you're considering include airliners flying into Dallas, Chicago and New York City. Isn't that a hint for the terrorists that in the end you are going to choose only New York City flights?"

"Maybe," answered Damitrov, a smug look on his face. "And then maybe not. The Star of Yakutsk is not a large, heavy piece of freight. It would only cost another few hundred American dollars to fly it to Chicago or Dallas, and then back to New York. We will pay whatever expenses are necessary to provide the best security, and confuse the Siberian terrorists."

"They seem to be aware of what we're going to do before we do it," the Colonel added. "We have secretly been talking to three airlines about transporting the Star of Yakutsk ... you, WorldAir and International Freightways. I'm sure you have heard that gunmen attacked the sales counter of World Airways in Zurich this morning, killing three people. The terrorists were screaming, 'Long live the Siberian people' in Russian, and so far they have all gotten away. How do the terrorist scum know our plans before we do? I want an airline that can protect this treasure, and deliver it to the United States." He looked hard at Fitzgerald. "I want to know ... can you do that?"

Lori had been too busy to read a newspaper for days, and had not even heard of the airport attack in Zurich. She shook her head, finding it all hard to believe.

"Sir, we can and will do that, if you choose to use TransGlobal" said Fitzgerald. "Inspector Lodge, can you give us an idea of where we are in locating and identifying the terrorists? "Well, sir, I'm afraid that's quite a mixed bag," began the Inspector. "The Colonel has arrested three members of the Armed Defense Brigade of the Siberian People here in Russia, and incarcerated them. Two Siberians were killed by needles thrust out of chart cases in Istanbul on an airport escalator. One of the men who killed them fell to his own death immediately afterward, and appears to be a Russian member of the same terrorist gang. We have no idea why the terrorists would attack their own people, unless there is a lot of discord within the organization."

"How about the two AfricanAir pilots Fyfer caught while they were trying to assassinate Captain McEllen?

"Once again," answered Lodge, "it's hard to decide whether they're terrorists or smugglers. They're guilty of smuggling. Fyfer has proved that. And it could have also been a terrorist act, considering the organization's original claim that the Captain is with the CIA ... which he is not. Neither one of the pilots Fyfer caught would say a word to explain themselves or defend themselves. They must be very afraid of somebody."

"They're terrorists," claimed Colonel Damitrov loudly. "They may smuggle to support their terrorist activities, but above all they fight the government with acts of terror."

As Mr. Fitzgerald asked for information from around the table, Lori Fyfer had more to say about her experiences than anyone. Everyone at the table congratulated her except Colonel Damitrov, who scowled at her as she continuously identified the troublemakers as smugglers during her report.

"They're terrorists," repeated Damitrov, "and the scum of the earth!"

"I wish we could have arrested this Skipper person and more of his terrorist cell," said Fitzgerald, "but this obscure little group of terrorists have gone underground in remote areas, and it will take time to dig them out."

"If Colonel Damitrov chooses to entrust the Star of Yakutsk to TransGlobal" concluded Mr. Fitzgerald, "TransGlobal has decided to confuse the terrorists even more by involving two aircraft in the inspection process. Flight 4427, which departs Kloten for LaGuardia tomorrow two hours after Flight 4416, will also be scrutinized just as 4416 will be. Giving two aircraft special inspections will leave the terrorists wondering which airliner will carry the Star of Yakutsk to the United States."

"We'll insure that every mechanical system on both chosen aircraft is in perfect condition, and we'll have our best people spend the entire night before both aircraft take off searching every inch of the airplanes from the nose to the tail to insure that everything's as it should be on board," he promised.

"And," added Fitzgerald. "Since we know that these terrorists have formed an unparalleled criminal conspiracy with legitimate employees of this airline so they can blend into the airport work environment, we will check all workers in the areas where Flight 4416 and Flight 4427 are being inspected to insure that the only people there are our best people, legitimate employees who have been with us for years. All this security may delay us a bit, but we'll have the whole night to get it right. And it's certainly a job worth doing. We want the world to know that we can protect our passengers and cargo in every way."

It's great to hear that the first exhibit of the uncut diamond will take place in New York, thought Lori. *Surely they wouldn't waste time and money flying into DFW, and then turn back to New York. That certainly improves my chances not to be on the airliner carrying the Star of Yakutsk. And thank goodness they're taking security so seriously, since I'm actually going to be on one of those airplanes, along with hundreds of other folks.* Lori sat silently in her seat while one of the FBI agents asked a question. But she wasn't listening. She was asking herself, *So why don't I feel more secure?*

CHAPTER SIXTEEN

It would be viewed with awe by crowds around the world while experts decided how to cut it.

The Skipper stood alone in the balcony looking down at the Star of Yakutsk. There was a crowd gathered around the glass case that displayed what was now the largest uncut diamond in the world. The Star of Yakutsk was the most popular exhibit at the Russian Trade Fair in Moscow that year.

Yet the actual stone was hardly spectacular. It looked like a large rock with streaks of translucent glassy interior visible below its irregular shale stone surface. Still, the crowd was awed by the size of the uncut stone. And it had been plucked from their own Mother Earth ... from the Russian steppes in faraway Siberia, of course ... but still from the Mother Earth of the Russian Federation. They were sure it would be cut into the largest diamond in the world, and were proud that even now in its rough, uncut state crowd surrounding the glass-enclosed kiosk that held at the marble and shale covered lump of gemstone.

Knowing that he would soon possess this unique wonder of the world excited him. He pulled his cell phone from his pocket, and punched in a number. Through the dark glasses he wore he glanced at the beautiful blonde standing across from him on the other side of the balcony just as she answered her cell phone, and said, "Perhaps I'll let you wear it around your neck after I have it cut, my dear."

"I think a rock this size and weight might strangle me, Emil," answered Aspen Mohr with a casual laugh. *Which is just what you want, you miserable animal,* she thought, *and you still don't realize I know it. But why should I be angry?* she asked herself, *when you're the one who's going to die this week, and I'm the one who will possess the diamond.* "I'll be quite happy with my share of the profits on this enormous bauble," she added aloud to the Skipper.

"Please, my dear, I have asked you many times to stop calling me 'Emil'. It is a security matter." Aspen was the only member of the Skipper's organization who had known him long enough to know his real name. He remembered that she had been calling him 'Emil' more often since he started seeing the beautiful French woman, Noelle Chabrun. Could Aspen be trying to irritate him intentionally? Was she jealous of Noelle? He knew Aspen had met Chabrun, and was aware that her diamond-cutting firm was going to cut the stone as soon as the Skipper's gang stole it. *But I have kept everything very business-like between Noelle and me,* he assured himself, *at least when others are around. Aspen cannot possibly know about the trips I've been taking with Noelle. She can't be jealous. She always gets a little nervous when we get closer to the time for action, as we are right now ... and then she becomes difficult, as she certainly is becoming* at *the moment.*

Well, he reminded himself, *I just need her for two more days ... just two more days, and then she will die, and this irritation will be over.* "Speaking of security," the Skipper asked Aspen, "have you been able to recognize any of the people who are surely following you?"

"No, they must be very good, and they probably change agents often," said Aspen. "But since Lori must have told them nearly a week ago that I'm at least a person of interest, I'm sure they're there."

"By the way, the whole cabin crew is nervous about the threats to any aircraft carrying this diamond. I'll use my brand new phone to e-mail them tomorrow morning with the rumor that 4416 got the job carrying the diamond. They'll never figure out where the message is coming from, but I'm sure several of them will jump ship to avoid any terrorist danger on that airplane. That way no one will think twice about my bailing out the next day before 4416 takes off for the States."

"Everybody will assume I'm just another chicken who didn't want to be on a threatened airplane, and that's why I bailed."

"The car will be waiting beneath the rest room window as we discussed," said the Skipper into the telephone as he watched a willowy brunette stride toward him across the balcony. "Climb out the restaurant window at exactly noon Tuesday. I've taken care of the rest."

"I'll see you in New York City Thursday," replied Aspen very slowly. The Skipper glanced at her face again, and saw that she was no longer looking at him, but watching Noelle Chabrun as she approached the Skipper from across the balcony. "Be careful," warned Aspen, emphasizing each word. "We are very close now."

Noelle Chabrun was a striking woman. Her pale skin reminded one of the white makeup of a Japanese geisha, against which her long mane of coal black hair contrasted sharply. She strode briskly across to where the Skipper stood alone, and embraced him tightly.

"Those sunglasses make you look like a movie star" she said with a grin as she looked up at him. The Skipper smiled at the compliment and pointed to the uncut diamond in the display. "This is what I wanted you to see," he said.

"Oh, how enormous it is," sighed Noelle. "I've never seen even an uncut stone as large as that!"

"It's the largest natural diamond ever found," bragged the Skipper, as if he owned it already. "And I'm sure it will still be the largest gem ever cut when your experts finish with it. Your diamond-cutting firm will be world-famous my dear, as soon as this particular business is completed in the next two or three days," said the Skipper hurriedly. "When they finish this piece. It won't be the gem the world thinks it is, but it will still be the largest diamond in the world."

"We will do a wonderful job for you, I promise," said Noelle breathily. "But my services will not stop there. I want to get to know you much better, Mr. Skipper. When can I see you again?" she asked, taking a deep breath so that her ample bosom strained against her jacket.

"I want to take you for a helicopter ride, handsome."

"A helicopter ride?" asked the Skipper, surprised.

"You know that I have offices and labs in both London and Paris," said Noelle. "You may not know that I find it very convenient to fly from one to the other ... and many other places, as well ... as I gather my gems together without having to ever pass them through a commercial airport. I, myself, occasionally pass through commercial airports, of course, to look very legitimate, but my stones don't. I can release them from the bottom of my helicopter in amazing ways, and they're just not there when I'm visited by customs."

"I've studied you for some time, handsome," Noelle added, "and I think we could do some wonderful things together ... some very profitable things."

At that moment the Skipper's cell phone rang. He pulled it from his pocket and looked at the face of the telephone. "I am very interested in exploring those possibilities, my dear. "You will hear from me soon, I promise. Excuse me while I take this very important telephone call."

Noelle Chabrun was used to adoration, not being shooed away while a man takes another call. Her pale white skin flushed a stormy pink as she stalked away.

"I hope you are not mixing business and pleasure, my friend," said Colonel Damitrov's voice loudly from the cell phone in his ear.

The Skipper replied, "Not at all, Colonel." He quickly scanned the crowd, and spotted the Colonel, in full uniform, standing alone along the wall some 30 feet back from the diamond exhibit. "This lady owns a firm of well-known diamond cutters in London and Paris, and she's going to make us all very rich."

"And make a nice profit, herself, I imagine." replied the Colonel.

"Yes, sir," said the Skipper. "As will we all."

"Of course," said the Colonel, his eyes scanning the crowd so no one might guess that he and the Skipper were talking to each other. The Colonel lowered his voice and said, "I just wanted to confirm that my men and I will fly to Kloten Airport in Zurich with you tomorrow, spend the night in the airport hotel, and appear again Tuesday at 10 a.m. with the Star of Yakutsk at Gate 8 on the International Concourse. That will be two hours before takeoff for the United States. You will give us a ride to the maintenance facility where the mechanics will be sweeping Flight 4416 from nose to tail to insure that there are no deadly devices hidden aboard as per Mr. Fitzgerald's promises. You will then pre-board my men and myself at the maintenance facility, and taxi to the gate where the rest of the passengers will board. We will be seated in first class in seats that will allow us to observe the rest of the aircraft in all directions. Am I correct about all that?"

"You are perfectly correct, Colonel," said the Skipper smoothly. "And as I assured you earlier, when the diamond is stolen from the museum in New York, it will be their responsibility for the loss, not yours. In fact, your men will be with the unit that takes the stone, so it will never actually be out of your hands."

"I hope you realize, Mr. Skipper, that when this diamond is stolen, the efforts to find it and get it back will know no bounds. Many Russian security agents around the world will be involved, and more police agencies will cooperate on this case than you have ever seen. It will be this year's *cause célèbre,* and if our parts in this are discovered, we'll never see the light of day again in our lives, which may also be very short, indeed!"

"As I explained, Colonel, the uncut diamond will disappear so completely that everyone in the world will accept that the diamond went down to the bottom of the North Atlantic in the tragic loss of Flight 4416. Colonel, let us talk again in the aircraft tomorrow," said the Skipper, "where we can speak of this at greater length and in complete security."

"You are probably right. See you tomorrow, Skipper. After the flight I hope you'll meet me for a few vodkas together in Dallas to toast our new affluence." "It will be my great pleasure, Colonel," said the Skipper with a smile, knowing that the Colonel was going to die with his men tomorrow and that there would be no victory drink.

* * *

Aspen stood alone near the front of the crowd surrounding the huge uncut diamond. Her eyes, though, had been riveted on the Skipper in the balcony above her with the clingy brunette hanging on his arm. Aspen realized that she was now so full of hatred for the man who was ditching her; it might very well be showing in her eyes when she was with him. She felt a nasal chuckle resonating deep in her throat. *I will have to start wearing dark glasses,* she told herself, *just like Emil, to camouflage myself. But not for long. After all, Emil is going to die in the same disaster he is preparing for everyone else ... and he now has only one day to live.*

CHAPTER SEVENTEEN

Irma Bedwell always wore her shiny silver hair tied in a knot at the nape of her neck, and always balanced horn-rimmed spectacles on the bridge of her small bird's beak nose. Her even smaller mouth was generally set in an unpleasant straight line.

But not this afternoon. This afternoon the ends of her tiny mouth quivered tentatively as they curved upward, actually approaching the muted exhuberance of the famous Mona Lisa smile. After all, Miss Bedwell was only a year away from retirement as Thomas Fitzgerald's administrative assistant, and she needed all the cash assets she could accumulate as quickly as possible, considering how little she had been paid for 27 years of dedicated service to that penny-pincher. Miss Bedwell had grumbled to herself when Fitzgerald ordered her to accompany him to Zurich, but the city in the Alps was proving to be a treasure trove. She was now making more money than she ever had before by taping Fitzgerald's calls and selling them to this Skipper person. There was something about them that must have intrigued the Skipper, because he had just sent her a very pleasant and very unexpected bonus delivered yesterday by one of his strange and somewhat menacing foreign associates.

"I'm taking a great risk making this call," Miss Bedwell began in a whisper, even though there was no one in the TransGlobal Director of Operations office anteroom except her. "I must hurry," she added. "Are you ready?"

"Yes, I'm ready," she could hear Aspen respond from more than a thousand miles away in Moscow, and Aspen sounded impatient, Miss Bedwell decided.

"Well, here it comes," Ms. Bedwell said as she pressed a button on the recording machine connected to her telephone. Both Irma and Aspen could hear the two minute, thirteen second conversation Irma had recorded. When Fitzgerald said "goodbye" to the TransGlobal security officer he had called, Aspen broke the silence, saying with some enthusiasm, "Very good, Miss Bedwell. I think you'll get another bonus for this one."

Irma Bedwell's small smile broadened even further when she heard those words. Corporate espionage was exciting, and so very profitable. But her smile wavered as she listened again to the tape she had just shared with Aspen, trying to understand what was so important. All Mr. Fitzgerald had done was order that some airliner the mechanics were due to inspect tonight when it arrived from Moscow would not taxi to the maintenance facility, but remain at Gate 8 on the International Concourse all night while the nose to tail inspection was done. Hardly earth-shaking information, thought Miss Bedwell. But she was happy this generous Skipper man was pleased.

* * *

Even as Elsie and Inspector Lodge were talking, Lori was soaring at 35,000 feet over the snow-capped Austrian Alps reporting the presence of TransGlobal Flight 4416 Heavy to the tower at Kloten Airport in Zurich, Switzerland, requesting landing in 45 minutes. Captain Travers and Captain McEllen were both in their seats, and Lori was seated in the jump seat at the rear of the flight deck.

Back at the far rear of the Tourist section Aspen Mohr looked at her watch. It was time. She was proud of how quickly she had reacted to Fitzgerald's decision to inspect Flight 4416 tonight while it sat at Gate 8 instead of having it inspected in the maintenance facility. *The Skipper will appreciate how I have nullified that pompous Fitzgerald's decision. This aircraft must spend the night in maintenance for our plan to work, and that's exactly where it's going.*

It's just as well for the Skipper that tomorrow is his last day to live. With that mindless geisha girl he holds at his side instead of me, he would go no further, anyway. I'm actually doing him a favor.

Aspen stood up and walked up the aisle toward the cockpit. She slowed as she reached the middle of the section. There it was, on the right side. The aisle seat the seating chart had said would be empty. Aspen bent over and pulled an aerosol can out of the life jacket container under the seat. It and two others had entered the aircraft last night in the tool bag of the only authentic TransGlobal mechanic in the Moscow station occasionally employed by the Association, and one of the crew who had performed routine maintenance on Flight 4416 before it departed Moscow. There was another under an unoccupied seat in Business Class, and one in First Class in case one of the aerosol cans was discovered and removed. To place the three cans on board the aircraft, the mechanic had been paid more than he made from his TransGlobal salary in a month, while being assured that they could never be traced back to him. Both cans were labeled 'CLEANER: All Surfaces' on a label that carefully covered the original label which read 'ARTIFICIAL SMOKE: Airline Mechanic Training'.

The passenger in the middle seat glanced up at Aspen as she extracted the can from under the aisle seat. She gave him a glowing smile, which he happily returned.

"Are you doing all right, Sir?" she asked.

"Yes, thank you", he responded enthusiastically to the lovely blonde who gave him another smile before she turned and hurried forward.

Showtime! Aspen told herself. *And so it all begins.* As the other flight attendants asked passengers to move their seats 'to the upright position to prepare for landing', Aspen did what she always did at that point ... she began checking the rest rooms for passengers who should already be strapped in their seats.

She pulled open the door to the Tourist Class restroom and entered. It took only seconds to spray the artificial and invisible smoke around the small room, and then walk rapidly down the aisle forward with the aerosol can tucked in a jacket pocket as she traversed all the different classes of the cabin area. By the time she had sprayed all the restrooms, and both galleys, Aspen was again in the rear of the aircraft, where she secreted the two empty cans in her luggage, and sat down to begin securing herself for landing.

"Aspen," said flight attendant Hillary Burns, as she sat down next to Aspen and prepared to strap herself in, "I smell something! Do you?"

Aspen lifted her long, straight nose, and sniffed of the air in the cabin for a few moments.

Before Aspen answered, Hillary said, "Something's burning! Where is that smell coming from?" She unhooked her seatbelt and stood up, looking around her. "It smells like an electrical fire!"

"I'll tell the Captain," said Aspen, adding softly, "Calm the passengers if they smell it, too!" She turned and hurried forward to the cockpit. "We're only minutes from touchdown."

* * *

Lori was speaking to Kloten ground control when she heard the polite knock on the cockpit door. As soon as she finished the conversation, Lori went to the door and listened as Aspen Mohr identified herself. She opened the door for Aspen, who had a concerned look on her face. *Uh oh,* said Lori to herself. *Now what is getting ready to happen?* "Thank goodness we're about to land," Aspen said to Captain Travers.

"We have a mystery in the back. There's an odor of smoke in the cabin. We can't tell where it's coming from, but it's pretty strong!"

Captain Travers kept himself focused on the landing protocol, never taking his eyes off the runway as it grew closer and closer. "We're almost on the ground. Lori, tell Ground Control we need to taxi to the Maintenance facility ... oh, and get buses out to the facility to transport all the passengers to Gate 14."

Even as Lori reached for her microphone, another voice on the radio broke the silence on the flight deck.

"This is Fitzgerald, calling from TransGlobal Operations in Zurich for TransGlobal Flight 4416 Heavy, Captain Travers, over."

Captain Travers keyed his microphone.

"Mr. Fitzgerald, this is TransGlobal 4416 Heavy, Captain Travers here."

"Captain Travers, I need to speak with you and your crew in the conference room where we met a week ago as soon as you've processed through TransGlobal Operations here at Kloten. We'll see you in a few minutes. This is Fitzgerald at TransGlobal Operations, Kloten Airport, over and out."

"Mr. Fitzgerald, TransGlobal 4416 Heavy, Captain Travers. Our flight attendants have just begun smelling the odor of smoke in the cabin. Haven't found anything that could be causing it, but we'll need to taxi to the TransGlobal Maintenance facility as soon as we land at Kloten. My crew will report to the conference room as quickly as we can after turning the aircraft over to maintenance. This is Captain Travers, TransGlobal 4416 Heavy, over and out."

"Captain, this is Fitzgerald again. Forget all that I just said. I'll see you in TransGlobal Maintenance here at Kloten ASAP after you've turned the aircraft over to the mechanics. This is Fitzgerald, TransGlobal Operations, over and out."

"TransGlobal 4416 Heavy, over and out," said Captain Travers. "Now what?" he said with a grimace as he watched the runway ahead quickly getting closer.

* * *

As the last passengers and cabin crew filed off Flight 4416 where it was parked in the TransGlobal Maintenance hangar at Kloten, and bundled themselves and all their luggage onto the three busses lined up next to the airliner, Thomas

Fitzgerald gathered with 4416's flight crew in the First Class section of the otherwise empty airplane. "First," began Fitzgerald, "I wanted to inform you that 4416 has been chosen as the flight to carry the Russian gem to the United States tomorrow morning. Due to the security issues we have with the Siberian extremists, there will be no announcement that this aircraft has been selected until after you have taken off tomorrow. In fact, we have agreed to treat another flight, 4427, departing two hours later for LaGuardia, exactly the same. There will be another team of Russian guards on it, and it will be inspected exactly the same as your flight. But your flight will be the one with the diamond. We're just trying to confuse any terrorists in the neighborhood in any way we can."

"Our mechanics here at Kloten will spend the night slowly and carefully inspecting every part of every mechanical system on your aircraft and on 4427 from nose to tail to insure that every part is in a-one condition, and that there are no foreign items such as bombs, toxic gases or other dangerous items secreted anywhere on the aircraft. Passengers boarding the aircraft tomorrow, along with all their luggage, will be inspected thoroughly, and there will be security personnel and bomb-sniffing dogs checking the luggage that has been stowed in the hold of the aircraft. In other words, we will insure that this airplane and 4427 will do their jobs safely. I'm not expecting that we'll find anything on either airplane, and that these threats will all prove to be a sham."

"In the process, we'll also find out what is causing the smoke odor on the 4416," said Fitzgerald, pausing a moment to sniff the air in the airplane. "There's still a subtle odor of smoke" he decided, "but it won't be here when you return tomorrow. I can assure you of that. Get a good night's rest tonight. I'm riding back to DFW with you tomorrow, and I'll drop by the flight deck to say 'hello' before takeoff. Are there any questions?"

The flight crew looked at each other, then all replied, "No, Sir."

However, it might have been nice if Fitzgerald had issued us all sleeping pills for the night, thought Lori as she glanced around at the serious faces of the crew. *Still, he is going with us. That says a lot for the man.*

CHAPTER EIGHTEEN

Francois D'Obere was a tall and lanky man with a dark scraggly beard and unruly hair down to his shoulders. He wore the burgundy coveralls of a TransGlobal mechanic, which he had actually been for seven years. He was very good at both that job, and the one he held as one of the Skipper's associates, where he was the only one of the Skipper's followers with a French accent instead of a Russian one. The Skipper called him Navigator, and paid him a lot more money than TransGlobal did. Primarily an oiler who lubricated the two huge GE90115B jet engines on 777's passing through Kloten Airport, he was a very competent mechanic who could work on many aircraft systems.

The Skipper had managed to get him selected to help other TransGlobal mechanics work all night examining Flights 4416 and 4427 to insure that terrorists had not disabled either one in any way. Telling his crew chief that he was going to check the oil in Flight 4416's two engines, D'Obere entered 4416's cockpit, pulling what looked like a flat cell phone from the pocket of his overalls. He seated himself in the Captain's seat, and pressed a button on the airliner's control panel. The control panel came to life, and exhibited information screens filled with data. He pressed another button, and the screen showed him the oil gauge. Then he held his home-made device next to the screen, and pressed another button. The oil gauge disappeared, then clicked back on. Done! It would now read full no matter how much oil was held by the two aviation oil systems in the engines. D'Obere flicked off the control panel and left the cockpit. He climbed the scaffolding that had been set up to make the mechanics' inspection jobs easier in order to reach the underside panel below the left engine cowling where excess aviation oil was occasionally allowed to drip out when the oil pressure became too great in the huge engine.

He inserted a curved shim in the opening so it would drip slowly but continuously. D'Obere knew that no one would pay any attention to the several drops that would stain the concrete before the pilot taxied this aircraft to the gate on the concourse where he would load passengers. But by the time the airliner was high above the North Atlantic, the engine would be starved of oil, even though the oil gauge in the cockpit still read full. And then the engine would seize up, and never work again. D'Obere also stuck a curved shim into the oil release valve on the right engine. Over the North Atlantic this airliner was going to become a very heavy and awkward-to-fly-glider. And nothing the pilot did would make these two engines run again.

But his most important job still lay ahead of D'Obere. He knew how smart he was, and how little he needed the Skipper. He was doing all the hard work himself to make the Skipper's plan work. He deserved the diamond, just as Aspen had pointed out. And now he was going to get it. The Skipper would be on Flight 4427, parked at the other end of the hangar, and being inspected just like 4416. With his hand-held device and two more shims in his pocket, D'Obere accelerated his cart across the hangar toward Flight 4427.

* * *

The Skipper adjusted his dark sunglasses, and peered around the dirty aircraft parts stacked against his dingy, dusty desk. From a nearly hidden niche along the maintenance hangar wall he could see the groups of men gathered around Flight 4416, the huge silver airliner parked across one end of the maintenance hangar. Then he turned and looked over his shoulder at Flight 4427, parked at the other end of the hangar. How funny. TransGlobal hoped that having two airliners both treated as carefully as 4416 and 4427 would confuse the terrorists menacing whichever flight would carry the diamond. But due to his association with Colonel

Damitrov, the Skipper had known for months which airliner would be ordered to carry the stone. It would be 4416 ... the flight that maddening little woman who kept getting in his way would die on today ... while he and Colonel Damitrov left Zurich on 4427 themselves ... with the diamond. He had watched men swarm over both aircraft all night ... inspecting, replacing, and searching for hidden dangers of any kind. He had made all this happen, and today in spite of all they were trying to do to stop him, he would become richer than he had ever expected to be.

From across the vast hangar the Skipper could see the TransGlobal maintenance manager approaching him across the acres of smooth concrete floor. *Of all times, Bill Tomlinson wants to talk this morning just as the action is starting? If he stops to talk, I may have to send him on his way very rudely!* Tomlinson was getting close to retirement, and for the past seven years the Skipper had paid him more than TransGlobal had, while all the facilities and vehicles and information had in turn earned the Skipper much more than he paid out.

Of course, the manager didn't know what the Skipper did with those assets he loaned out, or the inside information he passed on. The Skipper never let him know details. The lives occasionally lost, the diamonds torn from bloody hands and secreted on TransGlobal aircraft *en route* to TransGlobal sites in the States. All that would disturb him. The Skipper knew that Tomlinson preferred to think of himself as a well-placed businessman who was willing to cut some corners and break a few restrictive laws to promote the Skipper's business. In return, his association with the Skipper had sent his three children through very good colleges, and paid for several dream vacations for Tomlinson and his wife that they would never forget.

Tomlinson walked up to the Skipper smiling, and shook his hand. The man was dressed in a dress shirt and tie, and looked like a middle manager talking with one of his mechanics as he stood next to the Skipper, who was clad in somewhat greasy burgundy mechanics' overalls.

"Hope the accommodations are comfortable," said Tomlinson, as he looked around the small niche enclosing the Skipper's dingy desk. The Skipper could hardly be seen behind the piles of dirty aircraft parts leaning against the desk. Yet Tomlinson had charged him probably more than any arena seat in any sports contest ever held for the grimy little inset work station the Skipper currently occupied.

"Perfect, thank you very much!" replied the Skipper. "Far enough away to stay out of everyone's business, but still close enough to know what's going on."

"I'm actually a little nervous having you here during all this hush-hush security stuff," said Tomlinson, looking around the hangar anxiously. "If I thought you were planning to try to abscond with this gigantic diamond everyone is so concerned about, I'd have to ... well, that would be a deal-breaker in our relationship, Skipper." He took a deep breath. "That's way too high profile."

"You compliment me too much, my friend," said the Skipper with a broad grin. "I deal in transporting very small stones from remote sources to more lucrative markets ... nothing more."

"Then why are you here watching the inspection of these airplanes that are being threatened by terrorists for transporting a huge diamond back to the United States? "You know ... I could lose my job if anyone found you here. You need to leave, Skipper, before we both get in big trouble."

"My friend," growled the Skipper in a harsher tone, "it benefits my business to observe what areas of the airplane the authorities deem important, and how they inspect them." He was no longer smiling. "I have paid you a great deal of money to be here. Throwing me out of here will certainly attract attention ... I'd make sure it did. And after all is said and done," he added slowly, "you might have to pay for all those luxurious vacations, after all."

Tomlinson stared at the Skipper for a very long moment, his face working as if he wanted badly to say all sorts of things. But the moment passed, and he turned and walked back across the broad expanse of concrete toward his office.

Thought he was going to call my bluff for a minute there, thought the Skipper. *But he was so concerned about his own embarrassment if our dealings had come to light, he didn't even think about how much it would have cost me at this very critical time. I'd have actually had to back down for the moment if he'd pushed me. So he did us both a great favor by chickening out first, as the Americans say. Having to kill him right here and now would have certainly complicated things.*

* * *

To keep the mechanics comfortable all night while they worked on the two aircraft being inspected in the maintenance hangar, large air conditioning hoses had been connected between the two aircrafts' main air conditioning ducts to portable air conditioning units that had been moved next to each of them. The units were perfectly normal in every way, and were often used when mechanics had to work in confined spaces in fuselages parked on the ground. But the Skipper intended to use them as a weapon this morning, and had made sure they would be in place.

At exactly seven twenty-eight a.m. Francois D'Obere was kneeling on the cement floor of the hangar loosening a gasket on the air conditioning pump connected to 4416. No one around him noticed that he was adding an unusual feature. He carefully removed a small, light green gas cylinder from his tool kit, and connected it to the air conditioning pump. To introduce the gas in the cylinder into the air conditioning hose, he needed only to turn the connection key in front of him as he knelt on the cement floor.

The lanky mechanic glanced across the hangar at the figure of the Skipper on the other side of the vast concrete floor. The Skipper sat like a statue staring at the mechanic through his dark glasses. The mechanic had been attaching and detaching the gas cylinder partly to look busy, and partly, he admitted to himself, because he was getting more and more nervous. He looked at his watch for perhaps the tenth time in the last five minutes. It said 7:32 a.m., although the four Russian guards protecting the Star of Yakutsk were supposed to appear in the hangar at 7:30 sharp. *Where are they?*

At 7:36 a.m. a TransGlobal sedan turned into the hangar and pulled up next to Flight 4416. A TransGlobal operations executive under orders from D/O Fitzgerald opened the driver's door and got out. He then opened the doors for four large, bulky men to step out. The last man out carried a large box close to his chest. All the men stood and looked around the hangar for a few minutes before turning to the mobile ramp standing against the passenger entry area of the airliner. Two men climbed the steps and disappeared inside the airliner, then reappeared a minute later to beckon to the rest of their party. The man with the box climbed the stairs next, and the last man followed.

* * *

Russian Colonel Damitrov and his assistants had been welcomed by D/O Fitzgerald, and invited to stand by and observe the careful inspection of Flights 4416 and 4427, and he had been there all night. But the Colonel was becoming ever more impatient waiting for his own guards to arrive from Russia with the diamond. He and his four Russian assistants were all standing close to 4416 when the four Russian guards appeared, having finally arrived via Aeroflot from Moscow.

Yet the Colonel and his four-man entourage stood aside when the sedan pulled up in the hangar and disgorged the men carrying the diamond. Damitrov stood silently and let the guards mount the steps into the fuselage of 4416, while the driver got back in the car and drove out of the hangar.

Then Damitrov walked to the steps by himself and climbed to the airliner entryway. He was met there by one of the burly men who had just entered, and who suddenly stiffened to the position of attention when he saw the Colonel, and saluted. The colonel casually returned the salute, then walked into the First Class area reserved for the guards of the Star of Yakutsk.

* * *

The Skipper rose stiffly from the chair he'd sat in for more than ten hours. Now that the action was starting, he wished he could have had one of his men bring a camera and record what happened as it occurred. It would have been an exciting film to be watched over and over at his leisure in the years to come. But he needed his remaining crew to be part of the action, every one of them. He watched as the Colonel emerged from the aircraft, and stepped down the stairs of the steep mobile ramp, to reach the concrete floor below.

The tall mechanic the Skipper called Navigator had walked to the steps and waited until the Colonel reached ground level and passed him, giving Navigator a nod. The mechanic mounted the steps the Colonel had just descended, and carefully pushed shut the large passenger entry door until he heard the click from inside as it was secured. He turned and descended the steps carefully, and walked back to his air conditioning apparatus, glancing on the way at the Skipper's niche-in-the-wall office as he walked to see if there were any changes to orders or other signals the Skipper would give him. There were none.

The Skipper looked down at his own watch. One minute before eight a.m. A little later than he had planned, but of no matter. There was still enough time. The Skipper watched Navigator walk to his air conditioning apparatus, then turn toward the Skipper once more. But there were no more instructions to give. He leaned back and watched Navigator, and rocked in his swivel chair.

* * *

Navigator turned again to his equipment on the concrete floor, and nervously grasped the connection key with his right hand. The gas cylinder was tightly connected to the air conditioning pump. He looked at the open sliding doors on the East side of the hangar, then those on the West. One of the Skipper's men loitered at each door to insure as much privacy as possible. "I am ready," Navigator said into his cellphone. "Is anyone coming?" "Negative," reported the two Russian gangsters from both sides of the hangar. He glanced nervously around the hangar one more time. The mechanics still in the hangar all seemed absorbed in completing their tasks and going home. He glanced quickly across the hangar at the Skipper and Colonel Damitrov, then with his left hand holding the light green canister, he turned the connection key sharply to the right with his right hand.

Pure hydrogen cyanide was now mingling with the air conditioned air entering the fuselage of Flight 4416. He needed only thirty minutes to completely eliminate the Russian guards inside the airliner – fifteen minutes of the gas going in, and fifteen minutes to clear it out of the airliner. Both of the Skipper's henchmen standing at the opposite ends of the hangar began walking casually toward Flight 4416. They were in no rush to enter the gassed airplane. The dead bodies would wait for them.

Navigator was easily the Skipper's most intelligent henchman, and his longest associate in the smuggling ring, other than Aspen. Navigator was the one who had laboriously worked with the cylinders of hydrogen cyanide slowly and deliberately with a rapidly diminished pack of lab rats to insure he knew how to kill only the targets the Skipper wanted to eliminate, and not himself or any of the Skipper's gang. But he also had more imagination than his fellow Russian thugs, and he couldn't stop thinking about what the gas could do ... and in fact, was now doing.

Actually, Navigator couldn't keep his dark, deep set eyes off the air conditioning hose through which the gas was entering the 777 only a few feet away from him. *Hydrogen cyanide can enter through the mouth,* he recalled, *or the eyes or the respiratory organs; even the pores of the skin. Death will result in minutes,* he remembered the manual saying. *Keep the gas flowing through the hose for 15 minutes,* he reminded himself, glancing again at his watch.

The manual had instructed that to fill any enclosed area that matched the square footage of the interior of Flight 4416, the gas could be turned off after that time, and that normal air conditioning would clear the gas from the area in another fifteen minutes. *So,* he told himself, studying his wrist watch, *four more minutes. Then turn off the gas, and let the normal air conditioning of the aircraft cleanse the area. Another fifteen minutes, and the airplane will be completely free of gas. It will all have been vented safely into the air in the huge hangar by that time, if the manual's guidelines are correct. Then it will be time to turn off, and disconnect that gas canister.*

The Navigator raised his eyes from the apparatus on the floor before him, and glanced toward the Skipper in his little niche in the wall. The Skipper still stared through his dark glasses, slowly rocking in his office swivel chair. *He'll kill me without a second thought if I mess up this gas procedure and lose him that diamond,* thought Navigator. *Well, I'm doing it right for myself and Aspen, and I'm getting good practice, so I'll be sure to do it right to Flight 4427 in a few minutes, and get rid of the Skipper, as well as Co-Pilot and Engineer and about 300 other people. That's what they call collateral damage, I believe,* thought D'Obere, smiling.

But can I be sure of the gas being gone in fifteen minutes when I walk into that airplane? No matter, he told himself with a faint grin. *I know that pompous Colonel will be the first through the door to get the jewel. I'll hang back a little, and give him time to topple over if there's any gas still present. I can't be too careful with nasty stuff like this.*

* * *

In the meantime, the Skipper was waiting for the next step of his plan to take place. His wrist watch read eight thirty-six a.m. He raised his eyes to the closed entryway to the fuselage of Flight 4416. *What is going on inside that parked airliner? Did the gas do its job on those four armed Russian guards? And has the gas all been removed from the interior of the aircraft? Is it now safe to enter?* He watched Navigator disconnect the gas canister from the air conditioning pump.

We'll know soon, he assured himself, adjusting his sunglasses.

CHAPTER NINETEEN

Colonel Damitrov was indeed the first person to climb the mobile ramp, pull open the entry door and enter the fuselage of Flight 4416 with the Russian diplomatic pouch in one hand. But even the Colonel moved slowly and carefully. He pulled a handkerchief from his back pocket and held it over his nose as he approached First Class, where he had left his four guards. Two of them lay on the floor, one staring at the ceiling with glazed eyes, the other on his stomach. The last two still sat in their First Class seats. One had managed to pull his automatic pistol, which pointed vaguely toward the Colonel. None of them were breathing.

At first the Colonel was alarmed by the sickening odors that penetrated his handkerchief, and he flinched backward, colliding with D'Obere. "Nothing toxic about the smells," observed D'Obere with a small smile. "That's just the odor of dying. Both the men on the floor vomited a little, and all of them released their bowels in death." He had an air freshener in his hand, and walked through First Class spraying on both sides of the aisle.

The Colonel stared after him for a moment, then began looking for the Star of Yakutsk, still holding the handkerchief to his nose. He found it in the arms of one of the two guards still sitting in his seat. The guard's eyes stared at the stained hardwood box the jewel was in, his arms crossed over it like a football player trying to hang on to a loose football as he goes down on the turf. "Dorski," breathed the Colonel. "Always one of my best. You did your job well, old friend. Sorry it had to be this way." He pulled the box from Dorski's grasp, opened it and stared at the Star of Yakutsk for a long moment. Then he walked back to the entryway, stuffing the box down in the Russian diplomacy pouch. The Colonel walked quickly down the steps of the steep ramp, past the Swiss policeman at the bottom, and across the concrete floor of the hangar to where the Skipper now stood in his niche.

* * *

The Skipper nodded to the Colonel, and asked with a smile, "Is all well, my friend?"

"Yes... yes, it is," said the Colonel. "Everything proceeds as we planned. It's very hard, though. When I am again on the concourse, I will stop for a vodka somewhere."

But the Skipper's eyes were on the Russian diplomatic pouch. "Let's look for a moment at the Star of Yakutsk," he said.

But the Colonel only stared at him, then said, "I had to kill one of my best men back there," nodding at Flight 4416.

"Had to be done. But it reminded me how easily any one of us might die as this mad scheme develops. It made me think. Perhaps I should tell you, I've written down a full confession of what I've done, as well as your part in it – just in case I don't make it through to the end with the Star of Yakutsk in my hands. I left my confession with an old friend, to whom I've promised to send a very generous part of what our diamond earns for us. He has promised to destroy my confession as soon as he receives his portion."

The Skipper shot to his feet. "You fool!" he raged. "You would imperil all our plans by broadcasting to the world what we are doing? That's insane! I have no plans to harm you! You may have cost us everything!"

The cagey old Colonel studied the Skipper's flushed and livid face, and thought, *Looks like I was right, and probably spoke just in time.* Then he opened his canvas diplomatic pouch and allowed the Skipper to view the Star of Yakutsk lying on the bottom. The Skipper calmed himself a bit as he stared at the large uncut diamond. There were also two hardwood boxes in the pouch, and four sets of automatic pistols, complete with extra ammo clips.

"Time to distribute arms and treasures to my troops, my friend," said the Colonel, holding one of the boxes up for the Skipper to inspect. He carefully opened the lid, and exposed a ten-pound weight and a two-pound weight wrapped together tightly with duct tape so they made no noise, and with added tape wrapped around the weights to fit them tightly in the box. "My two substitute boxes each weigh precisely 12 pounds, exactly as the Star of Yakutsk does," said the Colonel smugly. "Excuse me while I motivate my men on Flight 4427 one last time," he said, turning away from the Skipper's niche in the hangar wall, and toward Flight 4427, where the other Russians were waiting. "I'll see you when we board Flight 4427 at noon at Gate Six."

The Skipper still had a frown on his face. The Colonel's revelation about the note he left with a friend had him reeling. He wondered if the Colonel was lying to him. He didn't think Damitrov had any close friends. Certainly none that he would tell about this operation. Would the Colonel give up a significant part of his percentage of the value of the Star of Yakutsk to protect his own life?

Certainly not if he could do it in any other way. *I should have anticipated something like this*, the Skipper told himself. The Colonel was an experienced old spy from the Cold War. This was yet another complexity for the Skipper to address.

At least the gassing had apparently gone well. Francois D'Obere was proving to be one man the Skipper could count on when he needed him. He couldn't see D'Obere anywhere at the moment, but he didn't need him for the next part of the operation, so the Skipper let D'Obere drop from his mind. *"The baggage carts for 4416 should be here by now,"* the Skipper told himself angrily. It had cost him another small fortune to arrange for the baggage-loaded carts to come to the airplane in the hangar, not at the gate. "Why is no one on time?" he raged, staring at his wrist watch. As if they had heard him speaking, two TransGlobal baggage handlers appeared, wearing burgundy mechanics' coveralls, and driving tractors with several baggage-laden carts attached and bumping along behind. Both men pulled up their carts next to Flight 4416, and together lifted the airplane's baggage doors, exposing the airliner's hold. Then they began tossing in luggage from the carts. When the baggage was all loaded, the handlers closed the doors of the hold, started the loud engines of their baggage cart tugs, and pulled away to get the luggage waiting to be loaded on Flight 4427. Co-Pilot and Engineer were already beneath Flight 4416, wearing black, doublebreasted TransGlobal pilot uniforms and walking around under theaircraft as if they were performing a standard preflight visual inspection of the underside of the airliner. They glanced across the hangar to where the Skipper was watching them. He nodded to them, and both men showed their ID's to the Swiss policeman at the bottom of the ramp, and climbed the ramp to enter the giant airplane.

Inside, they grabbed the bodies of the Russian guards and dragged them back along the central aisle to the trap door that led to the baggage hold below. Then they roughly tossed the four bodies into the hold, and closed the trap door. Now that the baggage was all loaded in the baggage area, no one would open the trap door during the upcoming flight, and after the aircraft's two engines seized up over the North Atlantic, no one would ever open it again. Co-Pilot and Engineer descended the steep ramp, and reported again to the Skipper.

The Skipper leaned out of his niche in the wall office, and nodded at the retreating figure of Colonel Damitrov as the Colonel approached his people standing around Flight 4427. "Keep an eye on the Colonel and the diamond in that Russian diplomatic pouch he's carrying," the Skipper ordered Co-Pilot and Engineer. "He's going to talk to his guards who will fly on Flight 4427 to the United States. Make sure he doesn't pass that diamond to anyone else. After he's talked to the guards on 4427 and come back to talk to the replacement guards on 4416, there should be nothing left in his pouch but the Star of Yakutsk. You know what you need to do on 4416 in a few minutes. When it's over, bring me the diamond in the diplomatic bag."

* * *

    Just as Elsie studied records, a host of mechanics continued to search the two airliners trying to find anything wrong before the airplane selected by Colonel Damitrov left to climb into the sky over Kloten Airport in Zurich with that blasted diamond on it, and turn west for the long flight back to the US. But Elsie still couldn't make the many clues she had collected fit together to tell her what evil thing was about to happen today -- or even to whom, exactly -- and that was making her extremely anxious. The authorities couldn't stop it if they didn't know what was going to happen, or even which airplane it was going to happen to. She and Lori might well be on board the victim aircraft, and so would many other living human beings. She wondered how ... even if she survived herself ... she would live the rest of her life if her friend or even complete strangers died in some sort of airline disaster because she and Lori hadn't been able to find the answers to this whole enigma in time.

Only one thing to do -- keep working. Elsie picked up the next folder she'd brought with her. It was all the records she had put together on Purser Aspen Mohr. Nothing jumped out at Elsie as she read about Aspen.

Then she noticed something strange from the records she had gotten from TransGlobal's Crew Scheduling office... or at least something unusual. For years ... ever since Aspen had been senior enough to get her choice of trip bids, she had selected the same flight over and over. She had flown Flight 4416 to Zurich, Istanbul, Moscow and back, and done it repeatedly.

Talk about a busman's holiday, thought Elsie. *If she loves the area so much, why doesn't Aspen live over here?* Then she answered her own question. *Because it's not the cities ... it's the travel <u>between</u> the cities. Aspen is a smuggler, and her job involves transporting items between some of those cities, maybe all of them. Elsie noticed that when she wasn't assigned to fly herself, Aspen volunteered for stand-by to work any 4416 flight when a flight attendant called in sick. They must be pushing a ton of diamonds through these cities for her to travel that much!*

But she never flew 'space available' at no cost to herself as a TransGlobal employee, Elsie noticed. *Why? Maybe because she could get bumped at the last minute when the flights were full, and that might mess up some smuggling plan arranged months ahead.*

Then Elsie noticed something else. For as long as the Crew Scheduling records went back, all the telephone numbers Aspen left for Crew Scheduling to reach her if someone called in sick were the same. Elsie recognized Aspen's cell phone number from other records she'd collected on Aspen. But wait a minute – a couple of months ago she left a different number for two nights. Could she have broken or lost her cell phone, and had to leave a land line number until she bought a new one? Or maybe it was a friend's cell phone number ... someone she'd be spending the night with?

But what if it's only a hotel room? Hopeful that it wasn't, Elsie grabbed her cell phone and called Inspector Lodge. "Lodge here," he answered on the second ring.

"Inspector, can you identify a Zurich telephone number for me?"

"Certainly," replied Lodge. "Is it important? Do you need it before you take off today?"

"If I'm right about this number, it could be very important, Sir!"

"Then give me your own number, and I'll get right back to you," said Lodge.

Seven minutes later Inspector Lodge called Elsie back. "It's a land line, and it belongs to a Francois D'Obere at 1820 D

Stromberg Place here in Zurich. Does that help?"

"Let me make one more call, Inspector, and I'll know. I'll call you right back, either way!"

Elsie called Samantha Arnold in TransGlobal Human Resources. She started the conversation with "I'm going to owe you even more, Sam. I need another favor." "No, you won't," replied Sam, sounding excited. "These calls are the most interesting parts of my day. Are we solving another mystery?"

"No, it's the same one, but it's a whopper, Sam, I kid you not!"

"Okay, let me have it!" said Samantha enthusiastically.

"Does this airline employ a Francois D'Obere? First try the Zurich airport."

"Bingo," said Samantha. "He works in TransGlobal maintenance at Kloten! He's been with us for ... uh ... seven years. Does that help?"

"Enormously, girl! Thank you."

"Wait a minute! Am I going to find out someday what mystery I've just solved?" asked Samantha piteously. "You wouldn't leave me hanging, would you?"

"Not only will I tell you, but if I'm right, you might even hear about it first on television! Bye, girl!" said Elsie, hanging up. *I sure hope I'm still around to tell you first, though*, she thought as she looked for Inspector Lodge's number.

Elsie called Lodge back, and said, "I've got another suspect for you, Inspector. Aspen Mohr has been doing sleep-overs at the home of Francois D'Obere ... well, at least two sleepovers I know about, but I'm guessing many of them."

"And why are we concerned with Miss Mohr's social life?" asked Inspector Lodge amicably.

"Because Mr. D'Obere is a TransGlobal maintenance mechanic at Kloten Airport here in Zurich," replied Elsie.

"Ahhhh, you forgot to mention that part, lovely lady. We will put him under surveillance immediately. Of course, it may just be a romantic attachment. We have not run across this man yet in all the time we have been following Miss Mohr.

"I'm beginning to think Aspen Mohr is too busy for romantic attachments, Inspector," considered Elsie thoughtfully. "You just won't believe how busy this woman is!"

* * *

Colonel Damitrov handed one of the carefully weighted stained hardwood boxes from his large diplomatic pouch to one of the guards preparing to enter Flight 4427. "Treat this box every moment as if it contained the Star of Yakutsk" he said. "Don't handle it casually as if it's an empty box. Terrorists may decide where the diamond is just by watching what you do with this box."

"Yes, Sir," said the Russian guard as he accepted the box, holding it carefully.

"I have shown you where to sit in First Class. Take your positions. You'll have some two hours before Flight 4427 taxies to Gate Six, but the airplane is air conditioned and comfortable. Stay alert. You will be met in New York by embassy personnel. Good luck!"

The Colonel turned and strode rapidly across the concrete back to Flight 4416. His four assistants still stood by the ramp to the entryway high in the fuselage. "Follow me" he ordered, as he climbed the ramp and turned left into First Class. The four assistants scurried after the Colonel, and gathered around him in First Class.

Co-Pilot and Engineer were still dressed in the black double-breasted uniforms of TransGlobal pilots, and further disguised by dark aviation style sunglasses. They remained in the aft section of the airliner as Colonel Damitrov ranted at his assistants in Russian from where he stood in the aisle of the aircraft holding the diplomatic pouch.

"I have found the four guards initially assigned to keep this stone safe to be completely incompetent," said the Colonel. "They are all idiots! They are not worth being part of this important mission. They are sitting in the rear of this aircraft, and are under arrest. They will be turned over to the Russian Embassy in Dallas when Flight 4416 arrives there tomorrow. In the meantime, you four will function as guards. Here are the firearms you will carry." He passed out the four automatic pistols in the diplomatic pouch to his four surprised assistants. "You have all administered this program from the beginning, so you know everything about the duties of the four guards, and exactly where they are to sit, and what they are to do until this airliner reaches DFW Airport. You will be met there by embassy personnel. Do your job well, and you will be recognized for it!"

Co-pilot loitered at the entryway between First Class and Business Class as the Colonel talked to his men. His brainbag sat at his feet as he began untying the fabric curtains that draped the door into Business Class. Engineer walked back to the entryway to the ramp where they had entered the airplane. There he leaned out the doorway to see if anyone was anywhere near the ramp on the concrete floor below. A Swiss policeman stood at the bottom of the ramp, but he faced away from the airplane, and seemed unconcerned about anything going on inside.

Without waiting for any questions from his new set of four guards, the Colonel concluded his remarks and turned to leave the aircraft. *Why am I briefing them?* he thought. *They'll all be dead before nightfall.* He shifted the diplomatic pouch containing the Star of Yakutsk to his shoulder just as he passed Co-Pilot, who was preparing to pull closed the curtains draping the entry to Business Class. By the time he passed through Business Class, and neared the entryway door to the ramp, Engineer was there, down on one knee, apparently intent on refastening the handles of his case. Just before the Colonel reached Engineer, CoPilot called out from behind him, "Oh, Colonel, do you have a moment, Sir?" Colonel Damitrov stopped and turned around to face Co-Pilot, who pulled down his aviation sunglasses so the Colonel could recognize him. The Colonel was surprised and vaguely alarmed to recognize that Co-Pilot was one of the Skipper's men.

"I'm actually very busy right now, as you should know," he said, looking down his nose at Co-Pilot with all the hauteur of a senior officer addressing a minion. The Colonel had opened his mouth to continue just as he felt the hardness of Engineer's brainbag in the small of his back. "Nyet" was all he managed to get out of his mouth before he felt the searing pain of the hypodermic syringe plunging deeply into his back. Then he felt the heat that diffused throughout his body from the point where the needle entered his back, then nothing at all as his body collapsed to the floor.

Co-Pilot replaced his sunglasses, and leaned over to grab the diplomatic pouch. He burrowed into it to search for the Star of Yakutsk. It was there; now the only item left in the Colonel's pouch. Engineer seized both of the Colonel's wrists, and hurried backward, dragging the Colonel's body to the trapdoor in the aisle. Co-Pilot lifted the cover, and helped Engineer push the body through the opening. While Co-Pilot closed and locked the trap door cover, Engineer tossed the diplomatic pouch over his shoulder and walked down the ramp carrying his brainbag, as well. Co-Pilot followed him, carrying his own brainbag. They headed for the Skipper's little niche-inthe-wall office.

As the Skipper watched them approach alone without the Colonel, he whispered to himself, *I just didn't believe you, my old friend.*

"Now what?" asked Co-Pilot, as they walked across the wide concrete floor. "Skipper wants the stone on 4427 with him since 4416 is going down in the Atlantic. The Swiss cops won't let anything onto either airplane unless it's either scanned by security or in the diplomatic pouch, and if it's in the pouch, it has to go to the Russian guards sitting in First Class."

"The Skipper will have a way," Engineer assured him with a chuckle as they reached the niche-in-the-wall.

"Let me have another look at it," ordered the Skipper. Engineer opened the Russian pouch so that the Skipper could gaze down at the dull crystalline rock that would become the Star of Yakutsk when it was cut and polished.

The Skipper was roused from his reverie by spotting D'Obere returning to the hangar. Across the maintenance facility he watched D'Obere park his oiler truck, jump out and begin the long walk across the broad floor to the Skipper's niche. "Give me the diplomatic bag" ordered the Skipper. "Change out of your uniforms, and meet me at Gate Six where we will board Flight 4427 at noon."

"Very well done, Navigator," the Skipper told D'Obere when he reached the niche. He pulled a small overnight bag from the dusty desk he sat behind. "I've just put the Star of Yakutsk in here. Take it to the baggage facility and use the bar code system to place the bag in the pile of luggage accumulating for Flight 4427. I don't want anyone remembering you putting anything into 4427's luggage bin yourself. I've already got the 4427 bar code label stuck on the bag. Just be sure the top side is up when you put the bag on the conveyor so it can read the bar code, and the conveyor computer will send the bag to the correct luggage bin. In case anything goes wrong, I've put Aspen's name and Dallas address on it. But it won't. This new system is very effective, and it's never failed me transporting diamonds to the right luggage hold on the right airliner."

"But do it *now*," the Skipper warned D'Obere. "You've probably got another thirty minutes before the baggage handlers empty the bin and load the airplane, but do it *now* to be sure! Then meet the rest of us at Gate Six at noon to board 4427. And have the baggage claim slip with you when I see you next. That will be the most important baggage claim slip in recorded history, and worth more than your very life! Good luck."

D'Obere nodded and took the little bag containing the Star of Yakutsk. He even made a show of jogging across the wide concrete floor to his truck, jumping in and driving out of the hangar. But he slowed once he was outside. He pulled to the side of the road, took another label out of his coveralls chest pocket, removed its adhesive backing strip and pressed it down over the Skipper's 4427 bar code label. The label bar code now showing read Flight 4456. *Aspen and I wouldn't want to send you to the same watery grave the Skipper's going to,* D'Obere told the fabulous diamond he held in his lap. *He separated the claim stub from the rest of the ticket label, and put it in his pocket.* D'Obere knew the Skipper would be searching the airport, and eventually the world, for Aspen and him when they didn't show up at noon.

Then he pulled back onto the road and headed for the main concourse terminal.

CHAPTER TWENTY

"How are you this morning?" asked Elsie when she called Lori at nearly ten in the morning. "Better than you, I'll bet," said Lori. "Did you get the least bit of sleep last night?"

"Nary a wink," said Elsie. "Too much to look at and study. I've discovered some things, and I'd ask whether you want the good or the bad news first, but I'm afraid none of it is good news, although what's left probably isn't bad enough to stop Flight 4416 from taking off."

"Go ahead and tell me while I drink my orange juice."

"Well," said Elsie with a sigh, "I'm afraid we've lost Aspen. She disappeared yesterday apparently out a restaurant restroom window, even with the police following her. So either she's working with the bad guys as you've thought for so long, and she knows there's something wrong with the airplane this leg of the trip, or she's innocent, but just afraid with all the terrorist threats. Crew Scheduling has already replaced her with another purser, along with replacements for two other flight attendants who also bailed."

"That is scary," agreed Lori.

"And I ran down a boyfriend she has apparently spent some nights with during the past year," continued Elsie, "and this morning found out the boyfriend is a TransGlobal mechanic who is so trusted by the company that he was one of the mechanics selected to spend all of last night searching 4416 for any bombs or unsafe conditions ... none of which he found, of course."

"That's comforting," said Lori.

"And there's one last thing that's just ... just strange."

"That sounds interesting. I'm all ears ... tell me!"

"Well," began Elsie, I watched the guards for the Star of Yakutsk arrive in a TransGlobal sedan this morning a little after 7:30 a.m. and enter Flight 4416. A few minutes later Colonel Damitrov entered, as well. But he reappeared and did stuff around the hangar, including briefing his guys on 4427, I guess, before reentering 4416 bringing another four guards with him. So now there should be eight Russian guards on our airplane, and the Colonel makes nine because he never left! As it was getting later, I decided to go ask him if he had changed the number of guards or something. I showed my ID to the Swiss officer at the ramp, and entered the airplane. But the Colonel wasn't there, and there were only four guards after all. I searched the whole aircraft, but couldn't find the Colonel or the extra guards. Then I checked the manifests of both airplanes, and that the Colonel is not flying with the Star of Yakutsk. He's booked to fly on 4427 to LaGuardia, and the diamond is going to New York later on another flight from Dallas. Can you imagine the Colonel not flying with his big diamond?"

"That is crazy," was all Lori could think to say. "I guess he really trusts those guards, but it does make you wonder if he's nervous about flying on this airplane after all the threats." "I don't even want to think about that. And the only answer I can think of for the disappearing people is that I missed some comings and goings," said Elsie. "There are multiple entryways on both sides of the 777, and the mechanics working on the airplane all night put up ramps to every entryway so they could move around and on and off both sides of the airplane quickly and easily. I guess I might have missed someone leaving on the other side of the airplane from where I sat. We certainly have had Russians all over the place."

"Well, we can let the Russians and our own flight attendants worry about who is where," said Lori. "That's a lot less important than the safety of the airliners, as far as I'm concerned."

"Me, too," agreed Elsie. "I'll see you on the airplane."

"Let's plan on it," said Lori. "As soon as we've taken off, and I've said 'goodbye' to Kloten ground control and talked to London center, then I'll have some free time. I'll wave to you as I exit the cockpit and head upstairs to the crew lounge. You'll be in First Class where you'll be able to see me, so come join me and we can talk for a while up in the crew lounge."

"Sounds great," agreed Elsie. "I'll watch for you."

* * *

Francois D'Obere punched the time clock in the maintenance facility and walked out to employee parking, still carrying the Russian diplomatic pouch. After working all night, he was now off duty for the entire day and night to come. As he crossed the parking lot, a grey Dodge sedan pulled up beside him, and Aspen rolled down the driver's side window.

"Where you going, handsome?" she asked.

"I'm headed for a brand new life of luxury," said D'Obere with a smile.

"What a coincidence," replied Aspen. "That's exactly where I'm headed. Want a lift?"

"Merci, ma chere!" said D'Obere. "Let's get this big rock headed in the right

direction, and then you can take me home to change."

Aspen drove around the airport to the main concourse, then pulled into a short term parking place, and got out of the car. "I'll take it in," she said. "My uniform fits in better here than yours does."

Aspen skirted the row of check-in counters, and walked back through to luggage conveyors to the back of the darkened facility, where she was the only person in the large, secluded area. As she passed through an entryway to the main conveyor room, the Skipper caught her arm and pulled her back toward the wall he stood against.

"I gave this bag to D'Obere," he said. "What are you doing with it?" He was still clad in his burgundy overalls, and rather incongruously held one of the deadly brainbags he usually carried with his pilot's uniform in his other hand. He pulled up Aspen's hand that held the bag holding the diamond. "Well, look at that," he said, grabbing the bag out of her grasp. "Somehow this bag has a new flight number on it. 4456! How in world did this happen?" he growled in fury.

Aspen grabbed the bag back from the Skipper, and tried to throw it on the moving conveyor belt. "You're going to lose it anyway, now that you've taken up with that stupid Geisha Girl of yours!" screamed

Aspen. She rolled onto the moving conveyor belt, and tried to crawl along it, but the Skipper swept the brainbag up and against her hip, and he fired the needle from his grip on the handle.

Aspen shuddered, then fell face down on the moving belt, where she lay still. The Skipper dropped the brainbag and ran beside the conveyor belt in order to grab Aspen's dress as the belt carried her toward the line of baggage vehicles at the other end of the building. He hauled her like a rag doll off the belt and down on the concrete floor. He stared down at her glazed open eyes for a moment, then pushed her body under the conveyor belt with his foot. "I don't want you found any sooner than necessary," he said, "so I think you'd better stay right here. It'll probably be after midnight when the cleaning crew comes through."

The Skipper carefully pulled away the Flight 4456 label on the bag holding the diamond, exposing the Flight 4427 label he'd put on the bag himself. "Much better," he said. "I knew I needed to be sure this bag got sent to the right place. Guess I shouldn't have been so surprised to find you here," he said to Aspen's body on the floor beneath the conveyor belt. "One just can't trust anybody anymore."

* * *

It was twelve o'clock noon when Lori and Eric entered the maintenance hangar where Flights 4416 and 4427 sat. There were a few mechanics still around the aircraft, and Swiss policemen still guarded both airplanes. Neither airliner would take off for nearly three hours, but Lori wanted to look over the airplane, and she had encountered Eric on the way. Lori was frazzled and nervous, and in no mood to be friendly with her airplane's co-pilot.

"I cannot imagine how you can associate with smugglers," she complained. "You've got the greatest job in the world and an excellent salary, and you're willing to become a crook in order to make a little bit more."

"It's not a little bit more," said Eric. "It's a lot more! Smuggling diamonds can bring in many thousands of dollars in income over a year's time."

Every time Eric defended smuggling, Lori got angrier. "I don't intend to fly with you again," she said. "And I'd appreciate your not speaking to me again."

CHAPTER TWENTY-ONE

An hour after Flight 4416 lifted off runway 36 left at Kloten Airport and turned west away from the snow-covered Alps of northeastern Switzerland, Lori completed her call to London Center informing the air traffic controller there that she would be in his airspace in another hour and twenty minutes. She gazed ahead out the 777's windshield, between the silhouettes of Captain Travers in the left seat, and Captain McEllen on the right. She wondered what awaited them out there in the future.

The TransGlobal mechanics who worked all night gave D/O Fitzgerald a detailed report assuring that nothing dangerous was hidden within the wings or airframe of Flight 4416 -- or 4427, for that matter -- and that all their many systems were working perfectly. But Lori had a bad feeling about the situation, and so did the rest of the flight crew, all of them sitting silently, saying nothing but what they needed to say. Director of Operations Ian Fitzgerald, himself, sat only a few feet away from the flight deck in First Class. He seemed somber himself, but he was nonetheless there supporting them with his presence.

"The Brit I talked to in London Center was civil as Englishmen always are," said Lori, "but I could tell he wished I were talking to someone else. Everybody in the world seems to be following our progress since you became so famous as the almost-murdered CIA agent, Eric, and that Swiss TV station pointed us out as the diamond-nappers who are going to get blown out of the sky by the Siberian mafia." Then she added, "I'll bet we make the morning news everywhere when we arrive in the States tomorrow morning."

"I don't mind at all," said Captain Travers, "as long as we do make it!" "I'm with you," said Lori. "Mind if I spend some more time looking at evidence with my buddy Elsie up in the crew lounge?"

"Please do," said Travers. "I'll feel much better if you can solve this whole thing before we're over the mid-Atlantic this afternoon."

"I'll do my darnedest," promised Lori as she unlocked the flight deck door. She spotted Elsie reading a book in First Class, and waved at her as she started up the stairs to the crew lounge. Elsie gathered up books and papers, and hurried after Lori.

When Lori closed the door to the crew lounge, and turned to face Elsie, she stopped and stared. "You look like you've just seen a ghost," she said. "You know something new, don't you? It must be really grim."

"It's Aspen," said Elsie. "She's dead. Some workers were cutting through the luggage room at Kloten where they have that brand new baggage conveyor belt system that divides up all the luggage and delivers it to different luggage carts. They spotted her under a conveyor belt. She'd been murdered. The Swiss police haven't had time to do a forensic exam yet, but Inspector Lodge said that she had not been undressed as if someone had sexually molested her, and she had money and jewelry on her body, so she probably wasn't robbed. He's going to get back to us as soon as they examine the body."

Lori sank into the plush chair across the lounge from the bed, and tried to think.

"And I've been thinking about those guards ... the missing ones," added Elsie hesitantly. "Could they have been killed when someone attacked them to steal the diamond? But we know they made it as far as the airplane. They had the diamond, and they were all armed. How could they lose the diamond without a shot being fired, and with people all around them in the hangar. It could have only been someone they knew."

"Like the Colonel!" Lori blurted out. "The Colonel!" she repeated. "The only one who could have replaced the first set of guards with the second bunch was the Colonel. He had to be involved! And he was probably the only one who could have somehow gotten that diamond away from the armed guards without violence. He was their commanding officer! No wonder he's not flying on Flight 4416. The diamond is no longer here, either. The Colonel has probably taken the diamond with him on Flight 4427, and he's flying with it to New York City right now."

"And he switched the guards so we'd think it's still here?" said Elsie slowly, a grimace on her face.

"Yes," although that will all fall apart when they question everybody after we get to DFW." A sickly look suddenly spread across Lori's face. "Unless we never get to the States," she said. "Unless we go down in the North Atlantic, and are never heard from again. That's the only way this scheme can work."

Elsie and Lori just stared at each other. Finally, Lori asked quietly, "The baggage was delivered to the hangar where the mechanics were inspecting Flights 4416 and 4427, instead of being loaded at the gates, wasn't it?"

"Yes, I was surprised it was sent there. How did you know?" asked Elsie.

"Because I think the guards are still with us," Lori said quietly. "I think that after the baggage was delivered, there was enough time to throw their bodies down the trap door into the hold before Captain Travers taxied to the gate to pick up our passengers. That's why you never saw them leave. And I imagine they're all dead." "Something is definitely wrong with this airplane! We've got to get Captain Travers to turn around and fly back to Zurich before something explodes or both engines fall off, or whatever is going to happen does," said Elsie, a note of panic in her voice. "We're living on borrowed time."

"But he won't do it without some kind of proof," said Lori. "He's got Director of Operations Fitzgerald sitting only a few feet away in our own First Class section, and he can't afford to cave in too fast or make any kind of a mistake. Somebody has to confess, or we at least have to find the diamond, or the guards' dead bodies, I guess."

"Let's go talk to the Captain," said Lori. "I want to keep him in the loop as we do this. To be sure we know what we're doing, we first need to get the guards to admit they don't have the diamond, and then we'll move on from there. And let's hurry," she added nervously.

* * *

"That's the most hair-raising tale I've heard yet," said Captain Travers. "And I would certainly like to make sure what you're saying is not true by taking a quick peek, but opening the trap door into the hold in full view of the passengers might set off a real panic. The Captain didn't add that doing so just a few feet from where TransGlobal Director of Operations Thomas Fitzgerald sat could increase the embarrassment. "I understand, Sir," said Lori. "How would you feel about it if the Russian guards we have on board were to admit to you that they don't have the Star of Yakutsk in that box they're guarding."The Captain hesitated a moment, then said, "If they were to admit that to D/O Fitzgerald and myself, then that's a whole new ballgame. Yes, I'd authorize searching the hold if they acknowledge that the diamond is gone." I'll ask them politely," said Lori, as she turned and left the flight deck with Elsie right behind her.

CHAPTER TWENTY-TWO

First Class was comfortable and spacious, and Lori and Elsie found the Russian guards gathered together conversing. As they approached, however, the conversation dwindled, and the men all focused on them. One of them even let his hand drop to the holstered automatic pistol he carried on his belt.

"Gentlemen," began Lori, "I need to talk with you in a more secure area. Will you follow me, please, to the crew lounge upstairs?"

"We were not told we would ever have to leave this area," said the only guard sporting a beard. "It is matter of security."

"Are you Mister Valin?" asked Lori, consulting the seating roster.

"No, I am Rostikoff," said the guard.

"It is about security that I need to talk with you," said Lori. "None of you are the guards Colonel Damitrov assigned to this duty originally. None of your names match our original roster. And the Colonel himself was supposed to be with you, but he isn't. It's actually Colonel Damitrov I want to talk about. I'm concerned that something has happened to him."

"What happens to Colonel?" asked the bearded guard.

"We need to go upstairs where we can speak privately," said Lori.

"I am not authorized to leave this area," said the guard.

Lori looked around the First Class section. Her uniform had drawn the attention of nearly everyone in the section when she had entered, but she and the one guard were speaking so quietly to each other now few of the other passengers were still paying any attention to them.

"Very well," she said, moving closer to the guard and lowering her voice even more to a whisper. "I don't think the Star of Yakutsk is still in the box you're guarding."

"Of course it is," said the guard, his voice rising.

"Your life depends on it, as do all the lives on this airliner," said Lori. "Please keep your voice down," she whispered.

"How so is that?" said the guard, now frowning at her suspiciously, but lowering his voice.

"Because I think the diamond has already been stolen," said Lori. "I don't think it was in the box when it was given to you. Did you see it?" the guard gave no answer, just glowered at Lori. "We have discovered a plot to steal the diamond, and crash this airplane in the middle of the North Atlantic so no one will know the diamond is already gone. Then it can be sold without anyone guessing it's the Star of Yakutsk."

"I do not believe this," said the guard.

"If the diamond is missing, you can tell the Captain," said Lori, "and he'll turn the airplane around so we can land somewhere before something happens to all of us."

"No, I do not trust you," said Rostikoff, his voice rising again, as he backed away from Lori.

"You don't have to show it to me," said Lori, trying to keep her voice down and slowly moving toward the man as he stepped backward. "Your life is at stake also. If you will open that box and look yourself, then I will accept whatever you tell me."

"I will tell the others what you say," said the guard. He began speaking in Russian to the others. Lori could see first anger and disbelief spread across their faces, then fear. Soon all of them were staring at the small hardwood box that sat in the midst of them.

The guards began speaking among themselves in Russian. Eventually, one of them said something sharply to Rostikoff, which was soon backed up by the others.

What am I going to do if they say 'no'? I don't even know if we have a sky marshall on this airplane ... and if we do, that's only one gun against four. We can't let this become the shootout at the OK Corral on an airliner with three hundred people on board!"

"I look," said Rostikoff, moving several seats away from Lori. One of the men even drew his automatic pistol out of its holster, and kept it pointed at the floor as he turned to face Lori and Elsie.

Lori could feel her heart beating in her throat as she stood stiffly waiting for the guard to open the box. *If the smugglers locked that box*, she thought, *they'll probably win at this point in the game, and we'll all die.*

But the box had changed so many hands, and the stone removed so often that when Rostikoff turned the metal clasp on the box, he was able to pull the lid open. Lori held her breath as he peered down into the box. When he removed two gymnastic hand weights taped together, she let out a long breath. The worst possible answer, she thought, but an answer, at least. Now they could start doing something.

"Mr. Rostikoff, this means that the diamond has already been stolen from the first group of four guards. Your group of guards are not the ones responsible for losing the diamond." Lori said to the Russian. "Will you tell the Captain that the diamond is gone, and that you are not the first four guards assigned to take care of the Star of Yakutsk? If you will do that, the Captain will turn the airplane around, and we can land somewhere before whatever the smugglers have done to bring down this airplane happens, and we all die."

"*Da* -- yes -- I do that. Yes," said Rostikoff, who seemed to be having trouble breathing as he stared at the two weights taped together.

Lori took Rostikoff to the flight deck, where he surrendered his pistol to Lori before entering the cockpit. He then showed Travers the contents of the box he thought contained the diamond. "Lori," said a visibly shaken Travers, "please ask D/O Fitzgerald to step in here for a moment."

Lori brought in the TransGlobal D/O, who also listened to the Russian's story of how they replaced another set of four guards in Zurich, and looked at the now empty box. But Lori was watching Travers, and decided he was using the time it took Lori and the Russian to recount the whole story to plan what he was going to do. After all, it's up to the Captain commanding an airliner to make all final safety decisions about his airplane. And he was ready when the Russian finally completed his entire account.

"Mr. Fitzgerald," said Travers, "If there are indeed dead bodies in my luggage hold I'm going to declare an emergency, and land at the closest alternate airport. I'm convinced that whoever stole that diamond intends to bring down this aircraft, even though I have no idea how they plan to do it!"

Fiztgerald said thoughtfully, "I agree we're in imminent danger."

"Eric," said Travers, "Would you open the trap door to the hold, and go down to confirm we have dead bodies down there?"

"Could Elsie and I accompany Eric, Sir?" asked Lori. "Elsie has actually seen these people, and will know who we're looking for."

"And you're the airline's chief inspector in this investigation," said Captain Travers with a small smile. "All right, gang. Bring up any wounded personnel so we can take care of them. Have the purser tell the passengers in First Class that we've -- uh, that" -- he looked at Elsie in her civilian clothes --"that we're letting a vet care for some animals in the baggage hold."

"Yes, sir," said Eric as he quickly slid out of his co-pilot's seat and left the flight deck with Lori and Elsie right behind him.

* * *

Curious glances followed the trio from the flight deck back to the small trap door in the middle of the aisle behind First Class. Two TransGlobal pilots in full black uniforms with headgear, and one woman in civilian clothing, all preparing to pass through the small trap door into the baggage hold below got nearly everyone's attention. But no one asked any questions, so no one had to lie.

Eric unlocked and pulled back the door, saying, "The hold is huge. It extends most of the length of the fuselage. We could be down here all afternoon," as he climbed down the ladder into the pitch black windowless baggage hold. He started to say more as he helped Lori down, but he gasped and said nothing as his foot reached the carpeted lower level. He motioned for Lori to follow, but stopped her on the lower rung of the ladder. Elsie ran into her from behind. Eric mouthed "Close the door" to Elsie, then reached for Lori's flashlight. When the door was closed, he turned it on so the trio could see the bodies heaped around the bottom rung of the ladder. Eric had stepped on one the moment he reached the floor of the hold.

"They just threw them down here," he said, his voice outraged.

"Where's the light?" asked Lori.

"Over by the door where the baggage handlers toss in luggage," said Eric, as he stepped gingerly among the bodies, and turned it on. The entire hold was suddenly brightly lit. The three people standing in the hold were obviously the only ones alive down there. Lori counted five bodies, all men in civilian clothes. The last body she recognized as Colonel Damitrov. His glassy eyes stared at her, and he had a ghastly look on his face, but his body bore no bullet wounds or any other sign of trauma she could see other than the bruises it had received being thrown from the above level into the hold.

"The Colonel had to be involved in this scheme," Lori said. "But it looks like the Skipper is even more violent and evil than he was, and this won't be over until we've stopped the Skipper." "Well," Eric said quietly. "That's shock number two this afternoon, exactly as our resident detective predicted it." Then he turned to Lori. "Okay, Sherlock," he said affectionately, "now for number three. What's getting ready to happen next?"

"Next, we're going to get out of here and tell the Captain what we've found," Lori said, still shaken. "And I hope immediately after … immediately, I say … he's going to turn this airplane around and get us back down to solid ground."

CHAPTER TWENTY-THREE

"We have alternative fields ahead of us in Greenland and Iceland," said Captain Travers, as much to himself as to the others in the cockpit, "but I think we're still closer to Shannon Airport in Ireland, which we just flew over half an hour ago. Would you check our position, Lori, to confirm that Shannon is still the closest alternate airport? Then notify London Center that we're turning around, and call Shannon -- if I was right -- to request approach instructions."

"Yes, Sir" said Lori, rising from her seat. But before she reached the cockpit door, Captain Travers added," Tell them we may need emergency services, but I might not be able to tell them what the emergency is until the very last moment!"

Eight minutes later, Lori reported back, "You were right about Shannon, Captain. They're currently 116 nautical miles to our east, and the closest of all the alternates. Shannon says they'll be ready for us. They're rolling out their fire trucks and ambulances just in case we need them."

"Super," said Travers. "Let's also notify London Center that we're turning around, and that I'm declaring an emergency. Also, tell them we have five dead bodies in the hold, and that we think the murderer is on Flight 4427. Oh, and that 4427 probably has sabotage on board that could bring it down any moment, just like us. And you might mention that we are missing a diamond worth some seventy million dollars!"

While Lori talked to Shannon Airport, Captain Travers released the autopilot and guided Flight 4416 on a long slow turn to the south. When he had completed the turn, Travers asked Lori to dial in the heading for Shannon Airport, and pressed his own intercom mike button.

"Folks," Travers announced to his passengers, "this is the Captain. We're going to have to spend a short time in Shannon, Ireland due to general terrorist threats — threats that we need to investigate. We have not yet found anything amiss with this aircraft or any of its systems, but we are landing to investigate further due to an abundance of caution. We expect an uneventful trip back to Shannon Airport about 120 miles to our east, but we'll let you know if we encounter any problems at all." He clicked off the intercom.

"I've probably scared everyone to death," Travers remarked, as much to himself as to any of the others in the cockpit, "But I had to tell them why we turned around. Now let's hope we're going to have a very pleasant, uneventful flight back to the green fields of Ireland." London Center connected

Lori with Inspector Lodge in Zurich. Lodge listened to Lori's report that the Star of Yakutsk had been stolen, and her description of the bodies in the hold of Flight 4416. Then he gave her some information, as well.

"Sounds like the rats are all leaving the sinking ship," he said. "We found tickets for TransGlobal Flight 4456 in Aspen's uniform dress pocket. We checked that flight, and found her seat companion was due to be Francois D'Obere, whom we arrested as he tried to board the flight. We have witnesses who remember D'Obere setting up the air conditioning for Flight 4416 that surely gassed the guards. Can you believe it? All this time I could never figure out what that gas canister of Zyklon B was going to be used for -- but that was it. The Skipper used it to kill the armed guards. Anyway, D'Obere realizes he's going to be indicted for mass murder, so he's looking for any mercy he can get, and answering all our questions as fast as we ask them."

"Does he know where the Skipper and the diamond are located?" asked Lori.

"He says they're both in the same place," said the Inspector. "He saw the Skipper leave the baggage transfer room where Aspen was killed as she tried to put the diamond on Flight 4456, instead of 4427, on which the Skipper was going to be a passenger. D'Obere claims that when he saw him, the Skipper no longer seemed to have the diamond. Apparently the Skipper had killed Aspen and sent the stone on that new bar-coded luggage system to the hold of Flight 4427, which is what he had ordered Aspen and D'Obere to do in the first place. D'Obere claims the Skipper had a ticket on Flight 4427 headed for the U.S., so I imagine that's where they both are right now. Just like you, First Officer ... somewhere over the North Atlantic."

"By the way," added the Inspector, "I'm going to order the pilot of Flight 4427 to land at Shannon Airport, which he is now approaching from the east. We found that a man paid cash and booked himself on that flight as Colonel Damitrov when we were searching for the Skipper, who D'Obere told us was on that flight, along with the diamond. But now that you've told me you have the Colonel's body, I'm going to assume that I have found the infamous Skipper masquerading as the Colonel and sitting in his seat on 4427. Irish authorities will take him off the airplane when it lands at Shannon, and extradite him back to Switzerland ... along with that diamond."

"And First Office Fyfer," the inspector said hesitantly, "I think you're completely right about getting that airplane down on the ground as quickly as possible, and you'll have my thoughts and prayers until you do. I'm on my way to Shannon. And please tell Elsie ... Miss Ponder ... that she also has my prayers, as well."

My goodness, how British, thought Lori. *That's about as emotional a remark as I've ever heard from the inspector! I think Elsie may have made a conquest. Let's hope she lives to enjoy it!*

CHAPTER TWENTY-FOUR

The flight deck was quiet and tense. The crew all wondered if their airplane was rigged for a disaster of some sort, and they suspected that it could occur at any moment. But everything seemed so peaceful. It was a beautiful sunny afternoon, and perfect flying weather.

Lori watched the indicator she had set showing remaining nautical miles to be flown to Shannon slowly drop from 112 to 110, then 108.

Eric McEllen tried to make light of the situation, pointing out that Shannon Airport was only some 50 miles from the famous Blarney Castle. "Maybe we'll get a chance to visit the place, and climb up to the tower where we can kiss the Blarney Stone," he said with a grin. "I could use a little eloquence now and then," he said. "Particularly when chatting with the ladies," he added, glancing at Lori, and still grinning. "My looks alone won't get me far."

Suddenly the entire airliner shuddered. The flight crew flinched, and all peered back along the fuselage to look at the right engine, which had suddenly seized up and flamed out. Alarms began sounding in the cockpit.

Captain Travers flicked switches, checking for fuel pump problems, while Eric tried to re-start the right engine. "No dice," he reported after glancing back at the engine blades, which had instantly crunched to a stop, creating even greater drag than if they had continued to 'windmill'.

Suddenly the crew was shaken by another jolt, and they felt complete loss of headway as the left engine also stopped, with its fan blades suddenly still and rigid like those of the right engine.

The nose of the gigantic airliner slowly eased downward. A metallic "bong" sounded in the cockpit, signaling that both engines had stopped. None of the pilots had ever heard that metallic sound, even when training in the simulator. It just wasn't part of the training Boeing provided. Boeing never expected any of their airliners to lose both engines. It only happens with any kind of airplane once every ten years or so anywhere in the world. And none of the crew had ever experienced the silence that engulfed them, as the engine fan blades on both wings hung rigid in their engine mounts.

Captain Travers sat staring at his instruments only a few seconds analyzing his problems before pulling back on his controls. The 777 climbed slowly as its air speed slowed even more. When the air speed had dropped to just over 220 knots, Captain Travers let the nose of the aircraft again drop slowly into an unpowered glide into Shannon Airport -- he hoped. Travers pushed the control stick slightly to the left, and was gratified to see the nose of the 777 turn slightly left, as well.

"I've still got some hydraulic power to the ailerons, elevator and rudder," he reported exuberantly, "so I can still turn left and right when I find that runway."

"Eric," he said, "drop all our gas immediately. It's just dead weight now. And Lori, please call London Center and Shannon approach. You can tell both of them what our emergency is now. And tell them to notify Flight 4427. They can now tell 4427 the problems they're probably going to have if they don't get on the ground in a hurry." "When you've dropped the fuel, Eric, please tell the purser to prepare the passengers for a hard landing. We just don't know at the moment whether it will be a ground landing or a water landing! Tell her to review both land and water crash procedures with the passengers immediately!"

When Lori had talked to both London Center and Shannon approach, she checked 4416's current altitude. In ten nautical miles they had dropped 5,000 feet to an altitude to 30,000 feet. That was a glide ratio of about 11:1. Shannon was still over 70 nautical miles to the east.

"Unless we get a really wonderful tail wind into Shannon, it's going to be too tight to call," predicted Lori. "How did those smugglers do this to us?" she asked. "What did they do to this airplane?" Squinting her eyes to stare back at the right engine, Lori said to anyone in the cockpit who was interested, "the fan blades are fixed and frozen in the engines, instead of windmilling like they would be if we were just out of gas or something. They've done something to the oil! Even though the oil gauges read full, we must be out of oil to make the engines seize up like that!"

Still a good twenty minutes away from landing anywhere, Lori could see Ireland as a dark smudge along the horizon ahead, with the land to the north apparently higher.

"The Cliffs of Moher," said Eric, looking over her shoulder. "Solid granite cliffs more than a hundred feet high that rise straight up from where the ocean explodes against them."

"Very picturesque, but we certainly don't want to butt heads with them. Farther south," he added, pointing dead ahead, "the valley made by the Shannon River will be much nicer."

As TransGlobal Flight 4416 descended steeply toward the ground, London Center continued to open the air lanes ahead of them. The armada of airliners headed toward the United States from Europe were diverted left and right out of the path of 4416, which glided down from 35,000 feet to 25,000, then lower and lower as the story spread among other pilots about the airliner in their midst that had become a gigantic, awkward glider, and would be touching down in either water or on land in the next twelve minutes. As Flight 4416 descended to 5,000 feet, the airliner was still sixteen miles out from Shannon Airport's longest runway.

"I'm going to have to land in the water," said Captain Travers. "But hopefully our forward momentum will get us very close to land. Lori, please tell the purser to have the passengers hold on for a short, wild ride."

"Everybody on the flight deck," he called, looking around the cockpit, "Belt yourselves in and hold on."

Travers knew that he had only one shot at this landing. There would be no do-overs. He was down to less than one hundred feet above the water. He could see the end of the paved runway less than two miles ahead of him. Since he was landing on water, he had left his landing gear locked up in the fuselage. His hydraulic power was almost gone, but he could still maneuver the huge airliner's wings slightly, keeping them level as the airplane's nose pointing at the upcoming runway. If one wing bit into the water before the other, the airliner might cartwheel out of control, and probably kill some of his passengers.

At the last moment, Travers raised the nose of the airliner enough that the tail hit the water just before the nose did, sending a massive spray of water smashing against all the windows of the cockpit and along both sides of the airplane. The wild ride lasted only a little over twelve seconds, then jolted violently against solid, irregular surfaces that began to tear apart the 777's nose. Lori was thrown forward hard against her seat belt. The front of the airliner came to rest on a grassy berm where water met land at the very end of Shannon Airport's Runway 14 left.

Lori could see blue sky above her through broken portions of the airliner's outer skin. The floor of the flight deck was actually broken into uneven portions that drooped to the right, holding Captain Travers on the left sitting higher than Captain McEllen. Lori hesitantly unfastened her safety belt and crawled across the broken, tilting floor.

"Is everyone all right?" Travers asked, looking around the cockpit. "Lori, please check with the purser to see if there are any injuries among our passengers." He started to tell her to inflate the rubber boats, then realized that he was looking through the flight deck windshield at a grassy knoll where the paved runway started. He had undershot the runway by only a few feet.

"Excellent controlled crash, Captain," said Captain McEllen. "I'll ride with you any day."

Lori leaned forward against an unbroken cockpit window to look down the side of the fuselage. While the nose of the aircraft rested on the grassy berm, the rest of the fuselage, from the wings back, floated in the River Shannon.

Lori opened the cockpit door and hurried into First Class. She pulled down on the bar that locked the main aircraft entryway door closed, and opened it to look twelve feet down at dry grassy ground. The door was still armed, and the emergency chute puffed out of the door interior, exploding larger and larger as interior air pressure blew it up like a balloon.

"Let's get everyone out this door," Lori called to the purser. "No need to deploy the boats unless a fire or something breaks out and requires that we empty the airplane faster."

The bottom of the door was only some 12 feet from the ground since the landing gear had not been deployed, and Lori helped passengers slide down the plastic chute the short distance to the ground. Knowing that they were finally safe, the passengers waved at the flight crew as they appeared, and cheered for Captain Travers. Thank God we're all still alive," said Elsie.

"Thank God we found those bodies in the baggage hold while there was still time, and turned around an hour ago" said Lori. "We'd have been in much worse shape floating in the North Atlantic. We might never have been found. Now, all we've got left to do is to find and put away the maniac who's responsible for all this. Nothing is over until we can do that."

CHAPTER TWENTY-FIVE

Elsie waited until there was a lull in passengers sliding down the plastic safety slide the twelve feet or so to the grassy berm it had crashed against, then sat down in the doorway. She reluctantly took off her beloved high heels, knowing they might punch holes in the plastic slide material, spread her legs to keep her balance, and pulled her mini skirt as close down over her legs as possible. She wasn't being modest.

She could still remember from flight attendant training that one time she wore a dress trying to scoot down the slide, and how that plastic burned the backs of her legs as she slid rapidly down to the tarmac. And holding her knees up off the plastic also helped keep her clasped hands a few inches away from the abrasive rubbery material zipping by beneath her.

She landed at the bottom of the chute in a heap just as a shadow flicked over the scene, and she heard the roar of aircraft engines. Another TransGlobal airliner passed nearby overhead to land on alternate runway 41 right as Elsie scrambled to her feet, and put her high-heeled shoes back on.

"That's got to be Flight 4427," she said. Elsie could see Lori near the cockpit section of the airliner giving first aid to a woman who looked like she had a broken leg. All the flight crew were involved in caring for passengers, along with the cabin crew, as well. There didn't seem to be any life-threatening injuries anywhere, and only a few less serious wounds. Each injured passenger seemed to have two or three people caring for them. Elsie could hear the siren of an ambulance on its way from the airport. Lori was kneeling in the grass some 20 feet away with the injured woman when she looked up, and Elsie caught her eye. "I'll check on 4427," Elsie called. "I'll be back as soon as I know they've got the Skipper!" Lori nodded, and returned to bandaging the woman's leg as the ambulance pulled up on the berm, its lights flashing.

* * *

Elsie hurried along the green grassy landscape of the airport, staying away from runways. Half way to the parked aircraft she took off her shoes, and began running in her panty hose. She could see the police car, its light flashing, parked beneath Flight 4427 where it stood on the tarmac. Two police officers in white shirts and black pants, with billed caps, were climbing the mobile ramp parked against the forward entry door. They were even armed, which was unusual for British officers. She still wore her TransGlobal executive badge on her chest pocket, and it gained her entry to the aircraft past the two flight attendants guarding the door. They weren't sure who the pink-faced, hard breathing woman with shredded panty hose and a high-heeled shoe in each hand might be -- but she was wearing an executive badge, so they let her in.

Inside the aircraft in Business Class Elsie felt sure she had found the Skipper almost immediately. She had never seen him, but she had heard Lori talk about him. She found him in Seat 22 on the right side of the aircraft wearing sunglasses with his cell phone in his hand, and the two policemen standing in the aisle talking to him. He had apparently just used his cell phone, and was returning it to his shirt pocket as he listened to the Irish constables.

Suddenly Elsie saw Engineer and Co-Pilot, as Skipper called his last two henchmen, running down the aisle from opposite ends of the packed airplane, and both were carrying brainbags in their right hands. As the officers talked with the man Elsie was sure was the Skipper, his two thugs came up behind them and thrust the chart cases hard against their backs. Elsie barely had time to scream, "No!" and "Watch out!" before she saw the smugglers fire the needles out of the brainbags into the officers' backs.

Both constables staggered and fell into the aisle. Elsie watched in horror as the smugglers dropped their brainbags, grabbed the officers' automatic pistols and ripped them from their holsters.

Elsie heard the Skipper say, "Get her!", and looked at him to see the dark sunglasses turned toward her. Engineer grabbed Elsie's arm and yanked her toward the Skipper. Most of the passengers in the forward sections of the airplane were now standing and yelling at the three men in the aisle, but Engineer and Co-Pilot turned around, pointing the policemen's guns at the crowd, and the passengers shrank back. The men hurried down the aisle pulling Elsie with them. As he left the airliner, the Skipper yelled, "My men will kill the first person who sticks his head out this door!"

The Skipper's two henchmen pushed a stumbling Elsie down the steps on the ramp toward the waiting police car until Skipper yelled, "Wait a minute. I'm not going anywhere without the Star of Yakutsk!" He ran to the entry door to the airliner's hold, pulled open the door and began sifting through the luggage stacked inside. Then he hoisted himself inside the hold and continued looking.

Co-Pilot and Engineer kept glancing nervously around the tarmac and toward the terminal building as the Skipper looked through the hold. "Skipper, we've got to get out of here," yelled Engineer.

"We can go now," said the Skipper calmly, looking at the small overnight bag he had taken from the hold, the bar coded label he had stuck on it himself slightly askew.

They jumped into the waiting police car, Engineer pushing Elsie ahead of him into the back seat. She managed to open the door on the other side, but Engineer grabbed the inside handle and pulled it closed before she could escape. He swatted Elsie hard across the mouth with the back of his hand, and she fell back against the seat, tasting blood.

As the police car peeled away from the airliner with the overhead lights still flashing, Skipper leaned forward, took off his dark sunglasses and smiled at Elsie from the other side of Engineer.

"Good to see you again, Elsie," he said smugly. "You and I met in person once under the AirTrans track where I lost one of my men. "But I still wasn't sure it was you, so I looked up your picture in the TransGlobal employee records, and it matched the one I already had from the Airliner where you photographed two of my men" The Skipper pulled his cell phone from his pocket, tapped it a few times, and showed it to Elsie. It boasted a full cover shot taken of Elsie from an aircraft door as Elsie retreated across the tarmac, looking over her shoulder anxiously at the two mechanics she'd found in the airliner galley repairing the aircraft's black box.

"You've been doing a lot of research calling airline employees," said the Skipper. "And a few of them were also my employees. You're responsible for a lot of my problems, and I intend that you find out how I feel about that," he said with a grim smile on his lips. Elsie felt herself shiver as she stared at the golden glint in the Skipper's right eye.

The police car had barely reached outer extended parking when the Skipper said, "Turn in here!" and the small sedan slid around a row of cars and skidded to a halt.

"Hot wire that Ford, and do it fast," he yelled. "We probably only have a few minutes. Then put this police car in the place of the Ford."

As they drove carefully out of the airport parking lot in the Ford sedan, they had to pull to the left to let three small white police cars rush in, their sirens screaming and blue emergency lights flashing. "Where are we going, Skipper?" asked Co-Pilot, who was driving.

"I'll tell you later," said the Skipper, looking over his shoulder at the police cars. "Now just get out of here."

CHAPTER TWENTY-SIX

"Stop the car," suddenly yelled the Skipper. Co-Pilot was driving rapidly toward the edge of the airport when Skipper spotted a sign on the edge of the airport campus. "A getaway airplane is better than a getaway car, even if they can identify the airplane," he said thoughtfully.

"Go down that street," he called, pointing ahead to a wooden sign that read 'McMaster Flying School'. "Everybody out," he growled when Co-Pilot pulled the car up in front of a wooden building marked by a canvas windsock dancing about on a flagpole in the breeze beside the small structure. As everyone, including Elsie, piled out of the car, the Skipper walked around the side of the building and stared at the three training aircraft parked in the grass.

The largest was a yellow Cessna Skyhawk, an American four-place high-wing aircraft, and beside it on its left side sat a smaller two place red and white Cessna 150, a standard trainer on airfields around the world, while on its right was a small red bi-plane, a British Tiger Moth trainer, popular for training new pilots in the British Isles since World War I.

A few seconds later a small man who had been inspecting the larger aircraft walked around the wing and stared at the Skipper, who was approaching him pointing one of the two pistols his henchmen had taken from the Irish police officers. "We'd like a ride in the Cessna," growled the Skipper.

After a long silence, the man managed to say, "It only seats four."

"Okay," said the Skipper, as he grabbed Elsie and slammed her against the aircraft. He pulled one of the pairs of plastic zip-ties they'd found in the police car out of his pants pocket, and fastened Elsie's wrists together behind her back. Then he pushed her to the ground and secured her ankles with the other, interlacing the plastic thongs of the two pairs of zip-ties to bend her knees and pull her feet up behind her back, connecting both pairs of zip-ties. He stood back up and rested a moment, staring down at Elsie, her body hogtied and helpless on the ground.

"What are you doing?" asked Elsie as she writhed uncomfortably in the grass.

"You're baggage," said the Skipper, opening the door panel to the luggage area of the Cessna located behind the cabin. "You better stay quiet back here," he added, "or I'm going to shoot you as soon as we land." He leaned over her, picked up her bound body, and stuffed it into the baggage area.

"Don't leave me like this," pleaded Elsie from deep inside the recessed area.

Skipper slammed shut the door, and said to the instructor pilot, "You're going to be a little heavy this trip. But remember, if you don't make it off the ground, you're going to die just as fast as the rest of us do!"

Co-pilot hid the Ford auto behind the flight school building, and scrambled into the right rear seat of the Cessna Skyhawk. Engineer took the left rear, leaving the seat next to the pilot for the Skipper. As the Skipper started to duck into his seat, he noticed the flight instructor walking toward the rear of the yellow aircraft, pulling out the chocks in front of the wheels, and eyeing the landing gear apparatus and the underside of the wings. "There's no time for a walk-around," he growled. "Is she loaded with fuel?"

"Yes, uh ... yes, sir," said the instructor. "The tanks are full."

"Then jump in and let's go!" said the Skipper. "And turn off the transponder right now. We're not going to leave a trail! I'm watching you!" He carefully observed the instructor flipping the switch that disconnected the small device in the aircraft that emitted a unique signature to inform all receiving stations in the area where this particular aircraft was at any moment. The instructor pressed the start button, and the propeller flipped to the right, then accelerated into a blur as the engine exploded into a roar. The entire aircraft shuddered, then began maneuvering out from between the other two airplanes and turning right toward the airport runways. The instructor pulled a set of earphones down on his head, as Skipper did the same with a second set. Then the instructor leaned forward to press his mike button.

"Don't touch it," growled the Skipper. "We're not going to talk to anybody!"

"But there could be aircraft landing," said the instructor. "This is a controlled airport."

"It's going to be the airport where you die if you keep arguing with me," said the Skipper. "I'll kick you out and fly this airplane myself if you want to stay behind with a couple of bullets in you," knowing the instructor couldn't know that the Skipper knew nothing about flying. Now take off straight ahead out over the ocean."

The instructor taxied to the end of the runway, looking nervously into the sky over his right shoulder for any signs of landing aircraft. He and the Skipper heard questioning calls in their headsets from the tower as they approached the main runway, calls that became more urgent and demanding as they reached the end of runway 14 Left. The calls turned to enraged orders not to move.

Even though the instructor pilot could still not see any approaching aircraft about to land, the tower controller began calling "American 610 Heavy landing runway 14 Left, ABORT! Abort landing immediately! Turn right and maintain current altitude. Contact tower on approach frequency 4510. All other aircraft continue holding patterns until contacted by this tower."

The instructor pilot stopped worrying about landing aircraft now that the tower had warned incoming airplanes, and concentrated on his takeoff, moving his throttle forward as his small airplane accelerated down the runway westward toward the open sea.

"American 610 Heavy aborting landing on runway 14 left," called an American voice with a Southern accent as calm and business-like as if he experienced the extraordinary maneuvers going on around him every day. "Will return to holding pattern and contact tower again ASAP. American 610 Heavy over and out."

CHAPTER TWENTY-SEVEN

By the time Lori and Eric found out what had happened at the Flying School, there were armed SWAT police officers standing around the two remaining training aircraft, and talking into radios and telephones. One constable raised his hand as they approached, and asked why they were there. Lori's telephone began ringing at the same moment, and she raised one finger to the officer, asking for a moment, as she answered the international cell phone she carried.

Lori listened to the voice on the line, then responded:

"Hello, Inspector Lodge! I'm afraid our bad guys have slipped away again, killing two Irish constables in the process. The smugglers are flying away in a small Cessna training aircraft from here at the airport, and they've got Elsie with them as a hostage ... oh, and the diamond, as well!" "No, sir, we don't think they've hurt her at all. She had just boarded the aircraft where the Skipper was in the process of getting arrested when his men showed up and killed the two Irish policemen. They used those same chart cases rigged with hypodermic needles they used to kill the two Siberian men on the escalator at Istanbul's Ataturk airport. Lori started to speak again, but listened for a moment. "No, sir," she said. "The police will put out an alert, and they'll be caught at any controlled airport they try to land on. Of course, if the instructor pilot they took with them manages to land in some remote area, we may lose them again."

The burly, ruddy-faced Irish policeman who barred Lori's way had stepped aside as he listened to the conversation.

"Yes, sir." said Lori, gazing at the two aircraft. "And I have an idea. I can fly both of these trainer aircraft still remaining. I'll bet the Skipper will do a 180 after flying out west over the ocean. He'll eventually try to fly east toward London if he wants another shot at getting that diamond to the United States. If I take off in one of these airplanes, I just might be able to get close enough to him to see where he lands. Just a bare chance, but the only possible thing I can do right now."

Then a smile spread across Lori's face. "Yes, sir," she said, "I hoped you felt that way. Would you speak to an officer here to get me approval to take one of these aircraft to go after them? And Sir ... as soon as I know anything about Elsie, I'll let you know!" "Yes, sir," she concluded. "I'll do my best, but I could sure use all the prayers you can come up with in the next few hours!" Lori handed the telephone to the constable standing next to her, and directed her next comments to him. "This is Inspector Lodge of Interpol in Zurich," she said. "He thinks it would be a good idea for me to go looking for these guys in one of those aircraft. Would you see if you can get me a quick approval to take one of them from whoever is in charge? Thank you!"

While the constable talked with Inspector Lodge and the senior Irish officer present, Lori turned to Eric. "I'm going to see if I can scout around in the 150 to see if I can find the Skyhawk. They've got Elsie on board. Would you tell Captain Travers or D/O Fitzgerald where I am?

"You don't have a chance," said Eric. "That Skyhawk is twice as fast, with a range twice as far as your little 150. You'll never even see it!"

"Except that I think I know where he's going," countered Lori, a little miffed. He took off heading westward out low over the ocean to confuse everybody, but I know he's got to head eastward to one of the big airports in London if he's ever going to get that diamond out of the British Isles." She turned away from Eric toward the aircraft.

"So I just take-off heading east, and I'm ahead of him to start with. Anyway, if there's anything I can do to save Elsie, I've got to try."

"And doing anything is better than doing nothing ... right?" said Eric, an understanding smile on his face. "Slow down. I'm coming with you."

"Someone needs to tell Travers and Fitzgerald," argued Lori. "Inspector Lodge is on his way to Heathrow, and maybe on to Shannon this evening. He's still after the bad guys whether we can help him from now on or not."

"The local police will tell them where we are," said Eric. "And it's always better to ask forgiveness later, instead of permission now. Besides, what if you actually came across these guys? You need a man with you, and I also have a gun I always carry in the cockpit."

Lori felt her backbone stiffen. "How do I still not know whether you're a smuggler? I still recall your eloquent remarks about them."

Eric looked frustrated. "You know I'm no smuggler. And I'm the senior pilot. I'll fly."

"Then you can take one of the airplanes, and I'll take the other, because I'm the one who decided to do this, and I'm flying."

"I'm taking the Cessna 150," said Eric, claiming the small but modern American-built trainer, and expecting the argument to end there. "Fine," said Lori, as she quickly began pre-flighting the Tiger Moth.

Eric was speechless for a long moment. "I can't believe you have experience in a biplane," he said grudgingly, while looking over the Cessna 150.

There was no answer from Lori. She had only flown an open-cockpit bi-plane like the Tiger Moth a couple of times for fun when she was still in training in Texas. And she realized that Eric would probably be a bit faster in the 150 than she would. But she didn't feel badly about it for long.

Within a minute Eric was staring at the gasoline gauge display in the 150's cockpit. "It's almost empty," he said. "The instructor must have just brought this one in, and hadn't refueled it yet. And I don't have time to refuel!" He strode around the wing of the 150, and climbed over the side of the Tiger Moth into the front seat.

"Good choice. The pilot usually flies a Tiger Moth from the rear seat due to weight and balance issues," said Lori, "and that's me. I do need you for one thing, though. Jump down and manually start the propeller." "You've got to be kidding me," said Eric, staring back and forth at her and the wooden propeller.

"No, I'd do it myself, but I'm neither tall enough or strong enough to swing it around effectively. If you won't do it, I'll call for someone. We don't have time to argue." Eric climbed down from the forward cockpit, and hurried around the left wing to face the propeller.

"The way you're facing the airplane, the propeller will turn clockwise. Be sure the chocks are set in front of the wheels so the airplane can't move forward, then grab the propeller as high as you can, and pull down. Step away from the propeller as you do it so you won't get hit when it starts spinning. You may have to do it several times before the engine catches. Then stay out of the way of the propeller, pull away the chocks and climb back up here. It will be very loud!"

Eric was mumbling as he reached high to grab the propeller. *"This is the craziest thing I've ever done in my life,"* he muttered softly to himself. He yanked it down and stepped back. It resisted him lightly, and stopped when he released it. He reached up and tried once more. This time the engine coughed loudly a couple of times, then suddenly caught, and the propeller exploded into a translucent whirling machine of roaring sound and violent action.

Eric stepped back two paces, then ran around the whirling propeller to pull away first the left chock, and then the right. The little airplane seemed to come alive, pushing against the brakes Lori was standing on to hold it in place. The police officers around them stood back from all the sound and fury, and watched as Eric ran back to step on the lower wing, and swing himself up into the front cockpit.

The Irish cops were talking among themselves, and there were grins on several faces as the constables watched the two pilots prepare the bi-wing trainer to fly.

Eric looked back at Lori, and he could understand the humorous looks going around among the Irish policemen. Lori was now wearing a brown leather pilot's helmet and pointing at his helmet hanging from the control panel. He pulled it over his head, thinking how much he must now look like Snoopy, the cartoon beagle. *I may never live this down,* he told himself as a rye grin began to meander across his own face. *Still,* he said to himself, *this little woman is determined do anything that has the slightest chance of saving her friend, and I guess I'll do anything that might keep her alive while she's doing it.* He surprised himself as he realized that for the first time he had no suspicions left that Lori Fyfer had anything to do with the smuggling.

Rising from the floor between Eric's legs was a wooden stick that he recognized as the 'joystick' pilots first used from the dawn of aviation to maneuver their primitive aircraft around the sky, often amid other primitive aircraft around them zooming and diving among the clouds. Lori's cockpit aft was equipped the same way.

Eric pulled the leather helmet down over his ears, and secured the strap buckle under his chin. He dropped the large pair of police binoculars a constable had loaned him to the floor of the small aircraft.

"Can you hear me?" asked Lori, sitting in the cockpit behind him. "Five by five," said Eric into the built-in mike held snug against his chin by the helmet strap. "You know," he added, "If this weren't all so serious, it could be a lot of fun."

"But it *is* so serious," said Lori. "We have no idea what's happening to Elsie right now. You did say you have a gun, right?"

"Yep," answered Eric. "I've got a small Beretta automatic I'm licensed to carry in the cockpit." He felt around his waist to locate the small pistol in its holster. "How about you?"

"No," said Lori. "I never decided to carry one. I do wish I had one right now, though."

"We'll share," commented Eric as Lori guided the little biplane toward the main runway.

"Shannon Tower," called Lori on the Tiger Moth radio, "this is Flying School biplane taking off to locate Flying School Cessna that took off without permission. It contains smugglers trying to reach London to fly out of the country. Our authorization is from your local police. I am First Officer Lori Fyfer from the TransGlobal Flight 4416 that just crashed at your airport. We hope to locate the smugglers when they turn back east to reach London. Do you read me all right, and is our transponder transmitting? Flying School bi-plane. Over."

Tinny words quickly poured out of the old-style microphone. "Aye, Flying School bi-plane, this is Shannon Tower. Your identification is 'AKM Shannon', and you're cleared for take-off. You find them bloody buggars, and we'll add a few more charges to the ones they're facing for endangering lives taking off without permission from this airport. Your radio and transponder both sending loud and clear. But before you get a hundred miles from here, squawk 7200 for London Information so as they know you're coming. And may you have a lovely day, lassie!"

"Thank you, Shannon Tower," replied Lori with a smile in spite of her stress. "This is AKM Shannon, taxiing for take-off, over and out."

CHAPTER TWENTY-EIGHT

The little Tiger Moth skirted the southern coast of Ireland at five thousand feet about two miles from the ocean as Lori and Eric flew east toward England. The fragile little airplane bounced about in the air flurries rising off the ocean, and made Lori remember how smooth a ride they'd enjoyed in the TransGlobal 777. An entire hour passed, and Eric and Lori saw only three other aircraft, all much larger airplanes.

Eric scanned the ominous dark clouds above, and wondered if they held rain that would soon drench the Tiger Moth. He looked down at the small cockpit he sat in, and wondered if World War I pilots caught in rainstorms had to worry about rain filling the little cockpits all the way up to their adam's apples while they were trading gunfire with enemy pilots. *I've got to look that up,* he vowed. *There are probably sites on the internet that can even answer that question.*

"Feet wet," Eric called to Lori, repeating the standard phrase military pilots use when the land they're flying over turns into water. "Ocean ahead of us as well as to the south."

"We've left Ireland behind," said Lori. "That's the Celtic Sea below us."

"We're going to be over the south coast of Wales soon ... a third of the way to London," she said so low Eric could barely hear her through the intercom.

"Maybe they're not going to do what I thought they would. I was sure they'd only fly out over the ocean to avoid being seen, then turn around. I thought we'd have them by now. And even if they ARE headed east," she added dispiritedly, "looking for them out here is like looking for the old needle in the haystack." Lori lay her forehead down on the control panel for a moment before raising it again to squint her eyes into the quickly darkening dusk ahead of them.

Eric agreed with her completely, but wasn't sure what to say. They flew on silently for a while until he could see land on the horizon. "Feet dry again," he said flippantly. "That's England below us now."

"They can't just pop into Heathrow," he added. "Probably all the police in the British Isles are looking for that Cessna, and half the military by now. Their only hope to avoid detection is to drop unseen into some uncontrolled rural airport somewhere, and make their way in some other fashion to London."

Eric felt uncomfortable mentioning what he had to say next. "You know, they're able to carry a lot more fuel than we are. They could actually make it all the way to London without refueling if they wanted to, but we can't. We've been flying at maximum speed, and have used up well over two-thirds of the gas in our tank. We need to land somewhere soon. It's beginning to get dark, and these smaller rural airports will be closing." Eric heard only silence over the intercom.

"I'm also going to call Shannon," he added, "and ask if we're flying into rain."

"Good idea," she replied. "It's getting mighty misty up here." But before he could make the call, Lori almost jumped out of her little cockpit as she pointed south. Wiping the misty wetness out of her eyes, she seemed very excited.

Eric grabbed the large, bulky binoculars and turned to scan the southern skies with his naked eyes before using them. But it was getting late and dusk was falling, and the skies to the south were as foggy as the skies ahead of them. Then he thought he spotted a yellow spot low on the horizon. He brought the binoculars to his eyes and found a small yellow Cessna out low over the Celtic Sea in the dark grey fog.

"Got 'em!" he said to Lori. "How did you spot them in all the grey fuzz out here, Old Eagle Eyes?"

"Just caught a split second of yellow in all the somber grey," Lori answered jubilantly, bouncing a little in her seat. She was so frantically animated, Eric decided that her seat belt and shoulder straps were all that was holding her in her cockpit. "I'm turning off our night lights."

"They probably won't spot us," said Eric thoughtfully, as he eyed the far-off Cessna through his binoculars. We're a dark red color, and they're not expecting anyone, anyway. Going a lot faster than we are, though, even with us at maximum speed. We won't be able to keep them in sight long." "As soon as we lose sight of them, I'll turn our lights back on, radio Shannon their location, speed and direction, and let Shannon tell the police where to be looking when they show up again," she said. "That's all we can do at the moment," Lori added wistfully.

"We've also got to be landing," said Eric. "We're almost out of gas. The instructor piloting their plane probably knows several airstrips ahead of them where they can put down in another hour or so. Maybe even some uncontrolled airstrips where they can land without anyone knowing. If Shannon notifies the police, maybe they can be waiting."

"Roger that" said Lori, and called Shannon's arrival frequency. She waited a minute, then called again. There was no response to her second call, either.

Lori sat silent for a moment, then called Eric on the Intercom, "I've waited too long. These radios only work within line-of-sight. The curvature of the earth would only allow us about a hundred miles at this altitude before we're under the curve, and Shannon can't hear us. I'm calling London center instead. I'm sure they're looking for that Cessna as hard as Shannon is by now."

"Right," said Eric, sounding distracted. He was leaning out of his cockpit to look into the hazy fog ahead. "Lori," he said, "the bad guys are right on the horizon now, and I think they're circling. They seem to be making tight circles over something on the ground."

Lori turned to look through her propeller at the foggy horizon ahead. By turning slightly to the south she was able to see more clearly without the wet windshield in front of her. The yellow Cessna ahead did seem to be slowly and tightly circling, spiraling downward toward the ground below. It soon disappeared, and Lori tried to memorize features of the hazy horizon ahead so she could remember where she had lost sight of the Cessna Skyhawk. She wondered if she could fly as far as the horizon. The gas needle on the instrument panel was already hovering near empty. She had to find a landing spot ... and fast.

But there were roads below her ... mainly empty ones. The south of England is mostly rural, so there were empty fields, as well as roads. And this was an emergency, so she'd find someplace to land in the gentle rolling landscape below when the time came.

I can do this, she told herself. And on she flew. Eric must have agreed with her, because she heard nothing more from the front cockpit.

But by the time the needle actually covered the word EMPTY on Lori's instrument panel she was looking down at fairly rugged country, a lot hillier than the rolling farm land she had left behind. And there was more forest covering the rocky ground, too. She would probably have to land on a road, and even the roads seemed to rise and fall, and curve sharply around the hills below. *I hope I don't wreck this museum piece of an airplane trying to land it among all the hills and valleys below. Surely they won't take the cost of this quaint old machine out of my pilot's pay*, thought Lori. *But Elsie's worth it, no matter what!*

And then she saw it. Eric saw it, too, and jabbed a finger down at the grey stone ruin of a castle below on a hilltop overlooking the ocean. It was taller than it was wide, with four peaked towers surrounding a central tower of rubble. Only two of the towers were still as tall as they once were, and rocks that apparently had once been part of the castle's architecture now lay tumbled around the lawn that surrounded the ancient building. The other towers looked like they, too, might fall to the ground if the scaffolding that supported them were ever removed. The structure was getting a major remodeling. Scaffolding helped support all four sides of the castle, as well as several interior walls.

Squinting her eyes in the growing darkness, Lori noted that a dark rocky ditch enclosed the castle campus just outside the decrepit walls, suggesting that the fortification had had an actual moat in its heyday.

But where were the bad guys ... and Elsie? Lori dropped to two thousand feet of altitude to study the castle, and made sure all her navigation lights were still off to remain as invisible as possible. There was some light showing from small windows in the rocky walls. She turned off her engine, and glided the light bi-plane around the rear of the castle silently to avoid making noise.

Suddenly she detected movement on the ground. There was a large parking area at the rear of the castle where sightseers apparently parked while exploring the castle ruins, and the instructor pilot must have managed to land there. Lori could still see the wings of the Cessna, even though most of the fuselage was already nearly covered with building materials. The bad guys were trying to disappear.

Lori glided silently around the ruined stone towers and back to the front of the castle. When she had put a mile of distance between her airplane and the ruins, she pressed the ON switch on her instrument panel. Nothing happened. She tried again, but heard only rumblings and scrapings as the engine tried to catch. But it had nothing to burn ... the gas tank was empty.

Lori quickly stuck her head out the left side of her cockpit. She could see dark, apparently empty fields on both sides of her, but she wasn't sure when she might encounter some small trees or a cow, or even a small shed in either field in the darkness. But lying directly below her was a narrow dirt road that curved down from the hill where the castle was perched. It would have to do.

"I'm going to have to land on the road below" she told Eric through the intercom. "That's what I'd try to do," he responded as he also stared down at the thin line that curved gently below them. "Don't forget to keep pressure on your left rudder to follow that slight curve to the left."

"What does he mean ... try to do? That's not very supportive, Lori told herself with a frown on her forehead. *"And why does he think I won't be able to follow a gentle curve like this one? Front seat driver!"*

By this time the light Tiger Moth had settled down to an altitude of about 50 feet over the narrow country lane. *"I wonder if it's very muddy, and if that will mess up my calculations?* Lori asked herself.

Lori sat the Tiger Moth down gently on the curving country lane, and found it was indeed muddy. So much so she hardly dared apply brakes for fear her wheels would stick to the surface of the lane, and cause her bi-plane's nose to be thrust down into the mud, as well, and stop the little airplane suddenly with its tail in the air.

But Lori had other, more immediate problems. The unpaved country road was so narrow that a copse of trees leaning over the lane on the right brushed strongly against the ends of the Tiger Moth's right wings as they whipped by. *What if next time there are trees on both sides, pressing in on the road*, she asked herself ... *will I be able to get through?*

Lori was finding it ever more difficult to see through the goggles attached to her leather helmet due to the misty rain making them more and more opaque. Suddenly, as she squinted through the wet goggles, she thought she could see something dark blocking the lane as it curved around the hill to her left.

She tore the goggles away from the helmet and stretched to her left to see around the small wet windshield in front of her. There was something ... something that filled the entire lane. And it was coming up fast in the darkness.

It was a bridge. A narrow stone bridge spanned a small creek ahead, and it was only a few feet wide across the narrow lane. The bridge consisted of a rock roadway with a rock wall extending up three or four feet on both sides of the bridge. Lori knew her upper wings were well above the height of the walls, but she wasn't sure about her lower wings. Lori pulled back on her joystick in hopes that she was still going fast enough to give her wings the lift to raise her a foot or two above the roadway of the bridge, and get her past those bridge walls.

But it was not to be. The Tiger Moth glided across the narrow stone bridge with the upper wings easily clearing the walls. But not the lower ones. They both crashed into the walls of the bridge on each side, and were torn off the fuselage completely in a violent explosion of torn metal sheets and wooden struts. The collision yanked Lori and Eric hard against their shoulder straps, which were all that kept the two pilots from slamming violently into their control panels.

The pull on the lower part of the airplane did what Lori had feared the mud might do. It brought the little bi-plane to a sudden quivering halt, and plopped the nose down into the mud, where the wooden propeller shredded itself in a frenzy of mud and water and rain. The tail end of the airplane was lifted high into the air, leaving Lori, in the back seat, some 10 feet off the ground.

The little airplane slid another twenty feet on the other side of the bridge before it finally came to rest. It was now a monoplane with only the upper wing remaining, while the lower wing it once had was lying in two pieces back in the lane still on the other side of the bridge.

Eric turned and looked up toward Lori, who was still in her back cockpit several feet above him. "Are you OK?" he asked.

Lori had removed her leather helmet completely by this time, and looked ready to cry. "I have wrecked two wonderful airplanes in just one day," she said. "That must be some kind of record!"

When Eric saw that Lori wasn't hurt, he stood up, clinging to the side of his cockpit and part of the fuselage. From that precarious position he managed to roll his pant legs up several inches above his shoes to protect his uniform from the mud, and clamored down the fuselage hanging by handholds like someone descending a tree trunk.

"I think Captain Travers will own up to being pilot of record for the 777 he did a very nice job of dropping into the Atlantic with no loss of life," said Eric, "so that leaves you with only one airplane down." Eric raised one hand to pretend to shade his eyes as he looked back down the lane and across the bridge, where the lower wings of the Tiger Moth still lay.

"I will say, however," he added with a grin on his face, "you did manage to litter quite a lengthy portion of this public roadway in the process of getting the second aircraft down."

But when he looked up at Lori standing in her cockpit, he recognized the anger, frustration and misery on her face was that of a pilot who has just lost an airplane ... and he managed to say exactly the right thing. "But you sure did a super job of following that left curve in near darkness and rain and forests on both sides of the road. If that stone bridge hadn't come out of nowhere, I believe you would have brought this airplane out of this as unscathed as we are. I'll fly with you anywhere, anytime, First Officer Fyfer!"

Lori carefully swung down from the airplane fuselage, and stepped daintily from the foothold toward the front of the airplane to the ground. The Tiger Moth would never fly again, but Lori still treated it with reverence. It had been a wonderful airplane, and had done all they had asked of it to get them here.

CHAPTER TWENTY-NINE

After a moment on the ground to get her bearings, Lori climbed back into the wreckage of the Tiger Moth and tried the radio. "Well, I managed to smash the radio along with everything else," she said. "All we've got are our cell phones now, but that should do the trick."

Both she and Eric pulled their phones out of their pockets as they walked down the dark muddy lane that led toward the castle.

"I'm calling Shannon," said Lori. "I know it's a country away from us now, but I don't know any local numbers. They can alert everybody."

"I'm calling 999," said Eric. "That's the Brit version of 911, and it'll have the locals here faster.

"Betcha," said Lori, as she punched in the numbers. 'NO SIGNAL', read the screen of her cell phone. "I have no reception," she said. "This valley, with all the hills around it, must be a dead zone. Do you have anything?"

Eric stared at his telephone, and shook his head. "Mine's the same," he said. "We'll just have to wait until someone finds our crashed Tiger Moth, and notifies the authorities. They'll ID the airplane, and where it came from. Of course, they won't know that we spotted the smugglers, and have them corralled in the local castle."

"We can't wait," said Lori, looking at him with big, solemn eyes. "The smugglers may be killing Elsie even as we speak."

"Lori, we've got to wait for backup," said Eric. "Our getting killed isn't going to help Elsie or that instructor pilot. The bad guys outnumber us and they're armed."

"But our advantage is that they don't know we're here. I'll go alone. Eric, give me your gun," said Lori.

"We're waiting for the professionals," said Eric.

"Eric, if you don't give me that gun, I'll never speak to you again."

"That's exactly what I'm afraid will happen if I DO give you this gun."

"Then I'll go in there unarmed," decided Lori. "If I get caught, I'll just tell them that they're surrounded by the police, and … how do you say it? … the jig's up … and they have no choice but to surrender. I'm certainly not letting them kill Elsie while we stand out here waiting for the police. It could take them until late tomorrow sometime to come looking for us and get here in force in a remote part of rural England."

"Remember," added Lori. "The smugglers have no idea that anyone is out here. They don't think that the police know where they are … which they don't … yet! If

I wait until there are SWAT teams hiding in the moat and police helicopters hovering above the towers, and probably TV crews pulled up in their vans broadcasting live, we'll have lost the element of surprise. The smugglers will use their hostages to negotiate with the police, and who knows where that will lead?"

Eric scanned the black silhouette of the ruined castle walls on the hill above them, and hesitated. "We may be able to use our phones at some point as we climb the hill," he said grudgingly, "and are closer to the castle."

* * *

While Eric and Lori were debating what to do, the Skipper had pulled his cell phone out of one pocket of his pants as he stood in what seemed the safest room of the ruined castle, and deep in another pocket located the now rumpled business card Noelle Chabrun had handed him as they studied the diamond at the Russian trade fair. He wondered if a woman so chic and attractive could actually fly a helicopter as well as she said she did. He thought a moment, then punched in her number. At this point, he had no choice.

"Noelle," he said softly when she answered the phone in her London flat. "I'm sorry to awaken you in the middle of the night this way."

"Skipper," she responded in a low, throaty voice with just a trace of sarcasm in it. "It is a pleasure. I am so pleased to hear your manly voice again so soon."

"I have come to see how valuable your skills could be to our operation, my dear. Are you still interested in joining us in profiting from the Star of Yakutsk that I showed you in Moscow?"

Still miffed at the brusqueness with which the Skipper dealt with her in Moscow, Chabrun was cool and reserved. "Perhaps, Skipper-man. How can I help?"

The Skipper started to warn Chabrun angrily about her familiarity with his title, then decided that this wasn't the best time. "I'm interested in using your helicopter," he said gently, "with you flying it, of course."

Chabrun hesitated a moment, then asked, "And when would you need my services, Skipper?"

"Tonight," said the Skipper. "Can you have it fueled and ready to fly into southern England and back to London tonight?"

The Skipper could hear Chabrun laugh through the receiver. "Skipper," she said, I'm already wearing a black lace negligee and drinking a margarita. This is the middle of the night. You are a bit tardy to propose a date with me tonight."

"I know that what I ask is difficult," said the Skipper, clenching his teeth and fighting to keep his tone pleasant. "But the rewards are immense," he said. "I am willing to give a tenth of the profits from the sale of the Star of Yakutsk for this service, and for the services of your technicians cutting the stone, as well. That would come to some seven million American dollars ... a handy sum."

"Handy, indeed," countered Chabrun coyly. "Handy enough that I bet there's more to this story that you haven't yet mentioned. Why aren't you in the United States with your diamond right now?"

Skipper let out a long sigh. "We have indeed encountered problems getting the gem to the States," he admitted, "and the police are probably aware that we are still somewhere in the British Isles with the diamond. But the police don't know exactly where we are, and I want to keep it that way. We intend to get to Heathrow Airport in London, where I have many contacts, and take the gem out of the area in a commercial airliner. I plan on putting the stone in a cache I've already prepared on one of the aircraft I've used before. I'll have one of my people take the stone out at DFW and hold it for me. Easy to do."

"In other words," Chabrun summarized, her voice now cold, "the diamond is extremely hot, with every cop in Great Britain looking for it and for you, and you want me to aid and abet you for seven measly million dollars, endangering everything I've amassed through the years. No thanks!"

"Wait a moment," said the Skipper hastily. "You're right. I really should make that a third the value of the stone ... that's some twenty-five million dollars for a short one-night flight and some work by your technicians!"

"No," said Noelle. "I'm going to get half, and you'll get half. I'm not interested in anything less. And I get a say in everything else you do with that stone from now on. I don't have time for negotiating ... the ice is melting in my margarita."

The Skipper took a long, deep breath. "Alright, my dear," he said evenly through clinched teeth. "I understand the chances you're taking, even though they're not as great as you think. The police have no idea where we are. They probably think we're still in southern Ireland. But I want you to feel adequately reimbursed for your efforts, just as I plan to protect you all along the way."

"Protection is an important thing to consider," said Noelle. "Protection from you, that is. My helicopter is a seven passenger Bell helicopter 206, and it carries a ton of useful load. I'll be flying it, and will have three armed men with me. That leaves you four seats, and 1,400 pounds of useful load. I don't care how your men are armed. My real protection will come from the calls on my cell phone one of my men will make every 10 minutes. If he is unable to make one of those calls, the people waiting for it will call the police identifying my helicopter and telling them exactly where it is according to the GPS system they'll be watching carefully from London. Now, I must go. I have much to do in the next few hours. Where are you?"

All that information left the Skipper a little dizzy. This female was as sharp as Aspen had been. She might indeed make a good partner in the years ahead, particularly as this diamond heist was costing him so much, he might not be able to retire as he had hoped, after all.

"I'm in Strathmore Castle, or at least that's what it says on the front gate," said the Skipper. "It's on the south coast of England east of Weymouth. It's a ruin, actually. It has one red aircraft navigation beacon on top of the main tower. Blink your landing lights at me when you get here, and I'll turn on all the lights around the large parking area behind the castle. Get here while it's still dark!"

"Just be ready to jump on board," said Noelle. "After you've shown me the diamond, that is. Get in on the right side in front, next to me, and show me that diamond. THEN we'll take off. Understand?" "I understand," said the Skipper, huffily. "I understand." *This woman might not live long enough to become my partner,* thought the Skipper. *After all, a man can only put up with so much. But in the meantime,* he sighed, *she's going to be a veritable lifesaver ... whether she likes it or not.*

CHAPTER THIRTY

Lori hadn't noticed how bad Eric looked until the moon came up behind the castle. He had a smear of mud along one sleeve, and his black uniform pants were speckled with mud in spite of his turning up the cuffs to avoid it. And his shiny black shoes were probably ruined with mud and water, as were her own, she imagined. Lori suddenly realized that she wasn't wearing her uniform hat, and guessed it was still somewhere in the cockpit of the Tiger Moth.

Eric's hair was so military-short that it still looked neater than the rest of him, but Lori imagined her own hair looked more like a tangled brown haystack at this point. They were both messes. Good thing it was still so dark, she decided.

"I think we stand a better chance of success if we wait another couple of hours before we attack the bad guys," said Eric, looking up at the castle. "They haven't had any more sleep than we have, and they're probably exhausted ... just as we are. Let's try to get an hour or so of sleep before we scale the castle walls ... or climb up the scaffolding, actually. Maybe we can catch them still deeply asleep."

"Do you think that's better than just trying the front door?" asked Lori hesitantly, eyeing the steep rocky walls that rose above the hill.

"There's no way to say for sure," said Eric, "but they're probably going to be napping on the ground floor guarding the front door. If we can get up the wall and into a window on the second floor we'll be in a better position to confront them than trying to burst through the front door, hoping they're all asleep. We only have one gun, and they have at least two."

"And I don't think it will be difficult to get in those second floor windows if we move quietly and slowly," added Eric. "There's no glass in them."

"Exactly where were you thinking of getting this shut-eye?" asked Lori, as she and Eric turned back toward the wrecked Tiger Moth. She was so weary she staggered a bit in the slippery mud, and even allowed Eric to insert his arm under hers and around her back to steady her. Even the mud at her feet looked fairly inviting on which to take a nap, although the wet grassy spots looked a bit softer.

"Can you stand here a moment alone while I build our bedroom?" he asked. "Sure", answered Lori as she stood in the light rain and tried to analyze what he had just said. She watched Eric pick up the largest remnant of the upper wing that had been torn from the Tiger Moth, and drag it across the bridge to where the fuselage of the airplane lay. He pushed it up under the rear end of the airplane that had been raised by the crash landing so that it provided a smooth metal surface on the ground, with the covering fuselage giving some protection overhead from the rain that was beginning to come down harder.

Rising on his tiptoes, Eric reached above his head to open the small door in the rear fuselage, still some six feet above the ground, and pulled a greasy tarpaulin from the airplane's storage area in the fuselage.

"This tarpaulin was stored in the back of the airplane along with some oil cans, and I thought it might make our boudoir cozier," said Eric proudly, with an elegant welcoming gesture to Lori. But when he saw how wobbly she looked as she plodded toward him in her muddy loafers, he hurried to her side and guided her under the raised end of the wrecked fuselage, and helped her collapse on the relatively clean surface of the metal wing.

He wrapped her and himself in the tarpaulin, and lay down beside her so that his nose nearly touched hers. Watching her dark hair blow lightly in the breeze, Eric removed his billed uniform hat and pulled it down snugly on her head. Then he pulled his I-phone out of a pocket, and set the alarm for two hours later. *I hope that's enough time,* he told himself. *No telling how much energy we're going to need in a few hours.*

* * *

Eric jerked awake when his telephone alarm went off at three o'clock that morning. He turned it off and lay still for a moment on the aircraft wing putting his thoughts together in the darkness. He became aware that someone's arm lay across his chest, and he quickly but carefully moved it to rest on Lori's chest, instead. He glanced up at her face, and realized that her eyes were open and staring at him.

"What are you doing in my bed?" she asked amiably, pulling herself closer to his body.

"Er ... uh, well ... actually I just thought I'd catch a couple of winks before beginning my chores this morning," stammered Eric, belatedly encouraged by the small smile that began to cross Lori's face.

"Too bad," she said, as the smile grew broader. "I was sort of hoping you might have some ulterior motive. It's such a lovely place to spend a rainy night," she said, patting the metal wing she lay on, "I really hate to get up. And you know ... I can't believe I'm saying this ... but if it weren't so important to save Elsie ... I mean, if you and I are both still alive after today ... I hope you'll find another place kind of like this where we can lie down next to each other ... and ... and continue this conversation."

"I can't wait," said Eric slowly, mesmerized by what Lori was saying. "I ...." Then he stopped trying to talk, and just studied Lori's face ... or the part of it that showed under his hat, which was pulled down over Lori's ears and propped up in front by her nose. "You're ... you're beautiful," he said finally.

Lori's lips continued to smile. "Right," she said, with only a little doubtful sarcasm.

"And, you know," he added. "There's something else I want to tell you now that I'm absolutely sure you're not a smuggler. Customs has been investigating this airline for some time, but they didn't have anyone to drop in undercover who could fly a 777. So they came to my Air Force outfit ... the 89th Airlift Wing at Andrews Air Force Base in Maryland, to get a volunteer ... me, as it turned out. We get so much time flying the President around in two 747's, it only took one intense month of 777 training for me to be certified as a TransGlobal 777 Captain."

"Customs was especially interested in you. Most of the smuggling seemed to be centered on this particular flight to Zurich, Istanbul and Moscow, and you seemed to be in the big middle of it."

"Especially when they found that you had flown it as a flight attendant eight years ago, as well. We weren't sure if the violence between you and the Skipper was inter-gang spats, or what. Then the smugglers seemed to think I looked good as a potential pilot-smuggler, <u>myself</u>, and tried to recruit me ... which is what Customs wanted."

"But someone in the Skipper's organization working in TransGlobal personnel must have started checking out my records at the airline really carefully, and apparently found something that looked strange to them. So, the smugglers just decided to have AfricanAir drop me ... literally, that is. If you hadn't saved my bacon, I'd have ended up in the Bosporus."

"I still can't believe you managed to stop my getting murdered pretty much all by yourself," added Eric, as he tried to look into Lori's eyes. But her eyes were now obscured in the darkness by the cap bill resting on her nose. He lifted the bill a couple of inches to find her eyes were closed.

"You heard all of that, didn't you?" he said. Lori opened her mouth, and a deep snoring sound came out of it for a moment before she reshaped her lips into a wide grin. Then she pulled back the cap, gave it to Eric, and grabbed his arm to pull herself into a sitting position.

"Yes, I heard all that," said Lori. "But all I care about is that you're no smuggler. I should also tell you, I usually look better than this in the morning. Now come on, dear. Let's go save Elsie."

"Do I get to call you 'darlin' if you call me 'dear'?" asked Eric.

"Yes, dear," said Lori. "Somehow it sounds a lot better now."

CHAPTER THIRTY-ONE

The rain had stopped by the time Lori and Eric started up the steep grassy hill that surrounded the old castle. But everything was still wet, and Lori felt she was sliding back two steps on the slick grass for every step forward she took. Eric noticed her plight, and grabbed her pants belt under her coat at the small of her back, and helped push her forward in the darkness.

They gradually got closer to the dark silhouette of the castle without any one inside apparently noticing. The only light present was a blinking red aviation beacon mounted atop the central tower far above the ground. The rest of the ruins and grounds were all black as pitch.

When they reached the old moat they slowly descended the small boulders on one side, feeling their way across the uneven bottom of the muddy ditch, and climbing as carefully and silently as possible up the rocks on the other side. "Saint Patrick chased all the snakes out of Ireland, didn't he? Hope he didn't dump them in southern England," Lori breathed quietly as they reached the other side of the rocky, bushy ditch.

"They don't bite when it's rainy," Eric assured her in a whisper as they stood studying the silent castle. "Do you have any bars yet?" he asked as Lori took out her cell phone and studied its face.

"No," she said, frustrated. Eric tried his phone, as well, just to be sure Lori's I-phone wasn't broken or somehow out of service.

"Then let's get even higher," said Eric. "There's a ladder leaning against the scaffolding on the closest tower."

Lori took the lead as they hurried across the wet grass to the first stone tower. She put her hand against the slippery cold, wet stones, and thought anxiously, *Oh me, this is going to be fun!*

"Wait a minute," she whispered to Eric as her foot struck something on the ground in the darkness. "There's equipment of some kind here. Buckets of stuff, and ropes and long-handled brushes."

"Did you say ropes? I was wishing we had some ropes," said Eric, forgetting for a moment to whisper. They both froze, and listened for a minute to hear if there was any reaction in the stillness. Nothing.

"Sorry" he whispered. "Let me get a feel of those ropes." Eric examined the ropes wound into small circular piles beside the ancient stone wall. "This will do," he whispered finally. "I'm an old climber, and I think it would be safer if we were roped together as we climb this wall. Come here a minute."

Eric wound the rope three times around Lori's tiny waist, and carefully tied it with what he called a square knot. Then he stepped back some 15 feet, and tied the remainder of the rope around his own waist.

"Did you learn to tie that knot as a climber?" asked Lori.

Eric looked thoughtful for a moment, then said, "No, I think I learned the square knot while sailing." "Ahhh," breathed out Lori with a smile. "Climbing and sailing, she whispered. "I can tell there's going to be a lot to learn about you."

"Not really," breathed Eric quietly in the dark. "Just a jack of all trades, and master of none. Let's do this. Ladies first."

Lori mounted the ladder, and climbed to the lower rung of scaffolding. Then she reached for the next horizontal piece at about her waist, and using a nearby vertical support, pulled herself up carefully on the higher thick aluminum bar, and then the next. She gripped each slimy wet bar of the scaffold tightly with all her strength so her hands wouldn't slip on the cold, wet aluminum.

At the thought of slipping, Lori looked down to see Eric just a few feet below her, and the dark muddy ground far, far below him. She felt her body freeze against the bar she was holding as fear quivered through her muscles. She squinted her eyes, and crushed herself as hard against the scaffolding as she could. A minute must have passed as she stood frozen on the scaffolding. Then, breathing heavily, but without looking down, she pulled herself up the aluminum bars until she reached the next level.

Lori was about to reach for the vertical bar next to her to heave herself up farther when she felt a hand on her shoulder. She was irritated at first, thinking that Eric had come to complain about her slow progress up the tower, but he didn't mention it.

"Let's move a little to our left," he whispered. "I think there's a window over there. Lori felt his strong left arm at her back holding her against the scaffolding as they side-stepped to the left along the wet aluminum rod on which they stood. When they got to the window they could see a cylindrical staircase and flickering light coming from down below. Eric motioned that they continue along the aluminum rod they stood on. They ducked below the window as they passed it, and sidestepped further to the left.

"I think we're on about the third level of the castle," whispered Eric. "We can't get in through any of these windows because they're all too narrow. They don't have any glass in them, which is good, but they're only about eight inches wide, which is impossible."

"They must have been built as ports from which to shoot arrows or throw spears down on the enemy below. No one ever intended to go in or out through them. We may have to climb all the way to the top of one of these towers to be able to access the interior. I think it'll only be another level up, or maybe two. We'll climb over the battlements at the top of the tower. Those are the teeth-like stone squares that run around the top of the towers." Even in the darkness Lori could tell that Eric was looking down at her anxiously. "Do you think you're up to it?" he asked.

"Of course I am," whispered Lori. "But let's take it slowly, okay?"

"Absolutely," agreed Eric, barely breathing out the words in the silence. "And remember, you're tied in with me. I'll hold you if you fall. Nothing bad is going to happen to you tonight as long as you're tied in."

Lori reached for the next aluminum bar of the scaffolding, and pulled herself up carefully. Then she did it again, and once again, with Eric right behind and below her. But when she reached up the next time she realized the aluminum scaffolding continued upward, but the tower stones didn't. She was now at the top of the tower actually touching the battlements with square spaces in between. She imagined soldiers wearing armor standing there hundreds of years ago poking arrows between the same battlements she was clinging to now, and firing them at the enemy down below. She started to look down as she thought of the arrows raining down on warriors besieging the castle, but she quickly reconsidered.

Instead, she hugged the scaffolding for a moment before pulling herself up and between two of the battlements, and dumping herself on the walkway behind them, where she lay panting, grateful to be lying safe on a flat stone surface. The rope tied around Lori's waist tugged and tightened for a moment, and Eric's head and shoulders appeared between two battlements as he propelled himself over the wall and down on the walkway next to Lori, breathing heavily.

They were much closer now to the aircraft beacon that bathed everything in red light atop the central castle tower, giving Lori and Eric a better look at themselves than they'd had all night. "You tore your coat," Eric informed Lori between breaths, pointing to the rip where a silver button had been torn from the elegant double-breasted tunic, leaving torn cloth behind. Lori grinned and pointed at Eric's coat. "You're a complete mess," she countered, shaking her head at the muddy smears on Eric's black uniform coat. Pulling her cell phone from her pants pocket, she asked, "Do you have any bars yet?" But before he could check his phone, and answer, Lori whispered breathily, "I've got bars ... I've got bars!"

"So do I," whispered Eric. "But I think you deserve the privilege, my lady. You tell 'em."

Lori pushed 999 on her telephone, the British version of 911, and was soon talking to a sleepy local constable she'd awakened. He listened to her explanation of everything that had occurred without any interruptions. When she finished there was a long silence. "You say the men who killed the two Irish officers yesterday are here locally in Strathmore Castle?" he asked incredulously.

"Madam, I must warn you. If this is a false report, you will be charged."

"Officer, let me first give you my name, Lori Fyfer." Then she spelled it for him. "I'm also giving you two other numbers to confirm who I am." She read off the Shannon number from a card still in her pocket, and Inspector Lodge's number from memory. "Inspector Lodge is with Interpol in Zurich," she added. "Oops", she said hesitantly. "Inspector Lodge is on an airplane about now flying into Heathrow. If you'll just call the number you have listed for Interpol, I'm sure they can refer you to him. And please come quickly."

"Things are happening very fast here."

Eric was making signs at Lori to let him speak on the cell phone as she finished. Constable," he said, "approach the castle from the seaward side, unless you're riding a bicycle. I'm afraid we crashed an airplane in the lane that leads to the castle from the inland hills, and it's not passable right now for automobiles. And bring guns ... plenty of guns. The murderers of those two constables still have theirs!"

Lori gestured to use the phone again when Eric finished. "I'm calling Shannon, as well," she said. "Wouldn't it be awful if the local constable went back to bed, thinking this was a crank call?" Lori called Shannon Airport, and talked with a policeman there to satisfy herself that she had indeed gotten out the word. "Now let's go save Elsie," she said quietly to Eric. Eric took Lori's hand, and they started toward the rubble that was the central tower. Suddenly Eric stopped, and Lori ploughed into his back. "Lori," he whispered, "I'm afraid we have another problem."

Lori peered around Eric's arm at the rubble-strewn top of the central tower. At this height the central tower and the four peripheral towers stood separately with only single stout logs joining the central tower with each of the others.

Lori felt ready to cry. "We can't get to Elsie," she said.

"Oh, we can," Eric assured her. "It's just going to be a little harder."

Looking down at the rubble below, Lori could tell that the towers rose up three levels of the castle from where the castle ruins were all one building. There was no way to access the rest of the ruins from the tower they were presently in except where they stood now, at the top.

And the only way at this point was a log. It was a heavy log, at least a foot thick, and it spanned a chasm some 50 feet down to the ceiling of the central building, and reached about eight or ten feet between each of the towers, and the rubble of the central building.

Lori studied the log, and decided it had probably been there since the castle was first built as it continued across the ceiling of the central building, where it looked like a ceiling beam, and joined the others in the center of the arched ceiling of the main area of the castle. It was formed with hatchet marks where the long-ago builders had hacked the round tree trunk into the more-or-less squared-off log it now was.

"Eric," whispered Lori. "I don't think I can do this. I just hate heights too much."

"No problem," Eric whispered back. "I'll find where they have Elsie, and go in with my gun, and you can go down these stairs to the ground floor after I've got her, and meet us there. I think that's a better plan, anyway."

Eric removed the rope from Lori's waist, and tied it on to the near end of the log that spanned the chasm below. He sat on the log, and pulled himself across the uneven surface to the central tower. When he got off the log, he turned to face Lori.

"Okay, darlin'" he whispered as loudly as he dared. "Untie the rope and toss it to me. Remember not to come down the stairwell until you're sure all's well below. "I'll yell up to you!"

"I'm coming with you." whispered Lori, surprising both herself and Eric.

"Lori, No. No, please stay here," he whispered.

She shook her head, and bent to untie the rope from the end of the log. She curled it tightly around her waist three times, and then tied the square knot she had seen Eric tie ... or at least, it looked like the one he tied. But Eric, standing ten feet away across the chasm, didn't like the look of it. He had her re-tie it three times before he said, "Alright, that looks good from here."

"Okay," whispered Eric, "let's do this right." Eric sat in the walkway at the top of the central tower, both his feet braced hard against sturdy outcroppings of stone. "On belay," he whispered, saying the ages-old words that told a climber about to put his weight on a rope that his or her partner was braced and holding the rope tightly.

"Climbing," whispered Lori, repeating the climber's response Eric had taught her telling her partner that she was proceeding, and that if she fell he would immediately have to deal with her weight on the rope. "Climb," he repeated quietly, indicating that he was braced and ready, as he settled back against the stones.

Lori tugged at her rope, making sure it was tight, and that the square knot was secure. Then she sat down on the end of the log. She refused to look down, but kept her eyes on Eric's face. Then she scooted herself across, inch by inch, feeling the dampness of the wet log through her uniform pants, and never taking her eyes off his face.

Suddenly, when Lori was half-way across the massive log, she noticed a whap-whap sound in the night air as an airship of some kind approached in the darkness, hovering closer and closer to them, its rotors pounding the air more and more loudly until Lori could hear nothing but the tornado of sound that surrounded her, as the bright flood lights on the airship turned the tower and Lori's entire world into bright eerie whiteness. *Could the police have gotten here so soon?* wondered Lori. *That's just not possible.*

All she could hear was the overwhelming whap-whap-whap, as the massive blasts of air from the rotors tore at her hands and body while she clung to the wet log. Lori felt like all the energy in the universe was pulling her away from the beam on which she sat, even with her legs squeezed together hard against the wet wood.

Lori grabbed the wooden beam more tightly, trying to squeeze it to her chest. But the rotors above grew ever louder until they sounded like a railroad train passing over her, its sound deafening. All she could feel was the maelstrom of air that was pummeling her, pulling her away from the beam she sat on. Then her torn fingers slipped loose, and Lori felt herself falling into dark space.

Almost instantly she felt the rope tied around her waist tighten, slide up to crush her breasts, then rise further up to squeeze beneath her arms. But there it held, and quickly slammed her against the smooth, wet stones of the inner castle wall. Her body bounced away from the wall, then crashed into it again, this time not so hard. Lori scraped her bleeding fingers against the smooth, wet stones of the tower, but found no hold at all. She looked up, but couldn't see Eric. She clung to the wet rope, trying to look at the square knot tied somewhere below her chin. She found it with her fingers. It seemed to be holding tight and secure. But it was so small. She knew that her life could rest entirely on that little knot she had tied herself with Eric's direction, and that knowledge frightened her to death.

Lori felt tugs on the rope, and realized that she was being drawn foot by foot up the tower. But the sound and fury and the blinding light were no longer directly above her.

The airship was landing. As Eric slowly pulled Lori upward toward the battlements of the main tower, she caught glimpses of it behind the castle. The bad guys had turned on lights in the parking lot, and seemed to be greeting a black helicopter that was settling to the paved surface behind the castle. Lori strained to see the word POLICE painted somewhere on the helicopter, but failed to see any words painted on it anywhere. All that was there was the aircraft identification BLU436, but Lori spotted it and memorized the characters ... saying them over and over to herself as she was drawn slowly up the tower wall.

CHAPTER THIRTY-TWO

Lori reached above her head, trying to cling to the taut, very wet rope that pulled her up. As she scraped her hands against the rough stones, she felt the top of the tower! Just to her left was an opening between two battlements, and she pulled herself through the opening and onto the flat walkway behind it. "You're bleeding," said Eric as he pulled her toward him.

"It just looks bad because everything up here is red," replied Lori hysterically as she threw back her head and stared up at the blinking beacon just above them, the red aviation marker on top of the castle's tallest tower.

"You're still bleeding," argued Eric, as he found a wet handkerchief in one of his pockets, and pressed it against Lori's scraped hands.

"Thank you for saving my life," she cried, her tears mixing with the rain on her face.

"It was just my turn," said Eric. "The way we're going, you'll get your chance to even the score in another minute or two."

Looking down at the helicopter parked behind the castle, its rotors still spinning, Lori's eyes widened. "Those are more bad guys. That helicopter must be full of them. And they must have seen us up here with all the bright lights shining on this tower. They'll be coming up here after us!"

"Or they'll just get away from here now that they have transportation," suggested Eric thoughtfully. "However, you may be right. They may decide to come after us, now that they suspect that you have the serial number on the fuselage of the helicopter. By the way, you do have it, don't you?"

"BLU436," said Lori.

Eric grinned. "I knew you'd have it," he said.

* * *

"Who are those people on top of your central tower?" screamed Noelle as the Skipper bent low to avoid the flashing rotors above him, and squeezed himself into the front right seat of the black Bell helicopter, holding the Star of Yakutsk in his right hand.

"What do you mean?" he asked. "There's no one up there."

"There's a man and a woman. At first I thought they were police," said Noelle. "They're wearing black uniforms with silver buttons. Then I recognized the hat the man has on. And they're wearing two rows of silver buttons on their coats. They're airline pilots! What are two airline pilots doing atop the highest tower of your castle ... in the middle of the night ... in the rain?" Noelle finished in disbelief.

The Skipper seethed with anger. He pulled a knife from his jacket, and held it up toward the tower, his hand shaking. Even Noelle cringed away from him, and her men in the back of the helicopter lifted up their small Uzi machine guns to point at the Skipper. The Skipper was screaming, "It's her again! I'll kill her! I'll kill her! I'll do it with my own two hands!!"

Noelle's mind was very fast, and she waved to her men to lower their weapons. Looking at the Skipper in utter disgust, she said, "I assume this woman is the reason why you are not in the United States with your diamond. And thus I agree with you completely. She has probably already noted the aircraft number on the side of my helicopter. So we cannot leave her here alive. But I think," she added with total contempt, "we'll have my men take care of this little chore for you. Maybe we can silence her before she is able to contact the police. It will only take a moment, and we'll be able to take off. Now, where are your men? We will soon be ready to leave!"

The Skipper pointed at his last two men, who were hurriedly leaving the castle through the main first floor entryway. Noelle stared for a moment at the woman one of the men carried over his shoulder. Both her wrists and ankles were bound with plastic zip-ties, and she was loudly berating the man who carried her to the helicopter. "Let me go!" yelled Elsie. "I can walk if you just untie me."

"She's a hostage," said the Skipper. "We may need her if we run into police!"

"She's very loud," said Noelle. "I don't like her noise, and I don't want her blood on my leather seats if I have to kill her to stop it."

"She rode over here in the luggage compartment of the Skyhawk I stole," said the Skipper with a grin. "We'll put her in your luggage compartment, too. She's that airline pilot's side kick, and the more uncomfortable she is, the better I like it."

Skipper gave the orders when his men got to the helicopter, and they carried Elsie to the helicopter's storage locker, and pushed her bound body inside.

"Don't do this to me again," wailed Elsie. "Please let me go!"

The Skipper's henchmen slammed and locked the luggage area door, and jumped into the helicopter.

"There is a ... there's another prisoner on the second level of the castle. A man in civilian clothes, who also needs to be killed," bellowed and wheezed the Skipper hoarsely as he tried to give orders in his rage. "All of them in the tower," he grumbled. "Kill all of them."

Noelle turned to her men in the back of the helicopter, and said, "Kill everyone in the castle tower. There should be a man in civilian clothes, and a man and woman higher in the central tower in airline uniforms. I didn't see any weapons."

"And get back here fast. We've got to take off as soon as possible. The police are probably on their way here now!" Chabrun turned back toward the Skipper, and a small revolver appeared in her right hand. She spit out between clenched teeth, "If you've gotten me mixed up with the police all for nothing, I'm going to kill you myself!"

Two of Chabrun's men jumped down from the helicopter and ran to the back door of the castle ruins, their Uzi's held at the ready. The third stayed where he was, only letting his Uzi move slightly to point generally in the direction of the Skipper's two armed henchmen sitting in the rear seat of the helicopter.

* * *

Eric and Lori ran down the winding steps of the tower stairs. Eric held onto the inner rails of the rocky stairs with his right hand while he pointed the little Baretta handgun in his left hand into the dark gloom ahead, and Lori bounded down the crude, uneven steps behind him. But within two turns around the conical tower, the way became brighter. They were approaching a lighted room.

Eric slowed down and grasped the small automatic pistol in both hands, holding it stretched in front of himself pointed at whatever danger lay ahead. It was a small room that curved the way the tower did. A middle-aged man sat on the floor, tied hand and foot with the plastic zip ties the smugglers had taken from the police car. He jerked around to peer at Eric and Lori as they rushed into the room.

"Where's Elsie?" cried Lori, as she carefully cut the man's bonds with her Swiss Army knife "What have they done with her?" she asked with terror on her face.

The little man was a bit wobbly as Lori helped him to his feet. "They took her with them on that helicopter that just arrived," he said. "But she's fine ... well, not fine, but as well as can be at the moment."

"I'm Ian McMasters," he said, holding out his hand to Lori. "I own the pilot-training school at Shannon Airport, and I want to thank ...."

"Mr. McMasters," interrupted Lori. "Before you thank me, I have to tell you that I crash-landed on a country road about a mile away from here, and I wrecked your beautiful Tiger Moth. I'm so sorry. It was almost dark,and ...."

"Lassie, lassie," interrupted McMasters in turn. "Considering the circumstances, and how you for certain saved my life this very night, I and Mrs. McMasters both forgive you many times over, and thank you from the bottom of our hearts. Now, let me look for a loo, or it's going to be too late."

"Thank you, Mr. McMasters, thank you so much," said Lori. "Actually, all we can offer you right now is some privacy. If you turn right out of this door,

I think you'll find that, at least." As Lori watched Mr. McMasters hurriedly depart, she noticed Eric standing by the door holding his index finger to his lips.

"I think we've got company," he whispered. "There are at least two of them because I heard them talking, and they're down just one level, I think. But we still have an advantage. They have to climb to our level, while we can stay exactly where we are, and concentrate on defending ourselves. Also, they don't know whether we have guns, while we know they're armed."

"That's all wonderful," whispered Lori. "But they still have two big guns to our one little one."

"Good point," breathed Eric with a smile. "But I intend to change that ratio as quickly as possible."

There were faint noises from the tower below them. Noises that kept getting closer. Eric pulled back on Lori's shoulder, and stepped in front of her to peer down the tower steps. He held his automatic in both hands, his arms extended in front of him.

Suddenly, an Asian man wearing a black watch cap and dark clothing sprinted up the tower steps from below, cradling a small black machine gun to his chest. As soon as he saw Eric, he opened fire. Eric jumped back as bullets sprayed the doorway, chipping the stone and ricocheting back and forth, spraying stone dust everywhere.

The man on the stairs took two more steps upward, and stumbled on the uneven stone of the next step. His miss-step caused the next shots from his machine gun to go wild. In that instance, Eric leaned forward into the stairway, and fired one shot from his Beretta before jerking back out of danger. Eric's single bullet caught the man in the neck and caused him to drop his machine gun and tumble down the stairs.

Eric rushed out on the stairway when he heard the man fall. He pointed the Beretta down the stairs and hurried to where the machine gun lay. As he bent down to retrieve it, he locked eyes with another man on the level below who immediately raised his own machine gun and started firing.

Eric grabbed the machine gun the first man had dropped on the steps, and cringed back against the wall of the stairway so it protected him from the shots below. He stayed close to the tower wall as he made his way back up the stairway to the room above as bullets showered the tower stones, ricocheting off them until the tower stairwell was so full of stone dust the air was nearly opaque.

"Are you crazy?" cried Lori. "I thought you were dead! Do you understand me? I thought you were dead!"

"Sorry," said Eric, coughing from the stone dust. "It had to be done." He held up the Uzi for her. "This is a fully automatic assault weapon. Eventually, their Uzi's would have overwhelmed our little 9mm hand gun. Had to be done. But now you can have this one," he said, handing Lori the Beretta, "and I'll use this baby," he added, admiring the Uzi.

"You do that again … you do that again, and I'll kill you myself," cried Lori, also gagging on the stone dust. "You totally stirred up a sand storm," she added, coughing, the tears in her eyes making it even harder to see.

"And also a smoke screen," said Eric thoughtfully. "Less chance now that anyone will try to climb those rocky, uneven steps barely able to see a pace or two in front of themselves with all this stone dust swirling around. And if they try, I'll just scatter some ricocheting bullets around the tower steps with my trusty Uzi, and that will start the dust swirling all over again!"

"It will be hell charging up the tower steps through all that dust into gun fire from above," he added, with a grim smile on his face.

Mr. McMasters strode back into the room, a relieved look on his face, at that moment. "There was no actual loo on the other side of the tower, so let me recommend that no one go to the other side of the tower until I get a chance to clean up the area," he said.

As Eric and Lori peered down the tower steps at their enemies below, Eric suddenly lifted his head, then walked to one of the strip windows in the tower. He gazed out, his eyes searching the dusky skies above. "Do you hear it?" he asked Lori quietly.

"I don't hear any … wait, is that another helicopter?" asked Lori, as she heard the distinctive whap-whap-whap of helicopter rotors in the early morning sky. "And I bet this one has the word "POLICE" written all over it," she added gleefully.

"Go slow," warned Eric. "These may be more bad guys, and even if it is the police, after having just had two constables murdered, these officers may shoot first at anything that moves."

"I don't expect the smugglers to come up this tower staircase again," Eric said to McMasters, "but it pays to be watchful. Lori and I hope we hear police helicopters above, and we want to go to the pinnacle of the tower to wave them in. We'd appreciate your standing guard for us here watching the tower steps until we get back. Are you familiar with firearms?"

"I was an RAF pilot many long years ago," said McMasters, "and we carried automatic pistols like the lass has."

"Lori," called Eric. "would you let Mr. McMasters have your Beretta to guard the stairway?"

"Happy to," said Lori. "I'll bet he's a lot better with it than I am."

"Good enough to keep the stairway empty," McMasters called after them as Eric and Lori climbed the stairs toward the tower pinnacle.

CHAPTER THIRTY-THREE

As Eric rose through the entryway of the central tower into the fresh air, he found that the rain had stopped and that a red and orange sunrise was spreading across the eastern horizon. And there wasn't just one, but two black police helicopters holding an oval hovering pattern above the central tower.

Eric quickly tucked the Uzi into the entryway opening of the tower, and stood up, raising his hands above his head. He counted six sets of eyes in each helicopter grimly watching every move he made as he crawled out of the entryway. Lori was right behind him, and as she stood Eric warned her "Raise your hands over your head, dear, and be very still. And stay away from the back side of the tower. The smugglers down by the helicopter parked behind the castle may open fire, also."

The two police helicopters continued their slow patrol above the tower for another few moments before the first helicopter dipped lower until it was hovering only 20 or 30 feet above the tower. Eric stared back at the faces in the helicopters eyeing him so closely above several British assault rifle barrels pointed his way. He couldn't identify them, but they were all larger than the Uzi tucked away in the crawl space at his feet.

A policemen wearing a battle helmet and other all-black Special Weapons and Tactics gear slid back the side door of the helicopter and sat down in the opening. He twisted to the side, and began to lower himself slowly toward Eric on a long, black rope ... at all times still watching Eric closely. Eric stood quietly, not moving, with his hands still raised, as the policeman slowly neared him until the British officer also stood on the tower top.

"Mr. McEllen and Miss Fyfer, I presume," the officer said, smiling at Eric and Lori, bowing slightly to keep his head low, and avoid being a target of the smugglers in the back parking lot. He pulled head and shoulder pictures of Eric and Lori from his pocket, and glanced at both their faces as he unbuckled himself from the rope, then smiled and shook their hands. "I'm Lieutenant Broderick" he said, pronouncing his rank 'Leftenant'. "Shannon Airport told us that two TransGlobal airline pilots were going after the perpetrators of the murder of the two Irish constables in an open air Tiger Moth ... in the rain yet! I must say, you yanks are a hardy lot! Hope you don't mind just a little help."

"Not at all," said Eric jovially. "You won't believe how glad we are to see you!"

"And forgive my not coming to the front door," added the police officer, still smiling. "We spotted you up here, and presumed that you preferred receiving guests from the top of the main tower, although I hope you'll tell me some day how that came about. I'm also presuming that the people milling about in your rear parking lot around that helicopter are not your best friends."

"I think the smugglers plan on escaping in that helicopter," said Lori.

"Very probably so," agreed the Lieutenant. "We've already checked the identification numbers on the side of their chopper. It belongs to a very shady lady from London who we've been watching for some time. This may be the time we finally have something on her. And speaking of that, we'd better get busy. How far down do you control the castle?"

"Down to the second or third level," said Eric. "Mr. McMasters, the flying school owner who was forced to fly the smugglers here in a Cessna Skyhawk is watching the stairs at that point. He has the 9 mm Barretta I always carry in the cockpit with me."

"Very good," said Lieutenant Broderick, hesitating only slightly, and politely not mentioning at the moment that Eric had been flying and running around the English countryside with a pistol he was not authorized to carry in England. "So that's all we need to know?"

"No. I'm afraid not," spoke up Lori.

"The smugglers have a hostage in the helicopter with them. Her name's Elsie Ponder, and she's a completely innocent TransGlobal employee who's been helping me track these monsters."

"I'm so sorry. That's a complication," said the Lieutenant. "I was going to ask you both to remain up here while we finish this operation, but since you know the hostage, ma'am, I believe you'd better stay close to us as we try to find a way to make her safe." Broderick turned away and gazed up at the nearest helicopter, making downward motions with his right arm, his fist closed. The helicopter again drifted closer to the tower top, and another man appeared in the sliding door of the helicopter, twisting out of the chopper and climbing down the rope like Broderick had before him.

* * *

"Those are police helicopters above the tower!" screamed Noelle. "I knew I should have turned you down as soon as you called me!" she said to the Skipper. "Get the hostage out of the baggage hold. But do it slowly, and let the police see that we've got her. Put her face down on the bomb bay doors, and tie a rope back and forth above her so she can't get up off the doors. I want the police to let us alone because of her, but I'm going to drop her out of the helicopter as soon as we get away from them to help both our speed and the distance for which we have fuel."

Noelle took a moment to congratulate her brilliance and forethought for having installed the doors years ago in what she called her bomb bay in the floor of the helicopter. She had used them several times over land and sea to get rid of evidence in the form of stolen diamonds. Once she even delivered diamonds carefully to the grassy area behind her own hangar as she flew final approach into an airport where British excise officers were waiting to check what she was carrying in her helicopter on a return trip from France.

Noelle turned to her men, and began giving orders in French, a language she knew the Skipper didn't understand. But understanding people had kept him alive for many years, and watching her face had already told him all he needed to know. The Skipper knew his relationship with this partner was probably soon to come to an end. He slowly glanced around the helicopter, studying the men and weapons surrounding him to gauge the possibilities available.

"And I'm going to drop the Skipper and his men with the hostage," Noelle told her men rapidly in French. "Have your knives ready for the moment I tell you to kill him. Jacques, put your knife in the Skipper's heart from behind him. Don't give him a chance to turn around. If there is a problem, use your hand gun. Henri, your job is the hardest. Use your gun to kill the Skipper's two men in the back with you. We will be too low to be bothered by the change in air pressure if we blow out a window, and I'm going to have to dump this helicopter, anyway." The enormity of what Noelle was losing because she had aligned herself with the Skipper hit her anew, and she began cursing wildly in languages even her own men did not recognize.

* * *

As Lori and Eric accompanied Lieutenant Broderick down the stairway that curled around the central tower, they carefully studied each turn ahead of them for ambushes by armed smugglers, but made it to the dusty ground floor without seeing another person other than Mr. McMasters standing faithfully at his post. As they carefully stepped through the back exit into the parking area, they could see the smugglers gathered around the helicopter some fifty yards away near the back fence. Elsie stood in the midst of them, although everyone else seemed to be trying to stand behind her. Lori turned to look behind her through the open corridor of the castle to the front door. She could see that the front of the castle was crowded with police cars and other official-looking utility vehicles. Lieutenant Broderick was talking to someone through his cell phone and scanning the area behind the castle when a policeman wearing sergeant's stripes on his sleeve called to him, "Lieutenant, Interpol on the line. It's an Inspector Lodge." Broderick took the phone and said, "Yes, Sir, Inspector. This is Lieutenant Broderick, Special Weapons and Tactics Officer out of Scotland Yard, London." He listened for a moment, then continued, "Yes, sir. We have records on Noelle Chabron, also. Never been able to get her for anything, though. Right."

"Right. Thanks for that information, Sir. I'll keep it in mind. Lori Fyfer? She's standing right here next to me, and I'm passing the line to her right now. In the meantime, I'll keep you posted, Sir!"

Lori reached for the cell phone eagerly. She said, "Inspector Lodge, is that you?"

"It certainly is, Ms. Fyfer," said the very British voice on the line. "I don't know how you've achieved all you have in the last two days, but if you ever want a position, please consider Interpol. Can you see Elsie at the moment? Does she look all right?"

"Well, Inspector," said Lori, looking at the group by the helicopter who were holding Elsie prisoner, "she doesn't look terribly happy right now, but she looks healthy enough to get through the moment."

"I'm very glad to hear that, Miss Fyfer," said the Inspector. "I'm authorized to follow this case to the end, and I have just landed at Heathrow on a flight from Zurich. I'll see you as quickly as I can get to your castle!"

* * *

Elsie squinted in the bright morning sunrise at the police helicopters overhead, and British constables ranging along the parking area fence with rifles. The Special Weapons and Tactics team members were still on the top of the tower with their automatic weapons, and ... and ... it was, she was sure it was Lori and Eric up there with them! She was so relieved to see them, she felt dizzy, and swayed in the arms of the thugs holding her.

Elsie had thought that Lori and Eric were still back at the Shannon Airport in Ireland, and seeing them here was a joyful surprise. *Maybe this is all going to work out after all,* she told herself as the two men holding her dragged her roughly toward the front of the helicopter, and into the airship. They pushed her inside, and down on the floor.

Elsie was forced to lie face-down on the floor of the helicopter in a rectangular metal recess in the carpeted floor. Rope was tied back and forth above her from hooks on one side of the recess to hooks on the other, forcing her to lie flat on her stomach in the recess, her arms still tied tightly behind her back by plastic zip ties.

* * *

As her men secured the ropes above Elsie so she could not sit up on the floor of the helicopter, Noelle turned to the Skipper and said, "My men and I are going to France to a remote chateau I have east of Paris. We'll have to sit down in some isolated place in England to wait for darkness before we cross the channel. But I have enough fuel to get to my chateau if I drop our hostage out of the helicopter as soon as we're out of sight of the police. You're welcome to join us if you like … you and your diamond, that is. Remember, we're partners now. I've lost everything because of that gem, and I'll need my half of its value to get started again. Will you join us?"

* * *

She is actually quite a good liar, thought the Skipper, judging Noelle as only an expert liar could. *I can see how she has done so well in her business. She's decided she wants the diamond all for herself, and she'll try to get rid of me in the near future. She's a lot like me, actually.* "Sure," said the skipper, bouncing the Star of Yakutsk up and down in his hand. "I appreciate the offer. Maybe I can also get a new start in France." The Skipper looked back at his two remaining henchmen. "Co-pilot", he called to one of them. "Hand me your weapon. I'm going to need it when we take off in a few minutes in case the police try to stop us in spite of our hostage."

* * *

"Lieutenant Broderick," asked Lori slowly. "Could I borrow those binoculars you're carrying with your gear? I can't see Elsie at all since those monsters forced her into the helicopter. They must have pushed her down on the floor, or they did something even worse to her. I'm going up to the top of the tower again to see if I can look down into the helicopter to see where she is."

"Good idea, Miss Fyfer," agreed Broderick. "I hadn't noticed that she disappeared."

"Wilton," he called to another SWAT commando who had just handed the Lieutenant a bull horn. "Accompany Miss Fyfer up into the tower, and report to me as soon as she has found out what our smugglers have done with the hostage. Her welfare is our first concern at this point."

Pointing the bullhorn toward Noelle

Chabron's helicopter, Broderick began speaking to the smugglers. "You are surrounded by armed police officers. Call me if you want to talk; otherwise, step out of the helicopter, raise your arms and approach me immediately." He asked his sergeant what his unit's cell phone number was, and repeated it to the smugglers. Five minutes later, the cell phone the sergeant was holding rang. The sergeant answered it, then handed it to the Lieutenant.

"English policeman," said Noelle Chabrun, when Broderick answered the telephone, "if you value the life of the woman who is our hostage, tell your *gendarmes* to put down their rifles, and we will depart! If we see another airship of any kind following us, we will kill the woman."

"You know I can't do that," countered Broderick. "How do I know that you won't kill the woman anyway?"

"You will just have to take my word for it," said Noelle. "You know she will be the first to die if we shoot it out here at the castle. We have no reason to want her dead, so we won't kill her if we don't have to. I will give you ten minutes to notify all your officers, then we are taking off. If even one policeman shoots at us, we will kill our hostage. Take it or leave it!"

The Lieutenant ended the call, and immediately received another one, this time from Lori. "I'm on level two of the castle," she said. "High enough to see past the pilots' seats and low enough that the roof of the helicopter doesn't cut off my view. I can see Elsie ... the hostage ... and she seems to be lying on the floor."

"Lieutenant, she's lying completely still, and she seems to have some kind of backpack strapped on her back. Could they have killed her already? She's actually lying flat on the floor and not moving!"

"No, I don't think so," said the Lieutenant. "Doesn't make sense. They still need her to keep us from firing at them. I have another call, Miss Fyfer. I'll call you right back!" He ended his call to answer the other one that was buzzing in. "Yes, Inspector," he said when he found the call was from Interpol."

"Lieutenant, don't let that helicopter take off under any circumstances!" began the Inspector.

"May have to, Inspector."

"I've been studying the files we have on Noelle Chabrun," said the Inspector. "There's really only one reason we've never been able to arrest and convict that woman. The evidence we've actually seen being put on that helicopter in the form of people or bags of diamonds or other evidence have always disappeared by the time Chabrun landed. That always seemed strange until I noticed that all the times we had her under surveillance it was after dark and she was flying over water. I think she has a way of ejecting people or other kinds of evidence from her helicopter without opening her side doors, which the pilots following her would have noticed. And since she's barely going to have enough petrol to get back to London after a round trip this morning, she'll certainly be wanting to lighten her load in every way she can. If you let that helicopter take off, I don't think we'll ever see Elsie ... the hostage, that is ... again!"

"Thank you, Inspector," said Broderick slowly and thoughtfully. "I'll get back to you soon, Sir."

"There's one more thing that makes this situation even more ominous, Lieutenant," continued Lodge. "I decided to look elsewhere into what we had on people who had disappeared from Noelle Chabrun's helicopter. and I just found one of them who has been discovered dead".

"There had been no referrals noted between Noelle Chabrun's files and those of the diamond fence I found dead because we had no idea they were connected." Lodge explained. "Part of his skeleton floated up on a beach. The authorities swept the underwater area farther out, and found the rest of him, which happened to be wearing a backpack full of rocks. The loaded backpack was too heavy to have ever floated to the surface. If he hadn't been dumped too close to a beach, and if his skeleton hadn't separated, we'd probably never have found him. I'm convinced Chabrun killed him by dropping him out of her helicopter."

Inspector Lodge hesitated for a moment, then added, "Lieutenant, I'm acquainted with that lady who's being held hostage. Please don't let that helicopter take off."

Lieutenant Broderick cleared his throat. "I understand, Sir. I'll certainly do my best." He disconnected the telephone, and stared at the helicopter, thinking for a long moment before doing anything. *Talk about being between a rock and a hard place.*

"Sergeant", he called. "Notify everyone. That helicopter must not take off. They are to open fire if the pilot tries to depart ... but only by firing at the tail rotor to cause the helicopter to go into auto-rotation, and corkscrew back down to the ground. But no one is to fire at the cabin," he emphasized. "Remind everyone: they have a hostage on board," he added. "No one fires at the cabin!"

* * *

Once we take off, Noelle will be in control of everything, because she will be the pilot, thought the Skipper as he tried to appear relaxed in his seat, letting the automatic pistol in his hand sag almost to the floor. *I must kill her while we are still on the ground.* He fondled the Star of Yakutsk in the right pocket of his jacket. It was as large as an orange, and felt hard against his stomach. *If I can use my hostage to get myself and my men to Heathrow in London, I'll still be able to get this gem to the United States, and I basically won't have to share with anyone.* The Skipper savored for a moment the thought that he was far smarter than the woman sitting next to him, and that this was the time to show it.

* * *

"All right, we go now," said Noelle Chabrun. "I don't think *les gendarmes* will fire on us because they know we have a hostage. But if they do, I'll set back down immediately, so do not open fire on them. We cannot win a fire fight with some fifty police officers."

"That is an order," she said, turning her face to the Skipper, and glaring at him. As Chabrun turned the throttle in her left hand to power up the engine and cause the rotors to rotate faster, the engine noise of the helicopter increased dramatically, and she saw the police around her stiffen and bring their rifles to bear on the helicopter.

SWAT commander Broderick, still standing at the door of the castle, brought the bullhorn to his lips and called out to her, "Do not take off, Mademoiselle Chabrun. I'm warning you!"

But Noelle pulled back hard on the collective control in her left hand, causing the rotor blades to change configuration and bite into the air above the helicopter, making it rise rapidly off the ground. But as the helicopter's skids cleared the parking lot surface, he turned his bullhorn toward his officers ringing the parking area. He yelled, "Open fire! Commence firing!", and bullets began spattering against the tail rotor of the aircraft, actually tearing away part of the rotor.

The Skipper realized that this was also his last chance to take control, and he raised his pistol and shot Noelle in the right shoulder. She screamed a strangled curse as the force of the bullet threw her against the left side door, causing her to suddenly yank the collective control to the right, throwing the helicopter to the right, as well. The helicopter had risen about twelve feet into the air, and it crashed back onto the parking lot surface at an angle, causing the right hand skids to hit the surface with the entire weight of the helicopter on them. The skids collapsed into torn pieces of metal as the helicopter smashed down on top of them. But the rotors were still spinning at full speed when they scraped against the parking lot surface with a horrific screech as they were torn from the body of the airship. The first rotor to hit the surface ripped away from the airship, and hurtled into the body of the helicopter, ripping a gash the full length of the cabin. The entire helicopter was instantly torn into a heap of ragged pieces of metal sprinkled with beads of safety glass.

All sound and movement in and around the parking lot ceased as everyone still alive stared in horror at what had happened to the helicopter. Lori stared at the splintered lump of metal on the parking lot, and began sobbing, tears running down her dirty cheeks.

A police car pulled up in front of the castle, and Inspector Lodge got out. When he saw the debris in the lot behind the castle he sprinted the rest of the way through the building and out into the parking lot.

"Where is she?" he asked Lori, who just buried her head into his chest and continued sobbing for a long moment. Then she suddenly pulled back her head and said, "It could explode any minute if the gas tanks are breached, and come into contact with hot metal. But I'm not going to leave her in there, no matter what. I'm going to get her out!"

Eric was at Lori's side before she had run half the distance to the heap of torn metal. "Stay back, darlin'. It could go any minute. There's no one left alive in there. Don't die on me for nothing."

"I can hear her crying," said Lori in an awed tone of voice.

"And don't go crazy on me," said Eric miserably as he caught Lori and held her.

"Listen" said Lori, as she fought to get away from him.

Eric's mouth slowly dropped open, and he stared into the wreckage as he released Lori. "She can't be alive," he said. The rotor had torn through the cabin horizontally, striking every passenger sitting in the helicopter seats, and horribly mutilating their bodies into bloody remains.

But Eric and Lori could still hear the sobbing. "It's Elsie," said Inspector Lodge, who had run with them to the broken helicopter. "It's Elsie," he repeated as he tore off his suit coat and used it to protect his hands as he pulled apart hot pieces of shredded metal, and dragged objects out of the cabin. When he and Eric had cleared the floor of the helicopter cabin, the Inspector called, "Elsie?" and heard the sobbing slow. Elsie still wore the backpack of rocks, although the ropes that had held her flat against Noelle's bomb bay doors in the floor had been torn and shredded by the force of the broken rotor that had passed just above her. "Ian?" called Elsie, using the inspector's first name for the first time.

"We'll have you out in just a moment," said the Inspector. He was carefully removing the backpack, concerned that Elsie's shoulders might have been broken. All seemed well, though, as he slowly pulled off the backpack and used an old staghorn knife from his pocket to cut the zip ties that still held her wrists tightly bound together.

"Inspector Lodge?" called Lieutenant Broderick from over his shoulder. "It could go any second, sir, if that fuel ignites."

"We'll only be a moment," replied Inspector Lodge, as he raised Elsie to her feet and swung her body into his arms to carry her away from the broken helicopter "We've found some treasure among the debris."

"You found the Star of Yakutsk?" asked the Lieutenant.

"No," replied the Inspector. "Far more valuable than the Star of Yakutsk."

THE END

ABOUT THE AUTHOR

John Sandel lives in North Texas with his wife Lorrie and his West Highland Terrier Fergie. He graduated from the University of Texas in Austin, and spent the next summer as a seasonal Park Ranger in Yellowstone. The next winter he earned a commission as a Lieutenant in the United States Air Force, and was stationed for the next three years in Oregon and Greenland. By that time he knew he wanted to write, and he resigned his commission and began creating news releases, newsletters, brochures and TV ads for an ad agency, public relations firm and many other clients. Deadly Contraband is his first novel.

John Sandel

Made in the USA
Lexington, KY
13 September 2017